THE ABRIDGER

A NOVEL
OF MORMON

THE ABRIDGER

A NOVEL
OF MORMON

ROBERT H.MOSS

Other Books by Robert H. Moss:

Covenant Coat
I, Nephi
Waters of Mormon
That I were an Angel
Title of Liberty
The Abridger
Valiant Witness
Celestial Child

1 2 3 4 5 6 7 8 9 10

3 6 9 12 15 18 20 22 24 26 28 30 32 34 36 38 40

ISBN: 1-55517-044-7

Printed and distributed in the United States of America by
ACME PUBLISHERS
1795 Ann Dell Lane
Salt Lake City, UT 84121

Lithographed in the United States of America

TABLE OF CONTENTS

PREFACE

Of all the heroes in the Book of Mormon, none had more influence on the book itself than did Mormon, for whom the book was named. Each of the chroniclers wrote his own book, which became a part of the whole, but Mormon was the chief scribe, the abridger, the chronicler. His commentaries, which add great insight into God's dealings with the Nephite people, appear in almost every book of that volume.

Mormon was a powerful man, both in body and spirit. Chosen to lead the Nephite armies while still but a youth, he fulfilled that responsibility for sixty years. Then, as an old man, he completed his most important role: that of scribe and abridger.

Record keepers have always been important to God's chosen people. They are today. I dedicate this volume to the record keepers—the chroniclers—those who faithfully put history on paper—or plates.

PROLOGUE

Cumorah, 385 A.D.

A faint moan escaped Mormon's lips. Consciousness slowly returned. He tried to roll to one side and pain sizzled him like a red-hot coal placed from the fire on his skin.

"Easy, Father," Moroni said. "You were badly wounded."

The voice was fuzzy. Moroni? Memory assailed him. The battle! Painful memories. He groaned in agony as he remembered: eyes glazed, sword arm heavy, his ten-thousand being decimated by the Lamanites, then the spear thrust and unconsciousness.

"I don't need to ask how the battle ended," he whispered hoarsely.

"No," Moroni replied.

"How did I get here?" His now open eyes surveyed his surroundings. He and about twenty other warriors were in a pit covered with branches.

Another voice was directed toward him. "Moroni and I found you after dark and brought you here."

Mormon looked to see who had spoken. "And who are you?" he asked weakly.

"Asubel," the person responded. "One of Moroni's officers."

He looked at Moroni. "How did you find me?"

Moroni knelt and put a skin of water to Mormon's lips. "I saw where you fell. I knew I had to find you before the Lamanites did. The Lord led us to you in the dark."

"Why didn't the Lamanites finish me?"

Moroni smiled. "The Lord has plans for you. Other Nephite warriors were killed and fell on top of you. To the Lamanites it was a pile of dead warriors."

Mormon was silent trying to sort his thinking. He listened to his own ragged breathing and could feel the erratic pulse in his neck. He raised his hand and felt his side where the spear had pierced, so close to his heart. Fingers met padded bandages tightly wrapped around his entire chest. He sighed. "May I see the battlefield?"

Moroni carefully poked his head through the protective camouflage. "The sun is at its high point." He pulled himself through the brush. A few moments later he lowered himself back through. "It looks clear. Lamanite armies march to their camps."

Carefully, so as to not start his wound bleeding again, they raised Mormon on his litter until he lay propped up on the slope above their hideout.

Mormon had no strength. Even the slight raising of his head brought a spell of dizziness. He struggled to catch his breath. I have lost much blood, he thought. I have no reserve to call on but I must not die until I complete the record. He looked out over the valley. An involuntary shudder shook his body.

"All dead," he whispered. He saw where his ten thousand had fallen, and where the ten thousand of Moroni's army had fallen. He turned his head slowly in an arc, noting sadly where each ten thousand and their commander had died. The bodies of his people, stripped of their weapons and armor, lay naked on the valley floor. Thousands of birds—crows, vultures, ravens and others—dotted the carcasses.

He thought of his great leaders: Camenihah, Moronihah, Antionum, Gidgiddonah, Shiblom, Shem, Josh and others. All dead. His whole family, with the exception of Moroni, wiped out. He closed his eyes as he thought of little Greta. Her name was on his' lips but he did not speak it. That would bring additional sorrow to Moroni. He felt Moroni's comforting hand on his shoulder. As if a fountain burst forth from the ground, tears sprang from his eyes and ran down his wrinkled cheeks.

He cried out in his anguish. "Oh, my people, how could you have departed from the ways of the Lord! How could you have rejected Jesus who stood with open arms to receive you! If you had not rejected Him you would not have fallen, but you are fallen and I mourn your loss. Oh, you fair sons and daughters, you fathers and mothers, you husbands and wives, how is it that you could have fallen!"

"I so loved you, my people," Mormon anguished. "But you are gone and my sorrows cannot bring your return. The day comes when your mortal must put on immortality and these bodies which molder in corruption must become incorruptible bodies.

Then you must stand before the judgment seat of Christ to be judged according to your works." He shook his head sorrowfully. "How I wish you had repented before this great destruction came upon you."

Wearily, his eyes clenched shut, he lay his head back on the pallet. He felt Moroni's gentle hands as they cradled his head. He murmured weakly, "But you are gone and the Eternal Father knows your state. He will do with you according to His justice and mercy." Unconsciousness brought relief from his anguish.

*****

During the next few days Mormon watched the warriors depart Cumorah. Soon he and Moroni were alone. Moroni moved him to the cave he had prepared. Supplies were cached in niches. A spring bubbled near the entrance. "You have done much since I was last here," Mormon said. "When?"

"The Lord whispered to me that your life would be preserved and we would need a place for you to work on the sacred records."

"The records!" Mormon said, attempting to sit up. He grimaced as pain forced him back on the pallet. "The records?"

"They are safe," Moroni nodded. "I check them daily."

Mormon sighed. "Thank you, Lord." He looked at Moroni. "And thank you, son."

Strength came slowly. Physically, each day Mormon felt better. His mental state was another story. Every night he awoke, sweating and trembling as he relived the battle before Cumorah. Only the Spirit's sweet message of peace soothed his troubled mind. He knew Moroni was feeling similar anguish. Often he heard his son moan in his sleep. Finally, the day came when Mormon felt like writing. "But I really don't know where to start," he said.

"Will you be writing about what happened during your life?"

Mormon laughed for the first time since the great battle, and laughing felt good after his sorrow. "I'm afraid there is not that much to write about my life."

Darkness came but sleep eluded Mormon. He thought of what he had told Moroni. *Lord, what is it you want me to do? There is not enough to write of my life; nothing but wars and carnage. You must have something more important for me to do.*

The Lord's voice spoke to his mind. *"My son, peace be unto you. Yours is a special mission. You are to abridge all the records of my people from Lehi down to your own day. Condense the plates so they can be carried to a faraway place, a place where a latter-*

day prophet will find them, translate them, and teach them to a new generation."

Morning finally came and Mormon faced his son. "Moroni, God has a great work for me to do. He commanded me to abridge the plates; the writings of all the prophets since Lehi left Jerusalem."

"That is a major task," Moroni said.

"My problem is that I don't know where to start. How does a man, seeing all the records before him, select those to include in an abridgment which will go to the gentiles and be the means of saving this people?" He sighed. "It is an awesome responsibility."

"But, with the help of the Spirit, a responsibility which you will accomplish."

Mormon smiled at Moroni's simple and beautiful faith. "Can you bring me some plates of those written by Lehi?" he asked.

Moroni seemed pleased at the request. "Gladly, Father," he replied. He was gone for an hour, returning with several plates.

Mormon sat against a rock, stylus poised above a blank plate. He took a plate from the stack and read the beginning of Lehi's account. Before he attempted to write, he prayed that he would know what to inscribe; what would be of most worth to future generations. The Spirit warmed his bosum.

His mind went to the beginning of the record.

The Nephite Chronicles really began with Joseph who was sold into Egypt. He was the first keeper of the records and laid the foundation for our entire people. The Lord promised him that his posterity would be a "branch over the wall." Jacob, who became Israel, blessed Joseph that a remnant of his posterity would be saved. Mormon sighed. *I guess that remnant must be the Lamanites. There are not enough Nephites left to be called a remnant: Moroni and I and the few who escaped into the land northward.*

Lehi, the first chronicler of the book, became the patriarch of this dynasty. Directed by God, he courageously left his native land and sailed to this land of promise. Though he was close to God he had rebellious sons. Laman and Lemuel refused to follow his counsel. Now their descendants, the Lamanites, have exterminated the Nephite nation.

Nephi was a stalwart and faithful man. He was obedient to his father and his God. Without his leadership the Plates of Brass may not have been obtained, Ishmael and his daughters may not have joined the caravan, the ship may not have been built, and the people may not have arrived here in the promised land. Obedience—that was the key trait.

Jacob, in his writings, gave a powerful testimony of the Savior. Enos, son of Jacob, was a man of faith. He talked to the Lord. Because of his faith and humility the Lord answered his prayers. That was so with each of the great chroniclers. King Benjamin is a good example. What a powerful sermon he gave to the people. What a sermon he lived. His life exemplified his saying, "When you are in the service of your fellow beings you are only in the service of your God."

Alma, the elder, had great influence on the course of Nephite history. What would have happened if he had not listened to Abinadi? Through him the priesthood and the leadership of this people progressed down to the present time.

And Alma, the younger. An angel started his process of repentance, but he had to accomplish the full task of repentance on his own. "Oh, that I were an angel," he cried. In his own way he was an angel; the most prolific scribe and writer. His writings are filled with God's words. He kept an accurate account of his work with the people, as chief judge, missionary, prophet and scribe. Some of his most important writings were his recorded blessings to his sons, Helaman, Shiblon and Corianton.

Mormon mentally ticked off the lineage: *from Alma, the younger, to his son, Helaman; to his son, Helaman; to his son, Nephi; to his son, Nephi, who lived when the Savior came. Then, the lineage continued from that third Nephi to a fourth Nephi, to Amos; to Amos, son of Amos, to Ammoron, brother of Amos; and then to me. Now I will pass that heritage to my son, Moroni. An unbroken chain of prophets since Alma repented and accepted the words of Abinadi. What an influence is one man!*

Helaman's writings, though primarily of wars and fighting, fill an important part of the chronicle. His leadership of the two-thousand stripling sons showed great faith and courage.

In all the chronicles—other than the Savior—Moroni, chief captain of the Nephite armies, was my favorite hero. I even named my son after him. Helaman wrote of him as being courageous, fearless, patriotic and defending liberty to death if need be.

CHAPTER ONE

Cumorah, 385 A.D.

"I am sorry to be so helpless," Mormon said.

Moroni stirred the broth over the small fire and smiled at his father. "My only concern is that you get well."

"After we eat, would you get me more of the plates of Lehi?"

"I'll get them now."

Mormon studied the plates; pored over them, read them several times, waited for the witness of the spirit, then carefully wrote his abridgment. Days passed quickly as he wrote. Each day his body became more responsive to his will. Though weak from his wound and stiff with age he was soon standing, and then walking.

Moroni sat beside him as he wrote, sometimes even doing some of the inscribing as Mormon dictated to him. But the responsibility was his and his alone. The abridgement must be completed, and the Lord had assigned him that awesome task.

When he completed the large plates of Nephi he searched through the records for the next part of the chronicles. He found another set of plates which continued the record from Jacob down to the reign of King Benjamin. Mormon wrote: *It is many hundred years after the coming of Christ. I have witnessed the destruction of almost all my people, the Nephites. Soon I deliver up the record I have made into the hands of my son, Moroni. I suppose he will witness the entire destruction of my people. May God grant that he survive, that he may write about the Lamanites and about Christ, that some day it may profit them.*

Now I write concerning that which I have written. After abridging the plates of Nephi down to the reign of King

Benjamin, I searched among the records which had been given me and found these plates which contained this small account of the prophets, from Jacob down to the reign of King Benjamin, and also many of the words of Nephi. The things upon these plates pleased me, because of the prophecies of the coming of Christ—especially since most of them have been fulfilled. Prophesies down to our day have been fulfilled, and those which go beyond this day must surely come to pass.

Therefore, I will take the remainder of my writings from the plates of Nephi, even though there are so many that I cannot write a hundredth part of the things of this people. But I shall take these small plates, which contain these prophecies and revelations, and put them with the remainder of my record. They are choice unto me and I know they will be choice for those who will read them. I do this for a wise purpose, for thus has the Spirit whispered to me. I do not know all things, but the Lord knows all things which are to come and he works within me according to his will. My prayer to God is that my brethren may once again come to the knowledge of God, even the redemption of Christ, that they may once again be a delightsome people.

Now, I, Mormon, proceed to finish my record, which I take from the plates of Nephi, and I make it according to the knowledge and the understanding which God has given me.

Light had faded so it was almost impossible for Mormon to see what he had written. He put down his stylus and wiped his eyes. "That's enough writing for tonight," he said.

"More than enough," Moroni agreed. "You are very tired and the writing can wait until you gain more strength."

Mormon shook his head. "No, son. The writing cannot wait. It is only a matter of time until the Lamanites find us. The writing must be completed by that time."

During the next days Mormon wrote of King Benjamin, of the two kings who followed Benjamin, both named Mosiah. He wrote of those who left Zarahemla and went back to the land of their inheritance: of King Zeniff, and the wicked King Noah. Tenderly he wrote of Abinadi and Alma.

"Why are you crying, Father?" Moroni asked.

Mormon chuckled. "Tears of joy, son," he said. "I am so thankful that Abinadi was such a courageous prophet. But I am even more thankful that Alma listened to him."

"Yes. Who can know the effect one man can have on a civilization?" Moroni said. "Through Alma came all the prophets even down to our time."

"Including you and me," Mormon said. "I am proud that Alma is my ancestor."

"What of his son, Alma?" Moroni asked.

"He was a wicked man in his youth," Mormon said. "But after he repented he became one of the greatest of prophets." He turned and took Moroni's hand. "I praise God, son, that you have always been faithful, that your life has been Christ-centered." He sighed. "I don't know if I could have been as strong and faithful as Alma—what pain he must have felt over his wayward son."

"Maybe it is like the pain I now feel over the loss of my wife, sons and daughter," Moroni said quietly.

Mormon squeezed his hand. "Much greater pain, Moroni. Armora and your children were faithful and you will have them again. But if Alma had died in his wickedness, then his father would have mourned in emptiness."

The next few days passed quickly as Mormon, with Moroni's help, wrote of Alma the younger, and of Helaman, his son.

"There was no greater man in the chronicles than Captain Moroni," he said as he laid down the stylus.

"You named me after him," Moroni said.

"I wanted you to be like him. He was courageous, fearless in battle, and most important, faithful and prayerful before God."

"From my youth you taught me the words he wrote upon his torn cloak when the freedom of the Nephites was threatened by Amalickiah." He leaned back and quoted from memory. "In memory of our God, our religion, and freedom, and our peace, our wives, and our children."

"Listen what I wrote about Captain Moroni," Mormon said. "Moroni was a strong and a mighty man, a man of a perfect understanding. He did not delight in bloodshed but his soul did joy in the liberty and the freedom of his country. He was a man whose heart did swell with thanksgiving to his God, for the many privileges and blessings which he bestowed upon his people; a man who did labor exceedingly for the welfare and safety of his people. Yea, a man firm in the faith of Christ, who had sworn with an oath to defend his people, his rights, and his country, and his religion, even to the loss of his blood."

"I'm impressed every time I read of that Moroni. No wonder he is your hero," Moroni said.

Mormon nodded, then inspired, swiftly inscribed with the stylus. *If all men had been and were and ever would be like*

Moroni, behold, the very powers of hell would have been shaken forever and the devil would never have power over the hearts of the children of men. He was a man like Ammon, the son of Mosiah, and even the other sons of Mosiah, and also Alma and his sons, for they were all men of God.

Mormon rested, but even when resting all he could think about were those great heroes in the records—like Helaman and his two thousand stripling sons. Helaman wrote so much about the wars, Mormon thought. Through his history readers may know that freedom is of utmost value; that liberty is to be defended no matter what the cost. He sighed. But now there is no one left to defend our freedom. We lie here in hiding, waiting for the time when the Lamanites will discover us and take our lives.

Mormon was tired but he couldn't sleep. He thought of Helaman, son of Helaman. *Helaman's time was so like my own,* he thought. *Wars fought for greed and power.*

He called softly. "Moroni, are you awake?"

"Yes, Father."

"Did you read in the plates of the sons of Pahoran?"

"Wasn't there a fight to see who would be chief judge?"

"Yes. Three sons contended for the judgment seat, Pahoran, Pacumeni and Paanchi."

"As I recall, Pahoran won the election."

"True, but that didn't end the contention. Pacumeni accepted the results of the election but Paanchi and his supporters rebelled. He was tried and executed for his ambition."

"Didn't Kishkumen then assassinate Pahoran?"

"Yes. And from him came the band of Gadianton robbers for which the people suffered even down to our time."

He lay there silently, thinking of Helaman and the tough times in which he lived, of Kishkumen and Gadianton and his band. Finally, he slept and dreamed.

*****

Zarahemla, Forty-first year; 50 B.C.

Zarahemla's marketplace teemed with noisy, smelly life. Stalls, pens of livestock, and small shops under roofs covered with huge leaves lined the edges of the plaza. Woven fabric hung from fibers strung before booths. Craftsmen displayed their metalwork—bronze worker and goldsmith flaunting gleaming wares in the late afternoon sun.

Piles of vegetables nestled between baskets of herbs and medicinal bark, their fragrances vying with each other, only to be overcome by the fine dust of the road and the heavy aroma of manure drifting from the sheep and goat pens. Voices young and old, cracked and sweet, sang their songs, inviting the onlooker to buy, denouncing the nonpurchaser as a scoundrel.

Market day, and the people of Zarahemla had come to buy and sell. Normally, Helaman would have enjoyed the activity. But not today. He sneaked a quick glance over his shoulder. The hooded man still followed. He climbed the steps to the temple and slipped through the portal. *He will not follow me here.* For the first time in hours he allowed himself to relax. Here in the temple, surrounded by his priests and guards, he and the precious records were safe.

What has our land come to, that the chief priest is threatened by hoodlums? He sighed. *First, Pahoran was killed by an unknown assassin and now our armies have joined together to repulse another Lamanite invasion. Moronihah and his army must prevail. Would the Lamanites, if they conquered us, allow me to keep the records. I'm glad I hid them. Neither Nephite robbers nor Lamanites will find them.*

In his room he slipped off his uncomfortable sandals and briefly massaged his tired feet. Barefoot, limestone floor cool under his feet, he crossed to his desk and picked up a roll of bark paper. He read over the last words he had written. Moronihah, son of Moroni, follows in the footsteps of his father. His love of country is unsurpassed in this land. To maintain our freedom, and without regard to his own life, he leads the Nephite armies against Lamanites and Nephite dissidents. He has placed his armies in the borders of the land.

"To arms! To arms!" Shouting from the square aroused Helaman from his thoughts. Temple priests crowded around him as he pushed to the open portal.

"Lamanites attack! Lamanites!"

Booths collapsed. Hawkers piled their wares on heads and carts and scurried from the plaza. Others drove sheep and goats before them. Within minutes the plaza was empty except for smells and litter.

Helaman was aghast. Lamanites attacking Zarahemla—the very heart of the Nephite lands? The small militia unit in Zarahemla was designed only to keep the peace, not to repel invaders. He watched as Pacumeni, surrounded by a host of soldiers in full armor, strode purposefully through the plaza and up the temple steps. Pacumeni was still a youth—not more than twenty-five years of age. He stopped before Helaman, brow furrowed with worry. Helaman noted again Pacumeni's strikingly deep blue eyes and chiseled jaw, set now in defiant determination.

"Helaman, you have undoubtedly heard the news. A massive Lamanite army is within a few hours' march of the city. They will probably attack before morning. Moronihah and his armies guard our borders. Only a handful of troops are in the city."

"What will we do?" Helaman asked quietly. "How can I help?"

"I have ordered all citizens to arm themselves and assemble before the temple."

Helaman nodded. He had seen the rag-tag forces assembling. Though some carried wicked-looking axes, spears and swords, most were armed with shovels, hoes, rakes and pitchforks.

"I have also sent fast messengers by boat to get word to Moronihah in the city of Moroni."

"Moroni is a three-day march from here."

"Moronihah cannot get here in time to save the city from attack, but if we can hold out long enough perhaps he can break the Lamanite siege."

Helaman asked, "How did the Lamanites get by the border army? How did they get here so fast, without any warning?"

Pacumeni turned and looked at the assembling citizen warriors. He shook his head sadly but didn't answer Helaman's question. "We have brought it on ourselves as a nation. If we had kept alert instead of squabbling among ourselves this would have never happened. As it is..." He spread his hands in a gesture of helplessness. "But we cannot look backwards. We must overcome the enemy." He turned to Helaman. "The biggest help you can give is to pray for us. Pray for our army. Pray that we can hold out long enough for Moronihah to save the city. Otherwise..." Pacumeni didn't finish the sentence.

Not all people in Zarahemla were worried and unhappy about the arrival of the Lamanites. Kishkumen and Laish watched the Nephites gather in the temple plaza. Laish still wore the hooded cloak he had worn when following Helaman.

"Ah," Kishkumen gloated. "This invasion could not have come at a better time. We'll turn it to our advantage." He drew Laish into a doorway to let armed men pass. "Tonight you and I will sneak from the city and approach the Lamanite commander under a flag of truce. If all goes well, we will be his hosts in Zarahemla." He chuckled as he considered the possibilities. "Then the temple gold and Helaman's gold plates will be ours."

Pacumeni waited on the steps with Helaman. "Our people, all who can bear arms, are here," he said. "Your blessing may give them hope." He grasped Helaman's right hand and raised their arms high in the air. A hush settled over the crowd.

Pacumeni kept his arms raised as he spoke. "In our entire history, Zarahemla has never been captured by the Lamanites. We are a strong people. Let us use our strength now to hold off the Lamanites until Moronihah arrives with the army."

A ragged cheer went up from the crowd.

"I have asked Helaman, the chief priest, to bless this people. He will bless our army, this city, and Moronihah." He dropped Helaman's hand.

Another cheer. This time more unified.

Helaman raised both arms high above his head, the richly-embroidered priestly robes falling in cadences around his trim body. Heavy jade necklaces hung in bold relief from his neck and a lofty feather headdress made him seem even taller.

"God of our fathers," he cried. "Bless this city in its affliction. Give strength and power to this people to overcome their enemies. Bless each person with determination and courage to overcome those who come against us. Bless Zarahemla that it may be preserved as a place where freedom abounds and men can live in peace under the Title of Liberty." He ended his prayer with the plea that Moronihah and his army be granted "the wings of eagles, that they may arrive here in time to save Zarahemla from those who would destroy it."

Complete silence greeted his prayer. Helaman lowered his arms and turned with downcast eyes to Pacumeni.

"What's the matter?" the chief judge asked.

"I fear for the city," Helaman said. "The Spirit's confirmation did not come."

Pacumeni looked at him in silence for a moment, then shook himself as if to throw off his own pall. "We must not lose hope. We will fight." He started down the steps.

Helaman grabbed him by the arm. "Stay, Pacumeni. Your life is too valuable to lose. The temple may be a sanctuary if the city falls. Stay here and preserve your life."

Pacumeni shook his head. "No. I must lead the army, such as it is." Flanked by his guards he marched down the stairs.

Helaman walked slowly inside. Even with Pacumeni's courage and leadership, he had little faith in the ability of Zarahemla's citizens to keep out a large Lamanite army. He called the temple priests together. "The temple is a place of peace, respected by both Nephites and Lamanites. If the Lamanites win the city the temple must be a sanctuary. Hide the temple gold and silver. Bring your wives and children. This may be the only safe place in Zarahemla for our families."

Following his own advice, he hurried home. Vareena, his wife, waited at the door, tearstains on her cheeks.

"You've been crying," Helaman said, embracing her. Then without waiting for her to respond, in his urgency he cried, "Pack quickly. We do not know how much time we have until the Lamanites attack. I shall move you to the temple."

"What of the boys?" she anguished.

He stopped and faced her. "The boys?"

"They went to join the warriors in the plaza."

Helaman was astonished. "Warriors? Twelve and ten-year olds are too young to be warriors. Nephi has only had one year of warrior training and Lehi has none."

Vareena wrung her hands and fresh tears ran down her cheeks. "I tried to stop them but they joined with other boys who were hurrying to the plaza."

Helaman shook his head. "I'll take care of them. Please get your things and come with me." He chafed at the delay, then hurried Vareena to the temple. He helped her inside and stepped back to the platform above the crowded plaza, Nephi and Lehi temporarily forgotten.

Vareena cried out to him, "What of our sons?"

"I'll find them." Helaman hurried to the plaza.

"I don't know why we can't fight with the rest of the warriors," Lehi said, dragging his feet.

Helaman smiled. "If you are out fighting, who will attend the school of the scribes?"

Lehi mumbled something under his breath.

Helaman understood. He was about Lehi's age when his father left with the two thousand sons of the Ammonites. "I'm sorry, son. There are more important things for you and Nephi to do."

"Like what?" Lehi asked sullenly.

"Like helping me care for your mother." He walked up the temple steps, a hand resting gently but firmly on each son's shoulder. He was concerned about Nephi who had not said a word since he found them. The boys were so different. Nephi, tall and lanky, who seldom spoke; Lehi, stout and quite garrulous.

Vareena was elated. "Oh, you found them. Thank God."

"Lehi, you stay here with your mother," Helaman said. "Nephi, come with me." He could hear Lehi's grumbling as he and Nephi walked into the temple.

"What is it, Father?" Nephi said, breaking his silence.

"We must protect the plates," Helaman said. "If the Lamanites capture the city, I don't want them to find the records. For hundreds of years Lamanites have sworn to retrieve the records which they claim were stolen from their forefathers, Laman and Lemuel."

"But where will you hide them?"

"The plates are hidden under the floor of the temple. I want you to know where they are in case something happens to me. You are still young, but if..." He didn't speak the rest of the sentence, not wanting to upset Nephi.

His son looked up at him without blinking. "I will protect the records," he said quietly.

Kishkumen and Laish mingled with villagers leaving the city through the east gate. Hidden under Kishkumen's cloak was a broad piece of white linen. Away from the city, he found a short sapling and tied the cloth to it. "A white flag," he said with satisfaction. He smiled, his crooked teeth giving him a sinister look. "The Lamanite army is camped upriver. If we hurry we can approach them before dark."

Helaman stood listening at the door of the temple. Ominous sound of Lamanite drums had beat dismally since the first light of dawn over the east mountains. Now they sounded closer. The night had been sleepless and the new day portended evil. Helaman continued his silent petitions for God to spare Zarahemla. *This is my city. Vareena and I love Zarahemla, with its warm-hearted, happy people.*

The city normally seethed with life and noise of living. Brilliant colors—clothes, houses, paintings on the temple, even the fresh fruit in the square on market day—were subdued or non-existent. Where normally there was movement and

activity—now it was quiet. No one stirred. It was as if the city
were dead, waiting its burial.

The answer to his prayers was the same: God would not
save the wicked city.

Drum tempo picked up; Lamanites were closer now. The
sun, a flat-hued ball, lifted sluggishly over the east mountains.
The morning was warm but his hands felt cold and his flesh
creepy.

An anguished shout broke the silence, followed by
clashing of swords and yells of triumphant voices. Screams
filled the air. A chill went up Helaman's spine.
Nephites—warriors and citizens—backed through the square,
weapons held at the ready for whatever pursued them. Helaman
ached to join them, to be part of the city's defense, but he
couldn't. His first duty was to family and precious records.

Bronze-skinned men ran screaming across the plaza,
venting their anger on any light skin that moved before them.
Horrid sounds—sounds of war: a cacophony of screams of fear,
anger and anguish; shouts as Lamanites encouraged one
another; measured beat of drums; the strident calls of
triumphant voices—rose to Helaman's ears as the Lamanites
burst through the city. He turned from the scene, tears
streaming from his eyes. But he couldn't shut out the sounds. He
listened to the great noise coming from his beloved city:
resounding sounds of rape, rampage and rioting.

"Why, Lord?" he cried aloud. "Why do they pillage and
rape?"

Afternoon breeze brought scents of charred thatch and
sounds of a puppy's lonely yapping. Sharp ring of metal swords
no longer echoed through the streets. A terrible stillness had
settled over Zarahemla, broken only by agonized cries of the
wounded and the occasional wailing of a motherless babe. In
the city many dead things lay unburied: dogs, chickens, pigs and
people. Foul stink of death hung over the city like a pall.
Helaman angrily brought thumb and forefinger to his nose,
pinching off the stench. A shudder passed through his body as
he thought again of the hundreds—perhaps thousands—who
died defending the city.

Coriantumr chuckled, watching Helaman's
discomfiture.

"You laugh, when so many lay dead and dying?"
Helaman asked. "And you a Nephite!" He spit out the words and
then turned away to hide his anger from the smiling conqueror.

"No, priest. I am not a Nephite. I am a true descendant of Zarahemla who first settled this city before it was taken by the Nephites."

Helaman looked more carefully at the large man standing before him on the temple steps. Coriantumr, leader of the Lamanites, had an angular, handsome face. His nose was thin, high-bridged over a mobile, ruthless mouth. It was the face of a man accustomed to get his wishes. His face and body—that part showing through armor and gore—were tanned until he was almost as dark as the Lamanites he led. He slouched now, leaning on his bloody sword. Helaman looked beyond Coriantumr, at the hundreds of Lamanites lounging in the plaza before the temple. He knew other thousands patrolled the walls and streets of Zarahemla.

Coriantumr's gravelly voice brought him back to reality. "Do any Nephite warriors hide in the temple?"

"No. Only priests and their wives and children are in the temple."

oriantumr nodded as if satisfied with Helaman's answer. "I want the gold and silver from the temple to take back to the land of Nephi. Tubaloth, king of the Lamanites, also ordered me to bring back the records stolen by Nephi."

"No." Helaman surprised himself with his own audacity.

"Who are you to tell me no, priest?" Coriantumr raised the point of his sword to Helaman's belly.

"What of Pacumeni?" Helaman asked, changing the subject.

"Pah. A weakling. I backed him up against the city wall and killed him myself."

Helaman thought of the young man—so vibrant and full of life—who yesterday stood on the steps from which Coriantumr now commanded . "What now?" he asked quietly. "What will happen to those who still live?"

"Many fled the city," Coriantumr said. "My Lamanites will hunt them down and kill them." He thumped his chest. "We kill all who oppose us. I will leave a small army here to maintain the city and then will conquer the rest of the Nephite lands."

Helaman thought, *His heart takes courage to have conquered Zarahemla. I pray that Moronihah will be able to stop him.* "And after you have conquered?"

Coriantumr grinned. "Tubaloth will be king of all the land."

Helaman asked a question which had bothered him. "Your warriors are mighty but how did you gain access to the city so quickly."

"Ha!" grunted Coriantumr. "Traitors are always available to a conquering army. Some of your good Nephite citizens opened the gate for us."

CHAPTER TWO

MORONIHAH AND HELAMAN

Cumorah, 385 A.D.

"Aieee!"

Mormon waked with a start before the echoes of the scream faded from the cave. He looked around, suddenly realizing the scream had come from his own lips. Sweat beaded his forehead. An uncontrollable chill shook his frail body. The recurring nightmare: again he stood on the plain before Cumorah, seeing his own children and tens of thousands of his people slain.

"What is it, Father?" Moroni asked, concern in his voice, as he raised half out of his blanket.

"Only a nightmare," Mormon sighed. Father, he prayed silently. Help me to finish the record so I can die in peace and join Merena and my children in Thy kingdom. Nervously he threw the cover back and laboriously rose to his feet. He shuffled stiffly to the mouth of the cave and out into the open air, away from the stuffiness of the cave. He looked at the moon. Almost overhead. He sat on a rock, worn blanket over his shoulders, enjoying the quiet stillness of the night. Moroni silently joined him. Stars, normally bright, twinkled pale and faint in the glistening moonlight. Smell of pine and underbrush filled his nostrils. He inhaled deeply. No longer sleepy, his thoughts wandered again to Helaman and Moronihah. He shivered and pulled the tattered blanket more firmly across his once-powerful shoulders. He breathed deeply of the night air and looked again at the panorama of the heavens spread above him from horizon to horizon.

When he lay down the night before, he had been writing of Moronihah. Moronihah, chief captain of the Nephites, was like his father, Moroni—dedicated to preserving the freedom of the Nephite people.

Moronihah, Forty-first year; 50 B.C.

"What will you do?" Captain Lehi asked, rhythmically stroking his sword with the sharpening stone.

Moronihah leaned back and steepled his fingers, gazing unseeing at his hands. "It's my fault. I misjudged the Lamanites," he said. "I thought they would attack the border cities." He shook his head. "That thinking may have cost many lives. We must act quickly so more lives are not lost."

Lehi absently stroked his sword as he waited for his commander to continue.

"As soon as the courier brought news of Zarahemla's fall I sent men to spy on the Lamanite army."

"So, what is happening?"

Pointing to the map, he said. "The Lamanite army captured Zarahemla, Melek, and Ammonihah. They march towards Noah which will open their route to Bountiful." Moronihah stabbed the map with his finger. "We will meet them there, in the center of the land." His voice was harsh as if the words came hard.

Lehi, knowing the mood of his commander, waited.

"Move your army quickly and head the Lamanites before they reach Noah. Your army is more powerful than Coriantumr's. Force him to retreat back towards Zarahemla." Moronihah smiled coldly. "I will force-march my army over the mountains to Sidom. We will cross the River Sidon and be on the west plains ready to meet the retreating Lamanites."

*****

Broken swords and bodies littered the plain. Sound of fighting was done. Moronihah wearily trudged to the riverbank, knelt down and with both hands poured water over his head. Even that didn't clear his head of the tiredness, the killing, the smell of death. He leaned over and dunked his head into the river, swishing it back and forth.

Sound of someone clearing his throat brought him out of the water.

Captain Lehi smiled at him. "A good time for all of us to bathe," he said.

"Even bathing never rids me of the stench of death," Moronihah said, water dripping on his lean body from wet hair. "I sometimes wonder why I'm in this grisly profession."

"For the same reason I am," Lehi said. "Because our fathers were warriors and believed in a strong and free country."

"I know," Moronihah sighed. "And the only way to have a strong and free country is to have a strong army." He shook out his hair, then smoothed it back on his head. Picking up his sword, he started back to the battle area. "The Lamanite army is no more," he said. "And Coriantumr is dead."

"Those who were not killed have surrendered. What do you want me to do with the prisoners."

"I'll take care of them," Moronihah said. He looked at the blue-tinted mountains in the distance. "Bring them here."

"You have trespassed on these lands," Moronihah shouted to the horde of prisoners. "For that, we could execute you. But there's been enough killing. If you will take an oath to return to your own lands and never trespass on Nephite soil again, I will release you so you can return to your wives and families after we have retaken Zarahemla."

Weaponless, bronzed warriors rushed forward to take the oath, until every prisoner had done so.

Lamanite warriors in Zarahemla, when they heard Moronihah's magnanimous offer, yielded the city without a fight. Moronihah, Lehi and the Nephite warriors watched as the remains of the once mighty Lamanite army, carrying their wounded with them, started southward for the Land of Nephi.

Helaman, Forty-second year; 49 B.C.

"We have a problem."

"I know," Helaman said, turning from the window and facing Moronihah. "With the Lamanite army destroyed I thought we could have peace, but it isn't to be. Nephites bicker with Nephites and there is still much contention."

Moronihah laid a friendly hand on Helaman's shoulder "But I think this is a problem easily solved."

"Oh?"

"Yes. What's needed is a chief judge everyone respects."

"There are still more sons of Pahoran. Whom would you suggest?" He caught Moronihah's look. "Oh, no, not I. I am already busy with record-keeping and governing the Church."

Moronihah leaned forward. "Helaman, you are the only one that can do it. The people respect you. None of Pahoran's other sons are capable. Other contenders will drop out when they know you are nominated. After the vote is taken we will again have peace in the land; bickering and contention will stop. Your grandfather, Alma, set the pattern, being both High Priest and Chief Judge—as well as keeping the sacred records."

*****

"I was right, wasn't I," Moronihah said. "The lesser judges voted for your appointment by a large majority."

Helaman nodded morosely. "But the people still have to ratify that appointment." He shook his head as if it were inconsequential. "Something else troubles me."

Moronihah looked at him expectantly.

Helaman looked up at him. "Two things. One, we have a traitor element within the city. Coriantumr told me someone inside opened the gates to the Lamanite army. I intend to find those guilty of treason.

"And, the other?"

"The lawyers, led by Gadianton, grandson of Pachus, lead the opposition to my appointment. Gadianton, like his grandfather, preached for a return to a kingship. His supporters chanted through the streets, 'we want a king.' 'What better time' the lawyers said, 'since there is no one to fill the judgment seat. Gadianton himself stood on the temple steps and shouted to the people that it was time for a change." He picked up a cup of sweet chocolate and took a sip.

"Your Gadianton," Moronihah said, "would like to appoint himself as king."

"How do you know that?" Helaman asked suspiciously.

Moronihah laughed. "I have my ears in the city. And perhaps," he mused, "your two problems are one and the same."

"I've been thinking that myself," Helaman said.

"What have you done about it?"

"What can I do? Because of the laws Mosiah established, we still live in a free land where people can express their opinions, even if those opinions are contrary to what is best for the country."Moronihah grinned.

Helaman looked puzzled. "What have you done?" he asked.

"Not much. I helped a trusted warriors to 'desert' the army He joined Gadianton's band and keeps me informed."

"Is it right to have spies?"

"Not only right but necessary."

"So what have you found out?"

"It is as I suspected."

"What?"

"Gadianton flattered his followers that if they made him chief judge he will place them in positions of power."

"Do they plan violence?"

"Gadianton is much too clever to resort to violence himself, but he will hire someone to kill you so he can take the judgment seat."

Helaman nodded. "That would be his pattern."

*****

"We must act now," the one called Laish said.

"It's too soon after the appointment of Helaman. People will be suspicious."

"No, I say. Helaman must be put out of the way before he gets firmly entrenched."

Moses pretended to stitch his leggings while he listened to the two conspirators. He had met the first man, Laish, but didn't know the other. They were part of the Gadianton group of which he was now a part. He tied off a knot and bit the sinew with his teeth. In the days he had been with them he had heard much of how the band intended to rob and murder to gain power over the people. Another man entered the room.

"Kishkumen," Laish said enthusiastically. "Hanihah and I are arguing about when to take care of Helaman."

Moses looked curiously at the newest arrival. The man's head was too small for his huge body. His face was thin with a high-bridged nose. His mouth, behind a ragged beard, turned downward ruthlessly. The eyes disturbed Moses most: cold gray like the spume of foam from the waves in the east sea. Now they searched restlessly around the room, seeming to take everything in.

"Helaman must be killed," Kishkumen growled.

"I know that," Laish said, "but when?"

Kishkumen raised his eyebrows. "The sooner the better."

Laish slapped the one named Hanihah on the shoulder. "I told you," he laughed derisively. "Kishkumen will get things started."

"Where's Gadianton?" Kishkumen asked brusquely, silencing Laish's laughter.

"He stepped out," said Hanihah.

"Well, I can't wait. Helaman must be taken care of tonight."

"But how?"

"How?" hooted Kishkumen. "You ask how? How was Pahoran taken care of? And the other judges who stood in our way?"

"But how will you get into the judgment hall?" Laish persisted. "Helaman has placed guards at all the entrances."

Kishkumen glanced again around the room, his eyes resting on Moses.

Moses stared back. "Perhaps I can help," he said.

The eyes of the conspirators all turned to him. Kishkumen grinned, exposing crooked teeth.

"I served with the guards. They don't know I have deserted. They will let me pass."

"You'll conduct me to the judgment seat?"

Moses nodded. "And then?"

"Then I will do my job."

He said it so matter-of-factly that a chill coursed up Moses' spine.

"We can't leave from here, though," Kishkumen said. "We want no one to trace our activity back to Gadianton."

"Where?" Moses asked tersely.

Kishkumen laughed. "A planner we have," he chuckled. The laughter was short. "We will meet in the avenue before the temple."

"It will be dark," Moses said. "How will you know me?"

"To avoid suspicion, I'll ask you to guide me to the judgment hall. You answer that you'll charge me a shiblon."

The next few moments were spent arranging routes, then Kishkumen and Moses left by different ways.

There isn't time to get this information to Moronihah, Moses thought. *I'll have to handle it myself.*

He was two blocks from the hall of justice when Kishkumen stepped from the shadows.

"Pardon me," said Kishkumen. "I have a message for Helaman. Would you guide me to the judgment hall?"

"For a price," Moses answered. "It'll cost you a shiblon."

"Agreed," Kishkumen said.

As they walked down the center of the street toward Helaman's office, Moses whispered to Kishkumen. "Wouldn't it be better to take Helaman prisoner instead of killing him?" Though it was dark, he felt the cold eyes of Kishkumen upon him.

"Killing is cleaner," the assassin grunted.

"Well, then let us go on to the judgment seat," Moses said. "I know exactly where Helaman's office is located."

"Good." Kishkumen sounded pleased at the prospect.

Torches lighted the entrance to the hall. Moses nodded to the guards as they passed, then walked quickly up the steps to the hall of justice. Kishkumen paced a half-step ahead, an evil, mocking smile twisting his face.

Moses reached inside his robe for the slim bronze dagger. With a grunt of rage he drove it home. Kishkumen fell without even a groan.

"Guards," Moses cried. He hurried up the steps, calling back over his shoulder. "Take care of him. I must report to Moronihah."

Helaman entered the office before Moses finished his report. "I heard you killed an assassin. What happened?"

Moronihah faced him. "There is not time to talk. We must stop this Gadianton and his robber band before he destroys all we have attempted to do for this people." He faced Moses. "Lead us to the house where Gadianton meets with his fellow conspirators. We must capture them all. If found guilty, they will be executed according to the law."

Moronihah and Moses swept the guards with them as they hurried from the judgment hall. Moronihah himself burst down the door of Gadianton's headquarters. Food scraps and clothing lay in disarray throughout the house. It was empty.

"They have escaped," Moses sighed.

"This Gadianton is smart," Moronihah said. "When Kishkumen didn't return he must have suspected we were on to them. Fearing their destruction, he led them away—probably into the wilderness. We may never find them now."

Cumorah, 385 A.D.

Dawn painted a rosy glow on the hillside. Mormon stood in the cave's entrance, thinking of Helaman—how he judged righteously, bringing prosperity once again to the land.

Mormon sighed. Helaman's wife, Vareena, must have been much like his own Merena. In his writings Helaman praised his wife for her loyalty, her devotion, and her love. He gave her full credit for raising their two sons, Nephi and Lehi—named after their forefathers who had come from Jerusalem so long before. Under Helaman's tutoring Nephi and Lehi trained as scribes—prepared to carry on their heritage as chroniclers of the Nephite record.

Mormon's mood soured. "Gadianton," he hissed and spat into the dirt. "Gadianton proved the overthrow, yes, almost the entire destruction of the people of Nephi," he said to himself. "Oh, if Helaman could have foretold the future, he would have pursued Gadianton and his band until they were destroyed from the earth."

CHAPTER THREE

NEPHI AND LEHI

Cumorah, 385 A.D.

Mormon walked outside the cave. Light of dawn struggled through the tall pines of Cumorah's hillside. He sighed and returned to his favorite writing rock. He sat down and turned the next plate. Firmly-carved characters, even in the pale light, told of Nephi and Lehi, sons of Helaman. *Ah, there were two fine young men,* he thought. *Blessed by their father, they led the missionary movement which prepared the Church for the coming of the Savior. Their experience...*

Zarahemla, Fifty-third Year ; 39 B.C.

"My sons," Helaman said, "Come closer. Before I die I want to give you a blessing." His voice choked with emotion.

Age lay heavy on the white-haired patriarch. Nephi and Lehi crossed the darkened room as Habnah, Helaman's servant, gently raised the old man to a sitting position and propped him up with a pillow. The old chief judge, scribe, keeper of the records, and chief priest looked at his sons with eyes dimmed by many suns.

Nephi and Lehi knelt before him.

"My sons, I am pleased with each of you. You make an old man proud. I have made a difficult decision. You are equal in stature and equal in your testimonies concerning the coming of Jesus Christ. If I could, I would ordain both of you to the holy calling of chief priest to serve our people. But I can't."

Nephi spoke. "Father, I will serve wherever I am called."

"Me, too," Lehi added.

Helaman nodded. "I know." He sighed. "Nephi, because you are the eldest I appoint you to succeed me as chief judge. However, the people must ratify your appointment. As eldest son you will also serve as chief priest and keeper of the records."

He placed a hand on Lehi's arm. "Lehi, you are to share equally in your brother's callings. Support him. When you do, your blessings will also be great. Like your brother you have been faithful from childhood in keeping God's commandments. Your work in the school of the scribes was exemplary."

Helaman laid both hands on Nephi's head. "Through the power of God and His holy priesthood I ordain you a High Priest and appoint you as chief priest and scribe." After Nephi's blessing, in which Helaman promised his eldest son great gifts of the spirit, he placed his hands on Lehi's head. "Lehi, I ordain you a high priest and appoint you as scribe. I bless you to serve Nephi as keeper of the records. Look to your elder brother for counsel. Seek the Lord in prayer as you fulfill your holy calling."

When finished with the blessing, Helaman patted the couch beside him. "Both of you please sit here. My time is short and I want to give you counsel.

"My sons," he said, "though called to separate callings you are to serve equally. Keep God's commandments. Declare His words to the people. Your mother and I named you for our first parents who came out of the land of Jerusalem. Let your names remind you of that first Lehi and Nephi and how they served. Do as they did so your descendants remember you as we remember them."

"Father," Nephi said quietly, "I honor your name as proudly as I bear Father Nephi's name."

"That is one of the greatest blessings a father can have," Helaman said huskily. He cleared his throat. "But more important than honoring my name is to honor your Heavenly Father. Do all you do for the glory of God, not to boast, but to lay up eternal treasures, especially the precious gift of eternal life."

"Father, I will faithfully help Nephi keep the records," Lehi said, "and will protect the plates with my life."

Helaman sighed. "That, too, may be necessary. Gadianton's followers will attempt to wrest the plates from you. They do not value the precious words on the plates but would melt the plates for gold with which to buy earthly treasures. Earthly treasures have no power to save but what is written on the plates has that power if people will apply the teachings to their lives."

"Like the words of King Benjamin?" Nephi asked.

"Yes," responded Helaman. "King Benjamin taught that there is no way for man to be saved except through the atoning blood of Jesus Christ who shall soon come to redeem the world."

"And the words of Alma, our great-grandfather, and his friend, Amulek?" Lehi reminded.

"Those, too," Helaman said. "Remember Amulek's words to Zeezrom in Ammonihah. He said the Lord would come to redeem His people but He would not come to redeem them in their sins."

"But He would come to redeem them from their sins," Nephi finished quietly.

"That is why your faithfulness is so important," Helaman said. "The power to redeem people from their sins comes from God only on conditions of repentance. The Father even sent angels to declare that only the Redeemer has the power to provide salvation for all men. Remember, my sons, that it is upon the rock of our Redeemer, who is Christ, the Son of God, that you must build your foundation. The devil will do all he can to destroy you. He cannot as long as you are built upon that rock. It is a sure foundation and if men build upon it they cannot fail." Helaman's voice was weak.

"Please rest now, father," Nephi said.

"Preach the Gospel," Helaman continued hoarsely. "Teach repentance and the plan of salvation. Serve your fellow men and you will be rewarded by celestial life."

Nephi could hardly hear the last whispered words. He cradled his father's bony shoulders in his hands and gently lowered him on the couch. He stroked Helaman's forehead, brushing the stringy, white hair from his eyes. Then he leaned over and kissed him. "Father, we will be true to our covenants and will spend our days in preaching and calling the people to repentance."

"That is good, Nephi," Helaman whispered. "The Savior comes in just a few more years. Be faithful. Be faithful." His eyes were closed, his breathing slow and measured.

"He looks so peaceful," Lehi whispered.

Helaman's breathing faltered, then stopped. Nephi and Lehi each held one of their father's frail hands.

Cumorah, 385 A.D.

Mormon adjusted his seat, moving a small rock which dug into his bottom. He contemplated what he had written. Nephi and Lehi lived in times so similar to his own. Even with righteous leaders, dissension prevailed. Some trouble was caused by pride as people became wealthy; other dissension came through jealousies and petty grievances. Many people joined the Lamanites and came against the Nephites in battle, finally driving them from the Land of Zarahemla into the Land of Bountiful.

"War," hissed Mormon. "Always war. And always brave men."

He thought of Moronihah, son of Captain Moroni, leading his courageous Nephite army against the Lamanites, and of Nephi, who would rather be a missionary than have the status of chief judge.

Nephi and Lehi, Sixty-second Year; 30 B.C.

Nephi tried to be patient but his thoughts still drifted. He pulled himself back to the words of the man before him. Petty complaints, complaints! The clamor in the hall continued as it had throughout the day, and the day before, and the day before that. Twenty people, all from a village outside the City of Mulek, had spent the day complaining that the government cared only about the cities. According to their complaints they were left without protection or help of any kind.

"Where is the army?" one asked.

"Our village was within the line of march of the Lamanite army and was leveled to the ground."

"My farm was destroyed."

"Plants were torn from the ground. Our crops were all taken by the Lamanites."

"My wife was raped and my children sent to the land of Nephi as slaves."

"Our best men were killed."

"Our sheep were stolen to feed their warriors."

Nephi's head reeled. "Move your possessions into the City of Mulek and I will see what reparations can be made."

*****

Lehi sat with him in his home. Charo, his wife, discretely stayed in the patio, away from the men's talk.

"Lehi, I can no longer serve as chief judge."

"But, why?"

"Those who choose evil are more numerous than those who are righteous. Our nation ripens for destruction."

Lehi nodded. "Yes, they are a stiffnecked people."

"Our laws are corrupted; people have lost respect for the law and I am weary of their iniquity." He sighed. "The judgeship requires so much time that I have neglected my church calling."

"The church is no longer an important part of many people's lives," Lehi said soberly.

"Many who were once righteous have lost their testimonies of God and his concern for them."

"You are right," Lehi said. "The Spirit of the Lord has withdrawn from many people. But why give up the judgment seat? You can help the people best by judging righteously."

"There is too little time for serving people's spiritual needs. I have decided I must devote my full time and energy to the ministry: teaching and calling the people to repentance."

"We will work together," Lehi said.

Cumorah, 385 A.D.

Moroni kindled a small fire in the cave and Mormon gratefully hunkered down next to it. His old bones welcomed the heat. He thought of his abridgment of Nephi's and Lehi's missionary efforts. After Nephi turned over the judgeship to Cezoram, they started preaching in Bountiful, Gid and Mulek. They were inseparable. From morning to evening they preached. Few listened. With little success in their homeland, they finally left their families and went south to Zarahemla.

Zarahemla, Sixty-first year; 30 B.C.

"For the first time since starting our mission, I feel that people listen to us," Lehi exclaimed.

"Isn't it interesting?" Nephi said. "In Bountiful we were scorned. Here, in the midst of the Lamanites and dissenting Nephites, we are welcomed with open hearts."

"Not only are the dissenters reconverted and rebaptized, they also try to repair the wrongs they did in the past."

"The Lord promised us success," Nephi said. "We thought that success would come in Bountiful and became discouraged because it didn't happen there. And all the time God wanted us here in Zarahemla. These are the people who were ready for the Gospel. We must learn to accept God's decisions."

"Even the Lamanites have been receptive." Lehi said.

"They are so willing to listen," Nephi agreed. "We follow the footsteps of Ammon and the sons of King Mosiah. Thousands of Lamanites flock to the Church and desire baptism."

"Can we handle the baptism without additional help?"

"We will ordain priests to assist us."

Morning dawned bright and cloudless. Before the sun rose over the eastern hills hundreds of people lined the Sidon's banks.

The white-robed Nephi and Lehi, followed by similarly garbed priests of Zarahemla, walked into the tepid river until the water was almost to their waists.

"I have goosebumps," Nephi said. "This river bend is where great-grandfather Alma baptized the followers of Limhi and citizens of Zarahemla."

"Now we thrill at baptizing the Lamanites," Lehi said.

Men, women and children entered the river and came out of the water purified, reborn and cleansed.

"With the church strengthened in Zarahemla, the people here are in good hands." Nephi didn't look up from the flickering fire as he and Lehi contemplated what had been accomplished that day.

"You are suggesting?"

"The priests in Zarahemla can continue our missionary efforts among the Lamanites here. Most Lamanites are still in their homeland, the land of Nephi. Our success here is but a prelude to our real mission."

Sparks rose from the fire as he stirred it. "I feel the Lord wants us to go to the Land of Nephi and preach to the Lamanites."

"We will be like the sons of Mosiah," Lehi said humbly.

Nephi clapped him on the shoulder. "You are a choice brother, Lehi. I could not ask for a better companion."

"I didn't realize we would be walking up so many hills," Lehi panted.

Nephi smiled as he walked. "Perhaps you will learn not to eat so much," he said. "This walk will take off some of that stomach."

"If I just had your long legs," Lehi puffed, "I wouldn't need to worry. I take two steps for each of yours." He slowed his pace and wiped his brow with the back of his forearm. "I have to stop," he said, plopping himself on a rock beside the path. "How much further?"

Nephi leaned on his walking stick. "The trail leads to a mountain pass from which we can see the city of Nephi."

Lehi nodded dumbly. He stood and moaned. "Let's go."

Single file they tramped upward along the well-beaten path through the sea of forest—the main route between the land of Nephi and the land of Zarahemla. Nephi, in the lead, thought of the thousands of Lamanite warriors and Nephite dissenters who had used the path to come from the land of Nephi to attack Zarahemla. The path was probably the same path on which Ammon and the Sons of Mosiah walked as they went on their mission to the Lamanites so many years before, and where Alma met them on their return.

"I'd like to see the sun once more," Lehi complained. "Even at midday it never penetrates the thick canopy of trees."

Nephi nodded and continued walking.

No breeze eased the clinging heat. Hordes of mosquitoes arrived with nightfall. Tall trees rose in tiered galleries—splendid cedars, mahoganies, and other hardwoods. As days passed and they continued climbing, hardwoods changed to several varieties of pine. Thick-stalked fireweed bloomed. Bees and flies buzzed incessantly around their heads.

The trail, intersected by gullies, wound ever upward. Underbrush thinned the higher they climbed. At last they broke out onto the crest of a hill. Below them spread a huge valley, broader than the valley of the Sidon. Nephi gazed at the distant hills—almost too far to see in the haze of the high valley.

"This is the land of our forefathers," Nephi said.

"What a beautiful valley," Lehi gasped. "I believe it would take a Nephite a full day just to cross it."

Nephi nodded, not taking his eyes from the valley before them. To the west two gigantic volcanic cones, one perfectly symmetrical, punctured the heavens. Tendrils of smoke puffed into the blue sky, as if the volcanoes prepared to cast hot lava and cinders upon the waiting valley. He took Lehi's elbow, guiding his eyes to the area below the volcanoes. Sparkling in the late afternoon sun were the white-plastered walls of a central city, surrounded by a broad expanse of thatched huts. "That must be the city of Nephi," he said. "Here is where Nephi established his people after leaving the land of our first inheritance."

"Praise the Lord," Lehi breathed.

For long moments they gazed across the valley. Little villages dotted the expanse before them, but invariably their eyes returned to the city nestled close to the western range of mountains. South of the city, and at a lower elevation, a meandering river ended in a sparkling lake. Beyond it a third volcano smoked lazily into the lapis lazuli sky.

"I wonder what kind of welcome we will receive from the descendants of Laman and Lemuel." Nephi shifted the straps of his pack as if to start down into the valley.

Lehi laid a hand on his arm. "Seems to me you won't have to worry about it," he said. "We have a welcoming party."

Nephi looked where Lehi pointed. Toiling up the hill towards them was a detachment of fifty or sixty Lamanite warriors, deadly purpose apparent in their demeanors. Hair was shorn from heads, faces were painted white—making dark eyes appear even more frighteningly dark. Loin cloths made sharp contrast with glistening bronze bodies. The leader wore a green-tinged tunic, with multiple strands of jade necklaces hanging to his waist. In addition to spears which all carried, he carried a feather scepter in his left hand—feathers iridescent red and green in the afternoon sun.

"Shall we run?" Lehi asked.

Nephi put a hand on his brother's arm. "We'll trust in the Lord. At least we will have an escort into the city."

As the warriors approached, Nephi noted that the leader, though tanned as dark as a Lamanite from the burning sun, was really a Nephite—blue eyes gave him away.

His voice was as gruff as his outward appearance. "Why do you trespass into our land? To do so is death!"

A tremor of fear passed through Lehi. He glanced at Nephi. His brother stood like a rock, leaning casually on his staff.

"We come in peace," Nephi said. "God has called us to preach unto this people."

"Yagh," cried the leader of the Lamanites. "We have heard enough of your God. We want to hear no more." He motioned to his men. "Bind them. We take them to Tubilah."

The smell was the worst thing: smell of urine and offal, smell of death and dying, smell of mildew and age. The dirt floor of the cell had been packed hard by the hundreds—or perhaps thousands—of prisoners who had been locked in the place. At least there was light. Inexplicably, the Lamanites left a torch burning in a wall niche. Nephi took the torch and explored each wall. The prison, old but solid, consisted of one large room which could have held a hundred prisoners. Names of countless prisoners were scratched into the walls.

"Lehi," he called. "Come here."

He traced the outline of several names. "Can you read the name? Ammon! This is the jail where Ammon was kept when he came to the Land of Nephi."

"Ammon, King Mosiah's son?"

"No. The Ammon Mosiah sent to find the people of Zeniff. King Limhi put him and his companions in jail until he learned their intentions. This is that jail."

"They are the ones who helped Limhi and his people escape."

"Yes, they and that wily warrior, Gideon."

Tread of heavy footsteps sounded outside the door.

"Maybe they are bringing something to eat," Lehi said.

"I hope so," Nephi said. "It's been more than a day since we had any food."

The plank door squeaked open on its leather hinges. A light-skinned Nephite, flanked by two Lamanite guards, stood in the opening. "I am Aminadab," he said. "Here is water."

"What about food?" Nephi asked.

The man chuckled unpleasantly. "No food for prisoners. You do well to get water."

"Why are we being held prisoner?" Nephi asked.

"Tubilah, son of Tubaloth, dislikes Nephites, especially Nephite missionaries."

"What will he do with us?"

Aminadab shrugged. "That I can't say. Maybe he'll kill you and hold the ex-chief judge for ransom—let your people pay to get him back."

"I demand that we see him," Nephi said.

A smile appeared on Aminadab's face, but was not reflected in his cold eyes. "You demand nothing in my prison." He took the torch from Nephi's hand and left, the two guards slamming the door behind him.

Darkness was oppressing. Days and nights blended into one, with a thin sliver of light under the door being the only difference between day and night. Nephi counted each day, scratching a line on the limestone wall against which he leaned.

"Nephi, I wonder if they are ever going to feed us."

"I have wondered the same thing."

"How many days has it been?"

"We have been here eight days with no food and barely enough water to wet our lips."

"Is there nothing we can do?"

"Pray. The Lord will not let us die. He will free us."

Lehi started an answer but Nephi shushed him. Sound of many footsteps and clamoring voices announced the arrival of a large crowd.

Nephi cried, "Lord, We pray for Thy protection."

Immediately the room became bright—as if filled with flames licking and leaping towards the ceiling, and yet there was no heat. Nephi reached up and felt his hair to make sure it wasn't burning. He turned to Lehi who still wore an incredulous look.

"The Lord answered our prayers in a miraculous way," Nephi said. He faced the door as it opened.

"Look, the prisoners are on fire," someone shouted. All just stood there as if struck with amazement.

Nephi stepped towards them with Lehi following. The Lamanites and dissenting Nephites backed up, keeping their distance from the flames.

"Do not fear," Nephi said. "With this holy fire God has stopped you from killing us."

Dust cascaded from the ceiling and the ground trembled under-foot as an earthquake shook the walls of the prison. Panic-stricken, the Lamanites turned to flee. Before they could move a dark cloud blinded them. Clamoring with fear they crowded into a corner of the huge room.

Nephi and Lehi listened to their cries.

A voice—a small voice, almost a whisper—penetrated to every corner of the prison. "Repent! Repent! Seek no more to destroy the servants I have sent to you."

Again the earth shook and the walls quaked as if they would fall. The cloud of darkness completely obliterated the Lamanites from Nephi's view.

Again the voice: "Repent ye! Repent ye for the kingdom of heaven is at hand. Seek no more to destroy My servants." As if to punctuate the utterance the walls trembled again and the earth shook as if it would crack wide open.

A third time the voice came, again punctuated with quaking and trembling, speaking to the Lamanites—words too wondrous for Nephi to record.

Nephi and Lehi no longer heard the anguished cries of the Lamanites. Their full attention was focused on the voice of the Lord as He spoke directly to them, praising them for their sacrifices in His behalf.

Aminadab, the jailer, stood on the fringe of the Lamanite crowd. In Zarahemla, before his defection, he had belonged to the Church of God. Now he remembered teachings he had once followed. Amazed, he turned about to look at Nephi and Lehi. Even through the cloud of blackness their faces shone, as if they were the faces of angels. Their eyes lifted towards heaven and their lips moved as if talking.

"Look!" Aminadab shouted. He shouted again, trying to be heard above the fearsome clamor of the mob. "Turn and look."

One after another the Lamanites looked where Aminadab pointed. The cloud lifted so they could see Nephi and Lehi. Voices hushed. Except for whispers the prison was silent.

"What does it mean?"

"With whom do they converse?"

Aminadab raised his hands above his head for silence. "They converse with God's angels," he said simply.

"What shall we do?"

"How can we remove this cloud of darkness from us?"

Aminadab, head and shoulders above most of the others, said, "Do what the voice said. Repent. Cry out and confess your sins. Ask the Lord for forgiveness. When you do this the cloud of darkness shall be removed."

A babble of voices filled the prison. Lamanites cried in anguish of spirit. The dark cloud slowly dispersed until the room was radiant with fiery flames encircling Nephi and Lehi. Fear was replaced with amazement, then indescribable joy.

"What is happening?" Lehi asked.

"I'm not sure," Nephi answered. "But I think we are witnessing an outpouring of the Holy Ghost upon these men."

As if from a great distance, yet seeming to burn from within, the quiet voice again spoke: "Peace be unto you. Because of your faith in my Beloved Son you shall have peace."

"Look!" Lehi whispered.

Nephi looked up to see angels descending, mingling and ministering to the Lamanites.

Again the voice engulfed them with its pervasive whisper. "Marvel not at what you have seen. Doubt not what you have witnessed but go forth and minister to your people. Declare unto them all the things which you have seen and heard."

Cumorah, 385 A.D.

Mormon set down the gold plate and sighed. "What a powerful testimony of God's goodness to men," he told Moroni, who had returned with quail for their supper. "Several hundred Lamanites and dissident Nephites were in the crowd in the prison. All witnessed the power of God; all went forth and testified of the things they had heard and seen. Thousands, converted, laid down their weapons and gave up their hatred for the Nephites. So powerful was their testimony that the king, Tubilah, gave the conquered lands back to the Nephites."

Mormon carefully replaced the stack of plates behind the loose stone in the wall. "I am going for a walk," he said.

"Wait. I will join you," Moroni said. They left the cave and walked cautiously to the top of Cumorah—looking down at the lights of a Lamanite settlement in the valley below.

CHAPTER FOUR

NEPHI AND LEHI, (Continued)

Cumorah, 386 A.D.

Mormon cut deeply with the stylus on the plate, then sighed. His heart wasn't in it. He was tired. He toyed with the stylus. Moroni was out hunting food. *I am so old and so tired,* he thought, *Besides, I have written the important things.*

"Bless Moroni, Lord," he whispered. "Preserve him so he can finish the plates."

Sighing again, he slid back several plates until he read again about Nephi and Lehi. His lips moved as he silently read his own words. After the conversion of the Lamanites in the Land of Nephi came a time of peace. Lamanites and Nephites mingled together with no enmity. Crops were bountiful and both nations flourished; the Lord truly prospered His people.

Time of peace was short. Mormon shook his head as he read of the Gadianton robbers coming back into power. Cezoram, the chief justice, and his son who succeeded him were murdered. Gadianton and his band, more than any other influence, proved the destruction of the Nephite people.

"No," Mormon muttered. "It wasn't Gadianton. Gadianton and his band were only tools of Satan. Oh, Lord, how patient You have been with this people. Every time they became righteous You blessed and prospered them. Then, almost without exception, they became wicked and lost their blessings."

Mormon read the words he had written in his abridgement of Nephi's record: "Thus we see that they were in an awful state, ripening for an everlasting destruction."

Zarahemla, Sixty-Ninth Year; 23 B.C.

"Oh, that I might have had my days in the time when Father Lehi first came out of the land of Jerusalem," Nephi cried from his tower. His heart was heavy; his spirit anguished. He had preached in the Land Northward until word came that his wife, Sharo, was ill. He had hurried home to Zarahemla. Part of his sorrow came from a feeling of failure—the people in the Land Northward totally rejected his teachings. Lehi was still there, teaching and preaching, hoping for a miracle like they experienced in the land of Nephi.

As he now knelt on his tower, tears flowed anew as he thought again of his wife's suffering. Sharo had been near death when he arrived in Zarahemla. Fevers ravished her body. One minute she would complain of the heat, sweat pouring from her face, and the next moment she would shake with chills which swept across her tiny, emaciated body. The doctor gave her herbs and medicines from tree bark but nothing seemed to help. Nephi frequented the marketplace, buying fresh fruits and vegetables, but Sharo became thinner and thinner as days passed. She expressed appreciation for his attention, but picked at her food, eating almost nothing. The skin of her hands became transparent, blue vessels which carried her life blood showing plainly.

Compounding the problem was Nephi's infant son. Little Nephi was not yet two. He did not understand why his mother could no longer nurse him. The baby cried so and Nephi was relieved when he finally found a mother whose infant son had died, leaving her not only with milk, but with a hunger for a baby. She promised to take good care of little Nephi until Sharo recovered.

Even priesthood blessings did not seem to help Sharo. Nephi spent much time on his knees in prayer. The rainy season passed bringing long, dry days. Flocks of birds flew overhead, returning to the land northward, and still no improvement in Sharo.

His wife's illness and concern for his young son were not all that weighed on his mind and brought sorrow to his soul. Gadianton's followers had usurped the judgment seats, encouraging everyone to lay aside God's laws. These corrupt judges condemned the righteous and let sinners go free.

Time came when he knew Sharo was dying. Her eyes burned dryly with fever.

"I am no longer beautiful for you," she said one day.

"You are always beautiful for me," Nephi replied, his eyes burning from the tears that filled them. He touched her hot forehead with the palm of his hand. She reached up and laid her hand on his, holding it to her face. A terrible sadness engulfed him, burning in his eyes and in his belly. He did everything he could to keep her alive. When she was no longer able to drink by herself, he held her frail body on his lap and held the cup for her. The weight of her on his lap faded day by day until there seemed to be nothing left but her spirit. In his heart she had died already, and days spent with her fading shell agonized him.

The day came when there was nothing left. Her eyes opened once, then closed to open no more in mortality. Nephi laid her carefully on her pallet and walked out into the dark night, silently thanking God for easing her pain.

Now here he was praying on his tower. "Lord," he cried, "I wish I could have lived in the days when people kept the commandments and hearkened to Your words." He opened his eyes and gazed again over this land he loved. "If I could have lived in those days my soul would have delighted in the righteousness of my people. But I am consigned to these days and my soul is heavy because of people's wickedness."

His prayer was interrupted by a buzz of voices. He stood and looked over the parapet of the tower. Several dozen people lined the roadway outside the gate to his garden. "Why have you gathered here?" he shouted bitterly to them. "Do you come so I can tell you of your sins?"

The people stirred restlessly. Several judges, easily identified by their colorful robes, pushed forward but Nephi gave them no time to speak. "I came to my tower to pour out my soul to God because of my sorrow for your iniquities. You heard my mourning and wondered. Why do you wonder? Because the devil has such a hold on you." He shook his head in anguish. "You follow him who seeks to hurl your souls down to everlasting misery. Why? Repent! Turn to the Lord before it is too late. He has forsaken you because you have hardened your hearts and do not listen to His voice. You have provoked Him to anger against you. Unless you repent, instead of gathering you to Him, He will scatter you forth that you shall become meat for dogs and wild beasts.

"Oh, my people," he mourned. "How could you have forgotten your God? You murder and plunder and steal and bear false witness against your neighbor to get the riches of the world or to be praised of men." He shook his head sadly. "God has told me that if you do not repent He will no longer defend you against your enemies. This great city and all the other Nephite cities will be taken from you."

An astonished murmur rose from the crowd. More people stopped along the highway, swelling the group to almost a hundred.

"You have received more knowledge but the Lamanites are more righteous." Another roar of discontent greeted these words. He ignored it. "Because you sinned against that knowledge they will be better off than you. The Lord will be merciful to them and will lengthen out their days and increase their numbers in the land. Unless you repent, blind and wicked as you are, you will be destroyed."

He glared at the judges in their bright, flowing robes and feather headdresses. Pointing with his finger, he cried, "You Gadianton judges are especially condemned because of your wickedness. You have corrupted the laws. The common people no longer get justice from you. You have become wealthy by bribe-taking and by interpreting the law in your own favor. You have desecrated the very laws you are sworn to uphold. Unless you repent you shall lose your riches and shall perish."

Angry shouts came from the judges. They stepped forward as if to come pull Nephi from his tower.

He raised his hand to stay them. "Hold. I do not say these things of myself. God has made them known to me."

Shouts and curses came from the judges. "Seize this man," one cried. "Bring him to be judged so he can be condemned for the crimes he has committed."

Another shouted, "Why do you let this man revile against our laws and our people?"

A robed judge pushed to the front and faced the crowd. "How can you allow this man to speak so?" he questioned. "He condemns all the people. He has predicted your destruction—that our great city will be taken from us. You and I know this is impossible. We are powerful and our cities are great. No enemy is strong enough to overpower us."

Angry men pushed forward from the highway to surround the tower upon which Nephi stood.

But other voices arose. "Let him alone. I believe he speaks the truth. What he predicts will happen if we don't repent."

"He testified truly concerning our iniquities. Unless we repent the judgments he has predicted will come upon us."

"If he were not a prophet he would not have testified concerning these things. Let him alone. He knows what things will befall us as well as he knows our sins."

The judges, fearing the crowd, stepped back, looking hatefully up at Nephi.

Seeing that some now listened to his words, Nephi continued. He told them the story of Moses whom God gave power to part the Red Sea. "If He gave Moses such power, why do you say God has given me no power that I may know concerning the judgments that shall come upon you except you repent. You not only deny my words but deny the words Moses spoke when he predicted the coming forth of the Messiah! Did he not bear record that the Son of God should come? Did he not predict that just as the brazen serpent was lifted up in the wilderness the Son of God would also be lifted up? Just as those who looked upon that serpent should live, so those who accept the Son of God shall have eternal life."

Nephi waited for quiet then again spoke. He quoted from many prophets concerning the coming of the Son of God. "Our father, Lehi, was driven from Jerusalem because he testified of these things. Nephi and most of your forefathers down to the present time testified of the coming of Christ and rejoiced as they prepared for that day."

He looked over the now silent crowd and sighed. "You know these things. You cannot deny them unless you lie. But even with all the evidences you have you reject the truth and rebel against God. For that you stand condemned. Instead of laying up treasures in heaven you have heaped up earthly treasures which shall bring you wrath on the day of judgment. Your everlasting destruction—brought on by your murders and wickedness—is already upon you."

He paused as if listening, then looked sadly down upon the crowd. "The Lord has just revealed to me that the chief judge has been murdered by his brother—even now he lies in his blood on the judgment seat." Murmurs of incredulity rose from those below. Nephi silenced them with a wave of his hand. "Both the dead judge and his brother, who seeks to be chief judge, belong to Gadianton's secret band." Seeing the looks of disbelief, Nephi shook his head. "If you don't believe me, go see for yourself."

Several men detached themselves from the crowd. "We will go," a man shouted. "We will find out whether this man is a prophet of God."

Another cried, "If he really saw in vision that the chief judge is dead we will believe his words. We will know God commanded him to prophesy and call us to repentance."

Five men ran to the judgment hall: Anton, Ezias, Chemish, Gilgal and Helam. Out of breath they burst into the hall and stopped, astonished. The chief judge, limbs askew, lay on the steps before his throne. His blood formed a scarlet rivulet across the floor, puddling in a low place before the dias.

"Nephi was right," Ezias whispered. He dropped to his knees.

"I didn't believe but he spoke the truth," Chemish said as he joined Ezias on the floor.

Helam knelt beside them. "I fear God's judgment, of which Nephi spoke, shall come upon this people."

They were so intent upon their deliberations that they didn't hear the voices of the king's servants and guards behind them. "These are the men who have murdered the judge. God has smitten them that they could not flee from us."

Roughly the guards pulled the five to their feet, bound them, and dragged them from the judgment hall.

The chief judge has been slain but his murderers are in prison, read the proclamation sent throughout the city.

The funeral was grandiose. Dignitaries from great distances came to pay homage to the slain chief judge. Befitting a noble of the Gadiantons, lavish displays of flowers, feathers, jade jewelry and gold surrounded the sarcophagus containing the corpse. Attendants killed the judge's wife and four servants and laid them beside him in ornate splendor to provide company for his journey. Bowls of food were placed in the tomb to provide nourishment as they made their way to the spirit world.

The judges who had been at Nephi's tower asked the guards, "When we heard the chief judge was dead we sent five men to investigate. They have not reported back. Have you seen them?"

"We know nothing about the five you sent but we have the chief judge's five murderers in prison."

The judges looked at one another. "Bring them to us," they commanded.

"These are not the murderers," one said as Anton, Helam, Chemish, Ezias and Gilgal, chained and bloodied by beatings, were brought before them.

"What happened?" a judge asked.

Anton answered. "We ran to the judgment hall as commanded. When we saw the chief judge dead we were astonished and fell to our knees. Before we could stand and report back to you the guards threw us into prison."

"Who murdered him?"

"We don't know," Chemish said. "We did as you desired and found him dead, just as Nephi prophesied."

"Prophesied? Bah!" the judge spat derisively. "Nephi conspired with someone to kill the judge and then declared it to us as if he were prophesying. He is trying to convert us."

"Or to exalt himself as a prophet," another responded. "We will make him confess his collusion and name the true murderer."

"How would he have done this?" Anton asked his friends. "He was on his tower since morning."

"I believe he spoke words of truth," Gilgal said quietly. "He is not a liar."

"I also believe him," Ezias said. "He is innocent of any wrongdoing. His concern is for us."

"Bah!" the judge said. "Guards. Release these five men. They are misguided but innocent of murder. The real murderer is Nephi or one of his associates. Bind him and bring him before us."

Nephi offered no resistance, submitting with quiet dignity. Cords bound his arms to his sides but he stood fearlessly before the judges.

"Yesterday," the judge said, "you predicted the murder of the chief judge. It is our belief you conspired with someone to kill him. Who is the murderer?"

A second judge spoke up. "Confess your fellow conspirators and we will grant you your life."

Nephi shook his head in disgust. "You fools, you uncircumcised of heart, you blind and stiff-necked fools, how long do you think God will allow you to continue in sin? You ought to mourn and howl because of the great destruction which awaits you. I testified to you of his murder as a witness to you that I know of your wickedness. Now you say I conspired with someone to murder your chief judge. You use this as an excuse to kill me. Let me show you another sign and see if you still seek to kill me."

He paused as if in contemplation. "Go to the house of Seantum, brother of Seezoram. Ask him if I conspired with him to kill his brother. He will deny it. Then ask him if he murdered his brother. He will act astonished and declare his innocence.

Examine him and you will find bloodstains on his cloak. Ask him where the blood came from, and if it isn't the blood of his brother, the chief judge. Seantum will become pale as a ghost. Accuse him again of the murder and in his fear he will confess. He will also tell you that I knew nothing concerning the matter. Then you shall know that God sent me to tell you these things."

Cumorah, 386 A.D.

Moroni had returned with food. Mormon watched as his son prepared some fruit to eat.

"What are you working on now?" Moroni peeled a papaya and handed it to Mormon.

"Abridging the writings of Nephi and Lehi. I was just writing of Nephi praying on his tower and of his prophecy concerning the murder of Seezoram by his brother."

"As I recall it happened as Nephi predicted. After Seantum's confession, Nephi and the five messengers were released."

"True." Mormon bit into the tasty, yellow and ripe fruit. He wiped his lips with the back of his hand. "Many believed Nephi after this demonstration of God's power. Some said he was a god because his prophecy came true."

"But the interesting thing to me," Moroni said, "is that most of the people continued in their wickedness. Satan really had a firm grip on their hearts."

Zarahemla, Sixty-ninth year; 23 B.C.

Nephi, once again a free man, waited as the people left the square. He walked towards his house, almost empty now that Sharo was dead. I must not think of her death, he thought as he walked. I must think of young Nephi and the future of this people.

His thoughts were dominated by the Nephites' secret works of darkness, murderings, plunderings and wicked ways. What do I do, Father? he breathed. How can I help this people to repent? My efforts seem so futile against all the wickedness and corruption.

His meditations were interrupted by a quiet voice speaking to his consciousness: *Blessed are you, Nephi, for what you have done. You have tirelessly declared My word unto this people, have devoted your life to My service and have kept My commandments without fear of others. Because of your steadfastness, I will bless you forever. I will make you mighty in word and deed, in faith and in works. All things shall be done according to your word, for you shall not ask that which is contrary to my will.*

You are Nephi and I am God. You shall have power to call down famine, pestilence, and destruction upon this people, according to their wickedness. If you say unto this temple, "Be rent in twain," it shall be done. And if you say unto this mountain, "Be cast down and be smooth," it shall be done. And if you say for Me to smite this people, it shall come to pass.

I give you power that whatsoever you seal on earth shall be sealed in heaven, and whatsoever you loose on earth shall be loosed in heaven. Declare unto this people that the Lord God, the Almighty, says, "Unless you repent you shall be destroyed."

The voice left him as suddenly as it had come. Nephi gazed around. He had been totally unaware of his surroundings but now found himself standing before the temple. Slowly he walked up the steps into his office. He carefully wrote down the words God had spoken to him. Power to seal on earth and in heaven! Power over this people! Power to bring famine as punishment for wickedness!

He looked down at his hands. They were still mortal hands, his hands, but now they held awesome, immortal power. He knelt on the stone floor. "Father," he prayed. "I will wisely use the power Thou has given me. I will not abuse Thy trust in me."

Start now! came the word.

Now?

He didn't go home. Calling for a runner he sent a note to the woman caring for his son, Nephi. Another message went to Lehi's home with excerpts of God's revelation. *I burn within to preach to this people,* he wrote. *I will preach repentance, hoping to prevent their destruction. Join me when you can.*

He walked back through the city, stopping wherever he found people gathered, preaching the word to them. "Unless you repent," he cried, "the Lord says you will be destroyed." To his horror none listened.

Cumorah, 386 A.D.

Mormon sighed as he abridged the words from the plates. He empathized with Nephi. He had felt similar frustration when he called his people to repentance and they had not listened. He wrote quickly with the stylus.

"Listen," he told Moroni, as he lifted the plate and read aloud the summary he had written.

"When Nephi declared the word unto them, they hardened their hearts and would not hearken unto his words. They reviled against him and sought to cast him into prison, but the power of God was with him and they could not take him. He was conveyed out of their midst, carried forth in the Spirit from multitude to multitude, declaring the word of God until he had declared it unto all the people in the land. No one listened and obeyed the word. Instead, contentions developed throughout the land and people began to kill each other with the sword."

Zarahemla, Seventy-second year; 20 B.C.

"Lord, stop our people from destroying themselves," Nephi prayed. "This fighting, brought on by Gadianton's robber band, has been almost continuous for more than a year. Thousands have been killed. Rather than let them continue killing each other, Lord, send a famine to the land that will stir the people to repent and turn to Thee."

Nephi's prayers continued through every awake moment. The dry season ended. Time came for rains to fall, but none fell. For months no rain watered the earth. Ground was parched. Nothing grew in the prepared fields. Only dry dust was harvested. Trees in the forest, usually filled with papayas and mangoes and coconuts, were barren. People stopped fighting among themselves and worked together to provide food for their families. Few traveled on the dusty roads and trails.

Nephi went between his home and the temple, suffering as much as anyone from the famine. "The land is an inferno," he said to his son. The younger Nephi was too young to understand but at least Nephi felt he had someone to talk to. "No birds fly—not even the buzzard. Dust haze hangs over the valleys. People stay in their homes, searching out every bit of shade."

The sun was directly overhead as he walked to the temple. Dust, whipped into frenzied dances, reached high into the brassy noon sky. The same dust filled his eyes and ears, scratched along skin already parched and burned. People lay in the street, arms and legs thin as saplings. Flies crawled in eyes, mouth and ears, searching for moisture. Scabby herds of goats and sheep, ribs prominent against taut skin, searched out bits of scant vegetation. Sand drifts in the streets covered mounds of trash. Overhead the sun moved dimly through a pale yellow haze.

He noticed the thin-faced children, grotesque, stomachs bloated, legs spindly as bamboo shoots, gazing unseeing into the distance. He shook his head sadly. Many children under two years of age already had died in the famine. *This is my doing,* he anguished. *Was I right? Should I have called down a famine upon this people? Perhaps they would have repented without it.* In the temple he knelt on the cool stone. *Lord, was I justified? Was the famine necessary? Should I ask Thee to lift it? Please, Lord, comfort my soul.*

"Nephi, my son," came the sweet but quiet voice into his consciousness. "The time is not yet. Wait. The people will yet repent of their iniquity and return to Me."

In the next months thousands died. Inexorably the survivors' minds turned back to God and his goodness.

"Remember Nephi's prophecies?" some cried.

"We must repent and call upon God," others whispered. "If we don't we will all die."

A delegation led by Anton appeared before the chief judge. "Please, your eminence, our people die like dung flies. We no longer have strength to even bury the dead. Nephi predicted the famine. He predicted our destruction if we didn't repent. He can ask God to end the famine. God will listen to him. Plead with Nephi to do so."

Ezias added, "Say to him we know he is a man of God."

"If he doesn't end the famine," said Gilgal, "all he spoke concerning our destruction will be fulfilled."

The judge, torn between his pride and the certain death of his people, went to Nephi's home. Emaciated and dressed in his cheapest clothing, he presented a sorry picture. Nephi, Lehi, and young Nephi, his eight-year-old son, looked at him with pain-filled eyes.

"I beg you, as a prophet of God, to turn away this famine," he said. "Our people die in the streets. Women no longer have suck for their babies. Our only hope is that God will have mercy on us and cause rain to fall."

Nephi, after the judge left, fell on his knees. Lehi and young Nephi joined him, prostrated on the floor.

"Father," he cried. "The people have repented. Gadianton's band is now extinct. Because of their repentance and humility, Lord, I ask Thee to turn away Thy anger. Send forth rain upon the earth that fruit and grain will once again grow and feed these, Thy people." For many minutes he prayed, asking the Lord to once more see if the people would serve Him. While still on his knees he heard the wind die. Light in the room dimmed. He looked out. Clouds, blowing in from the sea, obscured the sun. First tentative drops of rain spattered into the dust of the street.

Cumorah, 386 A.D.

Mormon sighed. "Oh, that the people would have continued in their humility," he muttered.

Moroni was sympathetic. "Didn't the people rejoice and glorify God?"

"For a short time. They even esteemed Nephi as a prophet, having great power and authority. But after three years of peace, contention again reared its ugly head. Nephi and Lehi, having daily communication with God, were able to put it down. But in a very short time dissident Nephites joined with wicked Lamanites in searching out Gadianton's satanic plans. Murder and plunder brought fear to the righteous. People once again forgot God and were ripe for destruction."

"That was only seven years before the Savior was born," he whispered. He turned the plate and wrote: "God in His goodness blesses and prospers those who put their trust in him. But at the very time in which He blesses and prospers them many harden their hearts and forget the God who has blessed them. Unless God chastens his people with many afflictions they will not remember Him. Men are quick to do iniquity and slow to do good."

Mormon handed the stylus to Moroni. "You write." He dictated: "I would that all men might be saved, but in the great and last day there are some who shall be cast out from God's presence. These shall be consigned to a state of endless misery, fulfilling God's words: They that have done good shall have everlasting life; and they that have done evil shall have everlasting damnation."

Mormon stared unseeing into the distance while Moroni waited. "Because of that same evil spirit," he whispered. "My people have all been destroyed."

Moroni took his father's bony and wrinkled hand.

Mormon, through his tears, smiled into his son's eyes. "But God sent even another prophet to call the people to repentance: the Lamanite, Samuel."

CHAPTER FIVE

SAMUEL, THE LAMANITE

Eighty-sixth Year; 6 B.C.

An insistent knock aroused Nephi. Grumbling to himself, he went to the door. A tall Lamanite stood there. His black hair, with some gray showing on the temples, receded over a high forehead. Below heavy brows, his eyes were obsidian black, deep and unfathomable. Exposed through his loose tunic was a bronzed, muscular body. Nephi was impressed. The man before him was the epitomy of strength and character. "What is it?"

"I have come from the land of Melek," the man replied. "My name is Samuel. I am great-grandson of the Lamanite woman, Abish, and Ammon, son of King Mosiah. My grandfather, Samuel, after whom I was named, was your grandfather's friend when he led the two-thousand sons of Ammon."

Nephi smiled, extended his hand, and stepped aside. "Come in. Welcome to my house." He stepped inside. "My father spoke often of his father's friend, Samuel. 'A loyal friend and mighty man of God.' Wait, I'll call my brother and son."

In a few minutes Lehi and the younger Nephi joined them. When all were comfortably seated, Nephi asked Samuel, "Why have you come to Bountiful?"

"The Lord has called me to preach repentance to the Nephite people," he said simply. "I want to pattern my life after your great-grandfather, Alma." The Lamanite face didn't show any emotion except intenseness of purpose.

"Tell me how the Lord called you," Nephi said.

A dreamy look came into Samuel's eyes. "I was on the way from Melek to my father's village," he said, "and ..."

*****

Samuel cowered on the ground; fear blanched his bronzed face. A dark cloud filled the air around him, stifling his breathing. Rumblings like thunder roared from the cloud. Shafts of lightning briefly lighted the surrounding air, then receded.

"Samuel!" The voice reverbrated the air like a thunder clap. Samuel looked up into the darkness. A light, glowing bright as lightning, centered in the cloud.

"Samuel." The rumbling voice came again. "Do not fear. I bring you good tidings. Rise up from the ground."

Quaking, unsure what was happening, Samuel stood on trembling legs. Darkness had been replaced by light, and in the center of the light, almost brighter than he could look upon, was the figure of a man.

"Samuel," the angel, or at least that's what Samuel presumed the personage to be, said his name for the third time. "The Lord calls you to cry repentance to the Nephite people in the city of Zarahemla. He said: Unless they repent I will take away My word and withdraw My Spirit. I will turn the hearts of their brethren against them. Four hundred years shall not pass away before I cause them to be smitten.

Still quaking under the angel's voice, Samuel tried to memorize the words as the angel continued to quote the Lord:

Wo unto Zarahemla. If it were not for the righteous who live there, I would cause fire from heaven to come down and destroy it. Most of the people of Zarahemla harden their hearts against me and will not listen. The time will come when the righteous are cast out. Then Zarahemla shall be ripe for destruction. Blessed are they who will repent, for them will I spare.

*****

"He said many other things and then he was gone," Samuel said quietly.

The young Nephi served Nephi, Lehi and Samuel cups of hot chocolate, then sat and listened with his father and uncle.

Samuel took a sip of the sweet drink. "I didn't realize how long I had been in the angel's presence until he was gone and I noticed the sun had set behind the mountains."

Nephi sighed. "Lehi and I have preached to this people for twenty-five years, calling the people to repentance, pleading with them to reconcile themselves to God."

"Some do become righteous for a few years," Lehi said drily. "Then something tempts them and they revert to their wicked ways. I truly believe Satan has a stranglehold on this people."

"What do you think, Nephi?" the older Nephi said to his son.

The younger Nephi shook his head. "I have seen few righteous people. Those few who are righteous left Zarahemla and came to Bountiful."

Samuel listened intently to what the youth said. "How old are you, son?" he asked.

Nephi looked at his father and uncle before replying. "I am almost twenty."

"Not much younger than your great-grandfather Helaman when he led the two-thousand sons. My grandmother's brother, Ammon, was one of those he called his sons. He was your age."

Young Nephi looked embarrassed. Nephi interrupted. "What of your people? Have they remained in righteousness."

"Yes," Samuel said humbly. "The people of Ammon keep the commandments of God according to the Law of Moses." He looked at the brothers. "Because you converted the Lamanite people, the angel told me to come here to see you. Now I go to Zarahemla."

"I'm glad you came here first," Nephi said. He looked at Lehi for confirmation. "We will accompany you. I have a home in Zarahemla which I have not seen in more than a year. Each time I go there I am saddened by the decadence which has claimed people. So I find excuse to stay in Bountiful."

"The Lord says some who live there are righteous."

"A few. Many people were converted and some have not backslid." He crossed his legs and leaned back on his stool. "As chief priest I suppose I should live in Zarahemla but I prefer Bountiful. More righteous people are here."

"I would like to go, also," the younger Nephi said.

Nephi nodded his head. "You have finished scribe training. I see no reason why you can't go with us. This will be your first missionary experience."

His son breathed a sigh of relief.

The trip overland took thirteen days. Nephi and Lehi had traveled the trail to Zarahemla many times, but everything was still new and exciting for the younger Nephi. He loved the chattering monkeys and raucous parrots. He was amazed at the tall pine trees and high mountains over which they hiked. The trail wound by a beautiful waterfall. They drank from the clear stream and bathed in its cool waters.

As they rested beside the waterfall, Samuel continued his story of the angel. Nephi was especially interested in the prophecies concerning the coming of the Savior. "The angel said the time spoken of by all the prophets is almost upon us," Samuel said excitedly. "He said we should see the sign of the Savior's birth in just five years."

"Five years," mused Nephi, "and the people so unready." He looked at Samuel. "What signs signal His coming?"

"Great lights in heaven—lights so bright that in the night when he comes there will be no darkness. It will seem to be only one day, though it will be one day and a night and another day."

"Will people know it's the time?" asked the young Nephi.

"Yes," replied Samuel. "The sun will rise and set so people will know of a surety that there are two days and a night, even though the night shall not be darkened."

"That is the night the Savior will be born?" Lehi asked.

Samuel nodded. "That is what the angel told me."

"Is that all?" Nephi asked.

"No. There will be many signs and wonders in the heavens," Samuel said. "Also a new star—one you have never seen before."

That was interesting to Nephi. He considered himself to be a fairly good astronomer and had built a tower in his own yard to view the heavens. "Alma and Amulek also predicted the Savior's death. Did the angel say anything about that?"

Samuel nodded sadly. "When He dies the sun, moon and stars shall be darkened and refuse to give light. There shall be no light upon the entire face of the land until He rises again from the dead."

"Alma said that would be three days."

"During the three days there shall be thunderings and lightnings and great tempests. The earth will shake and tremble. Mountains will become valleys, and valleys will become mountains. Highways will be destroyed; cities will become desolate. Graves shall open and the dead shall rise. Saints will appear to many people."

"What a glorious—yet terrible—time that will be," breathed Nephi.

The sky was cloudless as they entered the valley of the Sidon. From the foothills where they stood they could see the ribbon-like river, black under the noontime sun, meandering through the valley.

The four missionaries built a brush shelter on the river's banks near Zarahemla. They bathed in the Sidon's refreshing waters and lay on large rocks to let the sun dry them.

"We will have greater freedom of movement here and can avoid the city's pestilence," Nephi said, his eyes closed as sun and faint breeze dried the water from his skin.

"What are your plans?" Lehi asked Samuel.

"I will preach to the people wherever I find them." He rose to his feet, shaking water from his long, black hair.

The elder Nephi nodded. "The temple square in Zarahemla is always filled with people. The marketplace should be crowded tomorrow. We can start there."

"You're going with me?" Samuel asked.

"Of course," Lehi laughed. "We wouldn't miss the opportunity for missionary work. Why did you think we came?"

* * * * *

Flames reached skyward from the small fire before the shelter. The four men were silent. Few words had been spoken all evening—just the normal courtesies as they prepared supper.

Nephi sighed. "Preaching to the people of Zarahemla is as discouraging as our missionary journey to the land Northward."

"No one listened," Lehi said.

"I was most surprised by the rudeness," the younger Nephi said. "For the first time in my life I have been spit upon."

Samuel didn't say anything. They all looked at him. His eyes were downcast as he looked into the fire. He raised his head and glanced at the three, then lowered his eyes again. After a few minutes, he spoke. "The people of Zarahemla not only did not listen to me, but they cursed me and struck me. Among my own people I have never been treated so badly." He reached for a stick and stirred the fire. "This afternoon I was ready to depart for my home in Melek."

"And tonight?" Nephi asked gently.

Samuel stuck out his chin. "I am not a quitter. I will preach repentance to this people as the angel commanded."

Nephi and his brother smiled. "Good."

The younger Nephi was not so sure. "But why? They rejected the message. Why not shake the dust from our feet and have God destroy the city?"

"The Lord has not yet given up on Zarahemla," Nephi said gently to this son. "Neither should we."

The next day they stayed close to Samuel. "We can at least protect him from the mob," Nephi whispered to his son.

"Brothers and sisters, the Lord told me to tell you to repent, or He would destroy this entire city!"

Nephi listened intently as the tall Lamanite continued his sermon before the temple.

"Turn to God or be brought into bondage by your enemies. The Lord is a jealous God and will visit iniquities upon you unless you repent."

"Boo."

"Go back to your own land, Lamanite."

"Who are you that we should be judged of you?"

"Away with you. Leave our city."

Samuel stood on the temple steps, stoically accepting the verbal abuse from the hostile crowd.

Nephi was worried. He knew the temper of these people. He pushed through the angry crowd and stood beside Samuel. "I am Nephi, chief priest of God's Church in Zarahemla," he cried. "Listen to this man's message. It comes from God."

"We need no chief priest."

"Boo."

"Run him out of town."

"Lamanite lover! Run them both out."

"Since when does God speak to the heathen Lamanites?"

"Come, Samuel." Nephi gently took the Lamanite's elbow and propelled him past the hostile crowd, ignoring their glowering looks and raised fists. Lehi and the younger Nephi joined him, one before and one following.

"Not one person listened," Samuel said as they walked towards their camp. "The Lord called me to preach repentance to this people but I am having no success." He smiled wryly. "Yours are the only friendly faces I have seen in Zarahemla."

Nephi shook his head. "For over thirty years, ever since my father set me apart as chief priest, I have devoted my life to this people. My hair has become gray as I have preached repentance to them." He shrugged his shoulders and sighed. "And yet, the people are more wicked now than they have ever been." He looked into the opaque, black eyes of the Lamanite. "Samuel, your message is critical. Try one more day."

"You feel I do not waste my time?"

"No," Nephi said. "We do not waste our time when we preach repentance and the plan of salvation. Someone will listen." His eyes had a faraway look in them. "Abinadi preached a similar message almost one hundred and fifty years ago. As far as we know only one man listened to Abinadi and repented of his sins. That was my great-great-grandfather, Alma." He paused again in thought. "And his son, my great-grandfather, Alma—his message to the people of Ammonihah was also the same. Again, very few listened. One who did was Amulek who converted Zeezrom and those two became great missionaries of the Lord in spreading his word to the people. Samuel, you don't know whose life you will touch with your message. Your time is important, even if you only convert one soul."

"Destruction shall surely come to this people," Samuel cried the next day. "Nothing can save you except repentance and faith on the Lord Jesus Christ who shall come into the world and be slain for His people. An angel sent me to declare this to you."

The last words were drowned out by cries and hisses. A burly Nephite, dark-haired with full beard, climbed the temple steps to stand before Samuel. "We don't need your message, Lamanite." He spat in Samuel's face.

Samuel wiped his face with his sleeve and stepped back to stand between Nephi and Lehi. Angry men pushed up the steps, grabbed the missionaries and dragged them down the steps. Nephi's head slammed into the rock stair.

He woke up lying in the dust outside the city. He felt soft hands on his forehead and opened his eyes to see his son gently bathing his face. "What happened?" he groaned.

"You were carried by the mob and thrown through the gates of the city," his son said.

"Samuel?" Nephi asked fearfully.

"He was badly beaten but will live," his son answered. "They told him that if he came back to the city they would kill him. Lehi wasn't hurt. He went with Samuel to the river to soak Samuel's bruises. They left me to tend to you."

The four sat silently around the campfire nursing their hurts, engrossed in their own thoughts. No one cared to speak.

Samuel broke the silence. "I have decided to return to my people in Melek," he announced flatly.

"I don't blame you," Nephi sighed. "You have done all you could to follow the angel's instructions."

Nephi slept fitfully—not because of his aching head or
the uncomfortable bed, but because of the destruction he knew
must come to his people. He was awakened by a touch on the
shoulder. He sat up. The fire was dead, though a few coals glowed
like animal eyes in the dark.

A whisper came to him. It was Samuel's voice. "The Lord
spoke to me in a dream. He told me to return again to
Zarahemla and to prophecy whatsoever things came into my
heart."

Nephi smiled in the darkness. "Praise God," he
whispered. "He has not given up on my people."

The gates of Zarahemla were closed to them. No matter
how they pleaded, the guards would not let them in. "You disrupt
the peace of our city," they were told.

"Now what do we do?" young Nephi asked.

"Since I cannot go inside to preach, I will preach from
the wall," Samuel said.

While Samuel climbed the wall from the outside, the
three Nephites hurried around to the south gate. They had no
trouble getting inside. In the square they shouted to the people.
"Samuel, the Lamanite is on the east wall."

Nephites, some angry, others curious, milled towards
the wall. Samuel, silhouetted against the morning sun, had
already begun his discourse.

"I speak the words God puts into my heart," he shouted.
His voice carried clearly to the fringes of the crowd where Nephi
stood with his son. "He told me to tell you that the sword of
justice hangs over you and four hundred years will not pass
away until that sword falls. Then your people will be no more.
The angel said nothing can save you except repentance and faith
on the Lord Jesus Christ, who surely shall come into the world."
Samuel went on to recount all the angel's words which he had
previously told Nephi.

Nephi and his son, bark paper spread before them,
carefully wrote Samue"l's words, recording the message for
posterity.

"Because of your wickedness and abominations,"
Samuel continued, "the Lord of Hosts cursed this land. From
this time forward, whoever hides his treasures in the
earth—unless it is a righteous man who hides them up for the
Lord—shall find them no more. Hearken to my words, people of
Zarahemla. The Lord said you are cursed because you set your
hearts on your riches and did not hearken unto God who gave

them to you. God blessed you with abundance but you have forgotten who gave it to you. Instead of thanking God for your riches, your hearts swell with pride, bringing you to commit all kinds of iniquities. You are worse than the people of old who mocked and cast out the prophets."

Samuel continued to recount to them their sins. Perceiving their indifference, he cried, "Oh, you wicked and perverse generation—you wicked and stiffnecked people—how long do you suppose the Lord will have patience with you? How long will you let yourselves be led by foolish and blind guides? How long will you choose darkness rather than light? God's anger is already kindled against you."

He spoke again of the slipperiness of their riches and how they would lose all that they had. "Behold, your days of probation are past. You have procrastinated the day of your salvation until it is too late and your destruction is now made sure. You have sought happiness in iniquity, contrary to the nature of God's righteousness. I pray the Lord's anger will be turned away from you and that you will repent and be saved."

Samuel then predicted the birth of the Savior and the signs of his coming, the same as he had told Nephi. Then his voice softened. "Whosoever shall believe on the Son of God shall have everlasting life. The Lord commanded me that I should prophesy these things unto you. He said to me, Cry unto this people, repent and prepare the way of the Lord."

He waited until the noise subsided. "Because I am a Lamanite and have spoken to you the words the Lord commanded me to speak, and because it is hard against you, you are angry with me and seek to kill me." He raised to his full height. "But you shall hear my words. I came upon the wall of this city to tell you the judgments of God await you because of your iniquities, and that you might know the conditions of repentance; also that you might know of the coming of Jesus Christ, the Son of God, the Father of heaven and earth, the Creator of all things from the beginning; and that you might know the signs of His coming, that you might believe on His name. If you believe on His name, and repent of your sins, you will have a remission of your sins through Him."

He looked over the now silent crowd. "I give you one more sign, a sign of the Savior's death. For He must surely die that salvation may come. His death redeems all mankind from the first death—that spiritual death by which, by the fall of Adam, all men were cut off from the presence of the Lord and are dead both as to things temporal and things spiritual. Christ's resurrection brings them back into the Lord's presence. His death brings to pass the condition of repentance, that whoever repents is not hewn down and cast into the fire. Those who do not repent are cast into the fire, which is the second death, for they are cut off again as to things pertaining to righteousness. Therefore, repent, lest by knowing these things and not doing them you shall bring upon yourselves condemnation and this second death."

Samuel then recounted again the signs of Christ's death that he had shared with Nephi around the campfire. "The angel said that many shall see greater things than these. Because of these signs there should be no cause for unbelief among the children of men. Those who believe will be saved and those who will not believe will have a righteous judgment come upon them because they bring upon themselves their own condemnation."

He looked again over the restless crowd. "Remember that whoever perishes, perishes unto himself. Whoever does iniquity does it unto himself. God gave you knowledge of good and evil and made you free so you can choose for yourself. You may choose good and be restored unto that which is good or you can choose evil and have evil restored to you. About you, the Lord said, If they will not repent I will utterly destroy them because of their unbelief. As surely as the Lord lives these things shall be."

Nephi watched the angry reaction to Samuel's words. Judges, dressed in garish robes and headresses, moved through the crowd, inciting them, whipping them into a mob spirit. They angrily picked up stones from the street and cast them at the figure high on the wall. The stones missed. Arrows streamed at Samuel. They also missed. Samuel seemed to have a charmed life.

"It's a miracle," some said.

When the judges saw they could not hit him with their stones and arrows and the effect it was having on the crowd, one cried to the guards, loud enough for all people to hear. "This fellow has a devil which prevents us from hitting him with our stones and arrows. Take him and bind him and away with him."

Nephi watched as guards climbed the wall. Before they could get to Samuel he climbed down the outside and ran towards the river. Nephi guessed that Samuel would wait for them at their camp. Most of the mob stayed near the wall where they had last seen Samuel. The chief judge harangued them about "rabble-rousers" destroying the peace.

Nephi could no longer remain silent. He climbed the temple steps until he was above the crowd. "You have heard the Lamanite tell you of your sins. Now is the time to repent," he shouted.

By ones and twos, many thoughtful people left the crowd and worked their way across the square to the temple. With voices filled with wonderment they gathered around Nephi and Lehi and questioned them. The younger Nephi stood on the fringe of the group and listened to his father and uncle expound the Gospel.

Many had the same question. "I believe the words the Lamanite spoke. What do I do now?"

"Repent of your sins and be baptized," Nephi said. After giving instruction on repentance and baptism, Lehi and the two Nephis left the city and returned to their camp by the Sidon. Samuel, as Nephi predicted, was waiting for them. Nephi grasped the Lamanite's hands in both of his.

"You truly fulfilled the Lord's commandment, Samuel. The people of Zarahemla have now been warned. The responsibility for their repentance is on their heads."

"I feel like such a failure," Samuel said.

"A failure!" Lehi retorted. "Many requested baptism. Others consider your words and will repent and come back to the Church."

"Even if no one repented and was baptized as a result of your preaching," Nephi added, "you did all you could do. The rest is up to them. You can return to your land knowing you have fulfilled the angel's command."

Lehi laughed, as if at a private joke. "I think some were converted just by the fact that their best archers couldn't put an arrow through you."

Samuel smiled. "The Lord protected me."

Golden sun touched the Sidon, casting bright reflections on the people lining the west bank. Nephi, his son and Lehi waded into the water until they were immersed to their waists. Three lines of people extended up the bank.

The baptism lasted until the sun was at its highest point. When Nephi climbed from the water he was tired, but exultant. Those baptized waited on the bank, clothes dripping, faces radiant with the spirit of God. Nephi dried off as best he could and had the people sit before him. There was a natural amphitheater, formed by an earlier curve of the river which was now dry. The several hundred people listened as he expounded the plan of salvation and the coming of Jesus Christ. Those who were sick requested special blessings and he and Lehi laid hands on their heads and healed them. Lame men walked; blind men saw.

"My only regret," Lehi said that night as they sat by the fire, "is that Samuel did not stay and witness the baptism. That would have made him realize how much good his preaching did for the people of Zarahemla."

"He felt he had to return to his own land," Nephi said, his voice tired.

The younger Nephi looked at his father. Flesh sagged on his cheeks and neck. Firelight painted red and orange highlights in his white hair; skin wrinkled and checkered by countless suns gave him the look of an old man.

Father must be at least sixty, Nephi thought. I'm glad I have had the experience of being with him on this journey. This may be his last missionary journey.

Cumorah, 386 A.D.

Mormon dozed. Warm afternoon sun and sounds of flies buzzing and birds singing was all that was needed to make his eyes close. He waked refreshed, his finger still on the plate where he had been reading. He read again. The next five years passed quickly. With so many joining the church, Nephi and his son stayed in Zarahemla. Lehi had returned to his home and family in Bountiful. Though most of the people remained in wickedness the faithful members of the Church walked circumspectly before God. In the ninetieth year there were great signs given to the people. Angels appeared to men and declared glad tidings of great joy. Thus the scriptures were fulfilled.

Mormon shook his head. Still the greater part of the people hardened their hearts and refused to believe.

Zarahemla, Ninetieth Year of the Judges; 1 B.C.

Nephi called his son to his office in the temple. "Nephi, my son," he said softly. "The time has come to turn over the records to you." He motioned for Nephi to follow and shuffled down the hallway to the records room. The door squeaked softly open on leather hinges. Inside, by light of candle, Nephi saw the stacks of records and other mementos of the Nephite people.

"These are the records started by Lehi over six hundred years ago," Nephi said. "They were continued by that first

Nephi, he for whom my father named me and I named you," he said with pride in his voice. "King Mosiah turned the records over to Alma, who commissioned his son, Alma, to care for them. Alma turned them over to Helaman, who then gave the responsibility to my father, Helaman. Father commissioned me as the keeper of the records and now I call you to that position."

He stepped inside and ran his hands lovingly over the stacks of metal plates. "The care of these records is a sacred responsibility. One that cannot be treated lightly. They must be preserved. Write the history of this people." He stopped, as if thinking. "Yours will be the greatest responsibility but also the greatest opportunity of all. You will be here when the Savior comes. You will be able to write His words as they fall from His lips." He sighed. "Ah, that will be a beautiful time."

Cumorah, 386 A.D.

Mormon leaned back and looked at the evening sky. That was when Lachoneus was chief judge and governor of the Nephites. Nephi, son of Helaman, left Zarahemla and was never heard of again.

CHAPTER SIX

THE THIRD NEPHI

Cumorah, 387 A.D.

Mormon notched a stick and handed it to Moroni. "Another year has passed, son," he said. "Soon we will have been in this cave for two years."

Moroni shook his head. "The last battle seems like just yesterday." He walked to the entrance and looked out. "I am surprised the Lamanites have not found us."

"They won't find us until the work is completed."

"How much is left to abridge?"

"I'm to the time of the Savior's birth."

Zarahemla, 1 A.D.

"Fools!" the black-robed judge shouted. "There has been no sign. The time is past. You believed in a hoax."

Nephi did not know the judge's name, only that he was called "Prune" because of his pock-marked and wrinkled face.

The judge stepped up one more step to project his voice even further. "Samuel, the Lamanite, promised you the sign of the so-called Savior's birth would be in five years. Five years have passed. He lied!"

"He lied!" came a shout from a group near the judge.

"He lied! He lied! He lied!" Chanted the crowd.

Nephi looked sorrowfully at the unbelievers in the temple plaza. They chanted and danced—doubters who didn't want Samuel's words to be fulfilled because that would prove them wrong. The believers stood with heads bowed, feeling doubts, Nephi was sure, in the face of Prune's arguments.

No one likes to be proven wrong, Nephi thought. More especially those who have made speeches and taken a public stance. *Please, Father,* he prayed silently, *let the sign come. Help the righteous people to keep believing.*

"There have been so many signs," he told his wife, Zannat, that evening after supper. "The Lord has wrought greater signs and miracles among this people than at any other time in our history, yet many still do not believe."

Zannat sat by the window nursing her baby. "More than signs are needed to convince some," she said wisely. "I hope the sign of the Lord's coming is soon. Faith is fragile."

Nephi sighed. "That is why I must devote more time to teaching, but I hate to leave you and little Nephi." He chucked the baby under the chin, getting a smile for his efforts.

The next day he preached from the temple steps. "Watch steadfastly," he said. "Your faith has not been in vain."

A squat, broad-shouldered man, dressed in the dark robes and feather headdress of a judge, pushed his way to the front. It was Prune, the same lesser judge who preached to the unbelievers the day before. He pushed Nephi aside and looked with disdain at the crowd. "Know this," he cried. "We, your judges, have decreed that if the sign spoken of by the Lamanite, Samuel, does not come by tomorrow, all believers shall be put to death." He smiled evilly at Nephi and stepped back through the shocked crowd.

Nephi looked with sorrow upon the cowed people before him. Fear blanched their faces. A nervous babble erupted. He calmed it with outstretched arms. "This man is a follower of Gadianton," he told them. "Neither he nor his fellow lawyers have authority to carry out such a threat. I will seek protection from Lachoneus, the chief judge."

"Lachoneus is probably one of them, also," a man cried.

"No," Nephi said. "My father helped select him. He is a righteous man, faithful in keeping the commandments." But in his heart he knew the governor's power was small compared to those who followed Gadianton.

Lachoneus gave no help. "I can do nothing," he said. "I am a figurehead. As a believer I have been warned that I, too, shall be killed if the sign does not come by tomorrow."

"They cannot intimidate the chief judge and governor of the land," Nephi cried indignantly.

"Oh, but they can," Lachoneus said softly. "Not only can, but have."

"What about the army?" Nephi asked.

"The army is controlled by the lesser judges who follow Gadianton. The few officers faithful to me, such as Gidgiddoni, have been sent to guard the borders—insuring their absence."

Sorrowfully, Nephi left the judgment hall and sought the tower in his yard from which his father had so often prayed. All afternoon he pleaded with the Father. Nervously, he glanced at the position of the evening sun. Shadows of night would soon fall over the city. Still no answer. He longed to be with Zannat and little Nephi but forced himself to stay on his knees. As he prayed a quiet voice seemed to explode inside his head.

"Nephi. Lift up your head and be of good cheer. The time is at hand. Tonight will be the sign of my birth. Tomorrow I come into the world in fulfillment of the words of My prophets from the foundation of the world and to do the will of the Father."

Cumorah, 387 A.D.

Mormon set the plate—the abridgment of Nephi's writings—on the smooth rock and carefully inscribed his summary: *The sign came that night—at the sun's going down there was no darkness; night remained as light as mid-day. In the morning the sun rose again and people knew it was the day the Lord would be born.*

Mormon nervously tapped his stylus on his knee. "And yet," he told Moroni, "even with this sign, and myriad signs and wonders from heaven, people returned to their wickedness just as the hog returns to its wallow. Within just a few years both Lamanites and Nephites were faced with annihilation by the Gadianton band."

He glanced through his writings. His finger stopped on the name, Giddianhi.

Zarahemla, 15 A.D.

"Giddianhi?" Lachoneus said. "Why should the leader of the band of robbers write me?"

Timothy shrugged. "Here is his letter." He handed the bark scroll to the chief judge, obsequiously dropped his eyes to the floor and stepped back a pace.

Lachoneus unrolled as he read, incredulity written on his face. He sighed and put down the roll. "Timothy, call Nephi and Gidgiddoni to the judgment hall. I must talk with them."

His aide hurried out to do his bidding and Lachoneus returned to reading the letter.

"Our own iniquity has promoted the arrogance of the Lamanites and robbers," Nephi said solemnly. "If we were righteous they would have no power over us."

"True," Lachoneus said wearily, "but it still doesn't solve the problem." He waved the scroll in the air. "I called you here to help me decide what to do about Giddianhi's letter."

"Surely you are not going to give in to his demands?" Gidgiddoni asked.

Nephi looked at the brawny Nephite chief captain. I wonder if that is what General Moroni looked like, he asked himself. Gidgiddoni, son of Moronihah and grandson of General Moroni, was a broad man. Muscular, hairy arms ended in huge hands. Pale blue eyes looked out from beneath a heavy forehead, dwarfed beside a beaked nose. His eyebrows were so sunbleached they were almost unseen, but brown, curly hair cascaded from his head.

Lachoneus waved impatiently. "I have no intention to honor any of his demands," he said, "but I do need a plan. You are commander of the armies. What shall we do?"

Nephi interrupted. "Read again Giddianhi's demands."

"He demands total surrender!" Gidgiddoni said impatiently.

Lachoneus read. "I write this epistle to you and praise you for your firmness, and the firmness of your people, in maintaining that which you suppose to be your right and liberty. You do stand well, as if supported by the hand of a god, in defense of your liberty, and your property, and your country, or that which you call so."

Gidgiddoni said, "Empty flattery."

The governor looked up.

Nephi said, "Go on."

"It seems a pity, noble Lachoneus, that you should be so foolish and vain as to think that you can stand against my brave men who wait with great anticipation the word to go down and destroy you. I proved them in battle and know their unconquerable spirit. Because of the many wrongs you have done them they have an everlasting hatred towards you. If they come down against you they will totally destroy you."

"An interesting way to rationalize his aggression," Gidgiddoni said dryly.

Lachoneus nodded wearily. "His threatenings become even worse." He read again. "Give up your cities, your lands and your possessions or we shall totally destroy you. Don't just yield to us but unite with us. Become acquainted with our secret works; be our brothers—not our slaves—and partners of all our substance."

"Ha!" exclaimed Gidgiddoni. "They have no substance. That is why they desire to conquer us, so they can live off our labors."

"True," Nephi said. "They are a degenerate people who have forgotten how to till the ground and tend livestock. All they know is murder and stealing."

Lachoneus didn't comment but continued reading. "I swear to you with an oath that if you will do this you shall not be destroyed. But if you will not do this I swear unto you with an oath that in the next month I will command my armies to come down against you. They will not stay their hand but will slay you and all of your people.

"There is more," Lachoneus sighed. "The letter is signed simply, 'I am Giddianhi.'"

Nephi shook his head. "If the letter were not so threatening it would almost be humorous."

"It is certainly not a laughing matter," Lachoneus said. "Our entire nation is threatened with extinction by this lawless band." He saw Gidgiddoni's look. "But I assure you I am not frightened by Giddianhi's threats."

"What do you intend to do?" Nephi asked quietly.

"That's why I called for you," the governor said. "Nephi, you are the spiritual leader. Call upon the people to cry to the Lord for strength against the time the robbers come upon us."

He turned to Gidgiddoni. "Is the army strong enough to defend our nation."

"Strong enough to go against the robber band!"

"No. Their army is more powerful. We cannot defeat them in open battle.I have written a proclamation to the people."

"A proclamation?"

"It asks our people to gather all their possessions."

Nephi looked curiously at the governor. "For what purpose?"

"I have determined the only way to save our people is to gather together and set up effective defenses."

"With the Lord on our side, we can overcome them," Gidgiddoni growled.

"But at the cost of too many lives," Lachoneus said. "If our army is destroyed, who will protect us the next time the Gadianton band comes against us. They can retreat to the mountains and recruit more people. We are limited in the number we have available."

"It sounds as if you have given this much thought," Nephi said.

Lachoneus nodded. "Much thought and much pleading with the Lord while I waited for you."

"So you propose a gathering place?" Gidgiddoni asked.

"I was hoping that you had a suggestion," the governor said. "You know every city and its state of defense. What land would hold all of our people and be defendable against attack."

Nephi interrupted. "Will righteous Lamanites be included?"

"Yes. We will pull together the righteous of both peoples," Lachoneus said.

"Zarahemla is too small and not easily defended," Gidgiddoni, who had been thinking of locations, said. "Sidom is bounded by the Sidon and the mountains."

"What of Gideon?" Nephi asked.

Gidgiddoni shook his head. "Gideon has no adequate defenses and is too close to the lands controlled by the robbers. Manti and the coastal cities would be difficult to defend. The most defendable location is on the flat plains close to the land Bountiful—far enough from the mountains that the robbers will have difficulty finding supplies. Several cities there have defensive walls already built and would only need to be expanded to meet the needs of the increased population."

"Which would you suggest?" Lachoneus asked.

"Moroni."

"But that's so far," Nephi exclaimed.

"Why Moroni?" Lachoneus asked.

"Mulek, Noah, Gid and Nephihah lie in smaller areas or along major trails. All had their defenses seriously damaged during the wars my father fought against the Lamanites. Moroni is on the coastal plain where there is plenty of room for expansion, has the newest defenses of any city, and is right on the River Sidon which can be used to transport our people. Of all the cities, it is the most defensible."

"Nephi?"

"I feel the Lord's confirmation."

Lachoneus nodded. "Moroni it is." He smiled. "It is also
fitting that the city is named after your grandfather, Captain
Moroni." The smile faded. "Gidgiddoni, You are responsible for
organizing the defenses."

He turned to Nephi. "I need your help to gather the
people. Every village must be notified and must comply with my
proclamation. The land must be left desolate—no crops or
livestock left behind for the robbers to harvest."

"The priests in every city will be our cadre. We can start
by having them make announcements in the churches."

"When?"

"I'll send runners this very day."

Lachoneus nodded grimly. "Never has such an endeavor
been tried. Many thousands of people must be moved in a very
short time. Houses must be constructed, new defenses built, and
also storage places for our crops."

"As well as sheds and corrals for the flocks and herds,"
Nephi added.

"Thank goodness we have had excellent harvests during
the past years," Lachoneus said. "We have enough food to take
care of our people for the next seven years. I don't think the
robber band can hold out that long."

Cumorah, 387 A.D.

Mormon shut his eyes and rubbed them as he pictured
Lachoneus and his people. They gathered to Moroni, built
defenses and put their armies around them for protection. He
opened his eyes again when Moroni spoke to him.

"What happened to them?"

"The people repented and became very righteous,
praying faithfully to God to deliver them from their enemies."

"And the robber band?" Moroni asked.

"Giddianhi's robber band possessed the abandoned
lands but could not sustain themselves. Their livelihood came
from stealing and they were not prepared to plant crops. After
two years Giddianhi decided to attack Lachoneus' stronghold.
In the battle that followed Giddianhi was killed and the robbers
routed."

"Did that destroy the robbers?" Moroni persisted.

"No," Mormon answered tiredly. "After Giddianhi's
death, Zemnarihah, another dissident from the Nephites, led
the robber band. In a subsequent battle he was captured and the

robber band destroyed." He turned a plate over. "Here, let me read you what I wrote about Zemnarihah."

"Zemnarihah was hanged from the top of a tree. When he was dead they felled the tree. Righteous priests led a chant: 'May the Lord preserve His people in righteousness and in holiness of heart, that they may fell to the earth all who seek to slay them because of power and secret combinations, even as this man has been felled to the earth.' The happy people shouted, 'Hosanna to the Most High God,' and 'Blessed be the name of the Lord God Almighty.'"

Mormon set the plates down and accepted a handful of dried corn from Moroni. His teeth were so poor that he held the corn in his mouth to moisten it before he could chew it. As he munched on the corn he talked to Moroni about those years immediately preceding the coming of the Savior.

"People were very righteous for a short time." He read:

"Many great and marvelous things transpired—so many that they cannot be included in this book. This book cannot contain a hundredth part of what was done among so many people in the first twenty-five years after the sign of the Savior's birth. There are records which contain all the proceedings of this people." Mormon thought of the stacks of plates he had read and sifted through in making his abridgment. He read on. "I made my record on plates, made with my own hands, according to the record of Nephi, which was engraven on plates called the plates of Nephi.

"I am Mormon, named after the land of Mormon, where Alma established the first church among the people after their transgression. I am a disciple of Jesus Christ, the Son of God. I have been called of Him to declare His word among His people that they might have everlasting life."

Mormon's eyes misted as he read his words. "It is God's will that I make a record of those things which have been done from the time Lehi left Jerusalem until the present time. I make my record from the accounts written by those before me, until the commencement of my day, and then I make a record of the things I have seen with my own eyes."

"Being the Lord's scribe has been my greatest mission," he whispered, then read silently the words he had written. "The record I made is a true record. I am Mormon, a pure descendant of Lehi. As long as the children of Lehi kept His commandments He blessed them and prospered them according to His word. He shall again bring a remnant of Joseph's seed to the knowledge of the Lord their God.

"As surely as God lives He will gather the scattered seed of Jacob. Then shall they know their Redeemer, who is Jesus Christ, the Son of God. Then shall they be gathered in from the four quarters of the earth unto their own lands from whence they have been dispersed. As the Lord lives, so shall it be."

Moroni's voice was choked. "Father, that is a powerful testimony. Come lie down, you look very tired."

Mormon was tired. On his pallet he cradled his head in his hands and slept, his dreams vivid.

Moroni, 26 A.D.

"When do we return to our home in Zarahemla," Zannat asked. "Nephites and Lamanites leave Moroni daily."

"We are not going to Zarahemla," Nephi said as he repaired a sandal.

Zannat was surprised. "Not return home? Will we stay here in Moroni?"

"No," Nephi sighed. "The Lord has whispered to me that people will soon once again become wicked. He instructed me to take my family to Bountiful—to my father's house."

"But Nephi is only eight. What about his friends?"

"He will make new friends in Bountiful. Besides, he will be spending much of his time in scribe training."

Bountiful, 30 A.D.

Timothy, Nephi's brother, visited them. "The people prosper throughout the land," he reported.

"Yes," Nephi said. "They prosper because they were righteous and kept God's commandments. Now when they are returning to their evil ways God will destroy them."

"The Nephites seem to like unrighteousness."

Nephi, busily writing, nodded. He paused and looked at Timothy. "I wish I were wrong," He said. "Only thirty years have passed since the sign of the Savior's coming but new disputes break out daily. People begin to be distinguished by ranks according to riches and learning."

"What will happen?" Timothy asked.

"The Lord showed me the destruction which will come. All the cities being repaired, the new highways being built, will be destroyed." He sighed. "Why is it that our people—people who have been so blessed—return to evil ways?"

Timothy, knowing Nephi had more to say, did not respond.

"The end result is that the Church, which taught people to be humble and look forward to the second sign of which Samuel spoke, has become the church of the few instead of the many." Nephi shrugged. "But that is no excuse. We must still do all we can to prepare our people for the Savior's coming." He looked at Timothy, his eyes filled with distant visions. He whispered, "Angels visit me almost daily."

Timothy's voice was hushed. "What do they say?"

Nephi looked at him sadly. "They tell me the time is short until the sign of the Savior's death and that we must gather our families and other faithful people to Bountiful."

Nephi, Timothy and other faithful priests boldly preached repentance and baptism, but the powers of hell seemed to rail against them in their efforts. Even Nephi was discouraged. "Satan's lies seem more acceptable to people than the truths we preach," he commented.

Jason said, "Maybe it is the easier way."

"Satan deceives them by promising power, authority, riches and the vain things of the world."

Timothy nodded. "That's true. Yet there have been special manifestations from heaven. Many have seen angels." His voice dropped, as if in awe. "An angel even appeared to me, testifying of the sins and iniquities of the people and teaching about the redemption the Lord would make for His people through His sufferings, death and resurrection."

Nephi shook his head at Timothy's enthusiasm. "Many were secretly murdered—never heard of again."

"What can we do about it?" Timothy asked.

"I'm glad you asked, because I've been wondering the same thing. Perhaps we should go to Zarahemla to talk to Lachoneus, son of Lachoneus, who now governs the land."

Timothy started out the door. "I will be ready to go in an hour."

The boat trip upriver was without incident. Nephi and Timothy dressed as traders and were not disturbed. Nephi enjoyed the wild beauty of the black canyons and overhanging jungle growth, the brightly-colored parrots and river birds. When they docked at Sidom, they were shocked at the whisperings of a fisherman. "Lachoneus is dead. He was murdered."

"Has anyone been appointed as governor in his place?" Nephi asked the fisherman.

The man shook his head, furtively looking around as if in fear of his own life. "The Gadianton band wants no governor."

"Gadianton robbers were responsible?" Timothy asked.

The man nodded, whites of his eyes showing.

Timothy turned to Nephi. "Who will govern the land?"

Nephi grimaced. "If another chief judge is appointed, he will be appointed by the Gadianton band. It would be better to have no judge than a corrupt one."

"With no governor, each tribe would govern itself."

Nephi was nervous. "We should return speedily to Bountiful. To go on to Zarahemla is not only dangerous but a waste of time."

Timothy nodded. "You must be careful not to be recognized. Now that they have assassinated the governor they would be pleased if the chief priest also fell into their hands."

When safely back in Nephi's house, after an uneventful trip downriver, they both sighed with relief. Zannat and young Nephi were also glad to see them. Rumors of the assassination had preceded them and unruly mobs roamed the streets.

Nephi pulled out his bark paper. "I must record what is happening," he said.

"It has only been six years!" Timothy exploded. "Six years since the people were prospered because of their righteousness."

Nephi answered without looking up. "Yes, in six years Satan has gotten such a hold on this people that they no longer even have a government. The civilization our fathers and grandfathers formed and knew is no more."

"Our people have become as savage as the robbers."

"They have turned to evil like the dog to his vomit or the sow to her wallowing in the mire," Nephi said sadly. "Satan has never worked so hard to destroy a people." He pursed his lips and looked out of the window. His face was glum. "I'm afraid we've had our last chance. In fact," he said, "I am amazed the Lord has shown as much patience for the Nephites as He has."

"Never has a people been so willing to be destroyed."

Nephi sighed. "History repeats itself because men don't learn their lessons. They continue to live satan's way—the way of rebellion."

Timothy said hotly. "I guess they feel that's freedom."

"But it really isn't. Freedom is obedience to God's laws. We enjoy freedom when we submit our will to His. But man has a tendency to turn his back to revealed eternal truth."

Timothy sat thinking for a few moments. When he looked at Nephi his eyes were misty. "That's why we must turn even more strongly to the Lord."

Nephi nodded his agreement, touched that his brother felt so strongly about the church. "The most important thing we can do is to love the Lord and serve Him."

Timothy sighed, "Satan has marshalled his forces for war. With no government we have already lost many rights. Other families gather into tribes and elect a chief. Why don't we?"

"A good idea," Nephi said. "It is important that our family be together."

"Not only be together," Timothy said emphatically, "but have our own family organization and elect our own leader."

"That's good," Nephi said, still distracted by what he was inscribing. "Why don't you and your son, Jonas, take care of it."

Nephi was interrupted by Timothy's noisy entry. "Well, I've done it," he said.

"Done what?" Nephi asked, surprised by Timothy's tone.

"I've organized the tribe of Helaman," Timothy said.

"Tribe of Helaman?"

"Yes. All descendants of great-grandfather Helaman now have a tribal council."

"Who is on the council?" Nephi asked suspiciously.

"You and I, my son, Jonas, and several others."

Nephi could tell something else was on Timothy's mind. "What other news do you have?"

"News has come of a new robber chieftan," Timothy said. "A man called Jacob. The robber band calls him king."

"Jacob?" Nephi said. "What does this Jacob look like?"

"Tall, broad-shouldered with a face filled with pocks," Timothy said. "He denounced all prophets who testified of Jesus."

"Prune!" Nephi exclaimed. "He persecuted us even before the Savior's birth. Timothy, what of Jacob?"

"Other tribes outnumbered him so he took his people into the land northward. They have built several villages."

"Good riddance," Zannat sniffed as she came into the room. She placed a heaping tray of steaming shellfish on the table. Wicked people like that don't deserve to live."

Nephi smiled. Zannat was always willing to express a strong opinion.

Bountiful, A.D. 31

Nephi spent more time in missionary work. He went from house to house, calling upon people to repent and return to the church. His testimony was powerful but he was spat upon and rejected by many. Angels ministered to him and the Lord himself spoke to him. Nephi sometimes felt he was caught between two worlds—the world of sin and humanity, and the heaven where God dwelled.

Nephi's family was a great support and help. His son, Nephi, became his constant companion. The younger Nephi was skilled in writing and Nephi turned over part of the record-keeping so he could spend more time ministering to people.

"Nephi!" The strained shout was from Jonas, son of Timothy. Nephi left his room in the temple and stepped out into the bright sunlight. Jonas ran across the temple square as if his heels were on fire.

"What is it?" Nephi asked.

Jonas fell on the first step and gasped for air. "Father," he cried. "They have killed Father."

"Killed Timothy? Where? What do you mean?"

Jason pointed in the direction he had come. "On the road to Mulek." He looked up at Nephi, tear-stained cheeks attesting to his sorrow. "They stoned him."

"But why?" He grabbed Jonas by his tunic and hauled him to his feet. "Why? Why would they stone Timothy?"

"He called them to repentance," sobbed Jonas. "He listed their sins and told them they would enter eternal damnation if they didn't repent before the Savior came." He rubbed his arm across his face and looked at Nephi with pleading eyes. "They didn't give him a chance to finish his sermon. They scoffed at his words, then picked up stones."

"And you?" Nephi asked gently.

"Some stones hit me but the mob wasn't interested in me. They just wanted to silence Father."

"Let's go back where you left your father," Nephi said, as he started down the steps.

"But they'll kill you, too!" shouted Jonas.

Nephi turned to look at him. "No. God's power is with me. They cannot hurt me."

They found Timothy's bruised body in the weeds beside the road. The mob had left. No one was near. Flies swarmed on Timothy's almost-naked body; black and iridescent green bodies almost completely covered his bloodied face. Nephi brushed the flies away, placed an arm under Timothy's neck and cradled his brother's battered head against his breast, rocking back and forth in his sorrow.

Jonas hung back, avoiding looking at his father's body. Nephi carefully laid Timothy's bloody head on his lap. "Jonas, come here," he called gently. "We have the power and authority to raise Timothy. Help me give him a blessing."

The two men laid their hands on Timothy's head. Nephi prayed that his brother would again join them in the ministry prior to the Lord's coming. "Father," he prayed, "according to Alma's words, which he spoke to the people of Gideon, Thy Son will take upon himself our infirmities and our sicknesses. Angels have confirmed that through Him and His atonement the dead will rise. In His holy name I command Timothy's spirit to reenter his body."

Timothy's chest began to rise and fall with his breathing.

"He's alive!" Jonas cried.

Nephi smiled at his nephew. "The Lord heard our prayers. Jonas, get water and a towel so we can clean up your father."

While Jonas was gone, Nephi stroked Timothy's forehead and cheeks. With the wet towel, he washed off the blood and cooled the bruises.

Jonas stood by, astonished. "You brought him back to life!"

"Not I, but God," Nephi said humbly. "God promised us power to accomplish all things. That power, activated by our own faith, can literally move mountains, lower the water in the sea, or," he motioned towards the still unconscious Timothy, "even raise people from the dead."

Once again, with even greater commitment, Timothy went forth as a missionary. Nephi used his priesthood power often during the next months. In the Savior's name he cast out devils and unclean spirits, healed the sick, caused the blind to see and the lame to walk. Instead of believing and accepting, the wicked Nephites who observed these miracles angrily denounced him and turned even further from Christ and his teachings. That only increased his intensity. "The time is short, brothers and sisters," he cried. "Angels told me the Savior will be soon be here. When He comes, it will be here in Bountiful. Zarahemla and Moronihah and the other wicked cities will be destroyed. We must be righteous that we may be here when he comes."

A.D. 33

"The righteous are few in number," Nephi said as he watched Zannat dish monkey stew into three dishes.

"And never have there been so many signs and miracles," Timothy said. He blew on his stew to cool it.

"If signs would convert," Jonas said quietly, "all the people would be members of the church."

Nephi shook his head. "People will always seek for signs, not because they want to believe—but because they do not. Our members today, though few in number, are stronger than they have ever been. All are baptized and have received the Gift of the Holy Ghost. Many have testified that they have been visited by the power and Spirit of God."

"I am especially pleased about Mathoni and his brother, Mathonihah," Timothy said between bites. "They seem strong in their faith."

"Those we have ordained to the priesthood have all shown great strength," Nephi said. "Jumen and Jumenonhi, Jeremiah, Shemnon, Zedekiah, and Isaiah are young like Jonas and will be able to carry on after you and I are gone."

"Don't leave out uncle Jonas, after whom my son, Jonas, was named." Timothy put his hand on his son's shoulder and squeezed it affectionately.

"What about the wicked?" Jonas asked. "What will happen to them?"

"They are without excuse. So many signs have been manifest that they have become totally accountable."

Jonas said, "I guess the sign I want to see right now is dinner. I'm starved."

Nephi and Timothy laughed.

A.D. 34

"The thirty-third year has ended. When will the sign come?" Isaiah asked. "The unbelievers already scoff."

"They will always scoff," Nephi said, "regardless of any signs or miracles. We must be patient and believe."

"Three days of darkness," Timothy mused. "That will be a frightening sign for the unbelievers."

"Even the believers will become nervous," Shemnon said.

"Some church members have begun to doubt," Jeremiah added.

Nephi looked at those he had ordained to the ministry. They were so few. He sighed. "That is why we must continue teaching, calming people's fears, preparing them for the Savior's coming."

Jonas, Nephi's uncle, and oldest of those present, spoke up. "I feel a storm is on its way."

As if in response to his statement, a dust devil whistled through the patio, stirred the dust, whirled stinging particles into eyes and mouths. Nephi looked up. Heavy black clouds filled the western sky, obscuring even the close hills. Thunder throbbed menacingly; lightning spit at the earth.

CHAPTER SEVEN

THE SAVIOR'S VISIT

Darkness, A.D. 34

Wide-eyed, Timothy peered into the enveloping darkness. "Did you hear?" The voice, quiet as it was, could be heard over the rumblings of the earth and raging of the storm.

Nephi stood raptly by the window, eyes raised towards the unseen sky, finger to his lips. "Shhh."

"Wo, wo unto this people."

"There it is again," Timothy said. He shook Jonas awake.

"Wo unto the inhabitants of the whole earth unless they repent. The devil and his angels laugh because of My fair sons and daughters who have been slain for their abominations."

Timothy started to speak but Nephi stopped him. "Shhh."

The voice was not loud, yet it penetrated each person's consciousness. "Because of these abominations, I have burned Zarahemla and its inhabitants. Moroni and its people have been sunk in the depths of the sea." The voice went on to name all the other cities which had been destroyed. "You have been spared only because you were more righteous. My arm of mercy is extended towards you. Will you now repent of your sins and turn unto Me and be converted? Come unto Me and you shall have eternal life."

Nephi, his wife, Zannat, and those in his house were spellbound. All heard the voice—almost inaudible—a whisper speaking to their hearts. Nephi felt for brushes and paper—then remembered the heavy darkness which engulfed them. They hadn't even been able to light a fire. He silently repeated what was said, committing it to memory.

"I am Jesus Christ, the Son of God. I created the heavens and the earth and all things that in them are. I was with the Father from the beginning. I am in the Father and the Father in Me. In Me has the Father glorified His name. I came unto My own and My own received Me not. Now the scriptures concerning My coming are fulfilled. I am the light and life of the world. I am Alpha and Omega, the beginning and the end.

"Concentrate on what is said," Nephi whispered. "These words must be included in the record the Lord has asked me to keep."

"In Me the law of Moses is fulfilled. Offer up no more sacrifices of burnt offerings and shedding of blood. Instead, offer as a sacrifice unto Me a broken heart and a contrite spirit. Whoever comes to Me with a broken heart and a contrite spirit I will baptize with fire and with the Holy Ghost, even as the Lamanites, because of their faith in Me at the time of their conversion, were baptized with fire and with the Holy Ghost.

"I have come into the world to bring redemption and to save the world from sin. Whoever repents and comes to Me as a little child, him will I receive, for of such is the kingdom of God. For this I have laid down My life and have taken it up again."

"Whew!" Timothy said when the voice had stopped speaking. "The Savior himself just spoke to us."

Jonas seemed still in shock.

Zannat moved up and took Nephi's arm. Nephi could feel her shaking in the dark. He put his arm around her. "I feel this destruction is creation's response to the Creator's death. But now the Creator has again taken charge of the earth."

Outside, all was quiet. The wailing and grief-stricken shouts of a few minutes before were stilled.

"All who are still alive must have heard His voice," Nephi whispered. "I think only the righteous have been spared."

"I am grateful you insisted we leave Moroni and settle here in Bountiful," Zannat whispered back. "If we had not, we might have been destroyed with the rest."

Nephi squeezed her shoulders. "I'm glad God inspired me to have our family and friends come here to Bountiful. Almost every Nephite city has been destroyed."

"And some Lamanite cities," piped up Timothy. "Jerusalem, Onihah and Mocum all lay beside the Waters of Mormon in the land of Nephi."

Nephi nodded in the dark. "Judging by what happened here in Bountiful, even in the cities not destroyed there has been much destruction by the quaking earth. As soon as the Lord lifts this curtain of darkness, we must do what we can to help the injured and homeless. Meanwhile, let's rest."

Before they could seat themselves, the same voice continued.

"Oh you people of these great cities which have fallen, how many times have I gathered you as a hen gathers her chickens under her wings and have nourished you. How oft would I have gathered you as a hen gathers her chickens under her wings, and you would not."

Renewed wailing arose outside. Dust sifted into Nephi's room as the earth again rolled and trembled.

For three days Nephi and his family huddled in their home, not daring to venture out. Darkness was total. Every effort to even strike a spark failed. Then the trembling stopped.

The First Day

Morning came; new light dispersed darkness. Rocks stopped their grinding and rending. The tumult ceased.

Nephi cautiously stepped from his house, followed by his family. From homes up and down the street others emerged to view the glory of the morning. Sky was cleansed and renewed. Dust and haze lay in the valleys but not a cloud detracted from the sky's blueness. Never had the sun looked so beautiful.

Wails changed to shouts of joy as people realized they had been saved from the holocaust. Survivors gathered before Nephi's house, looking to him, their chief priest, for direction. Awed by the terrible destruction around them and the voice they had heard, they filled the air with questions.

"Nephi, what has happened?"

"Nephi, did you hear the voice? What does it mean?"

"Are we to be destroyed?"

"What do I have to do to be baptized?"

Nephi, leaving the questions unanswered, called his son to him. "Nephi, take Timothy and Jonas and gather the priests. Send them and able-bodied runners throughout the city. Encourage all who are alive and can walk to gather in the square before the temple. Hurry, there is little time."

After they left to carry out his instructions, Nephi spoke to those who had assembled in the street. "Go to the temple plaza," he called to them. "Gather your families before the temple and your questions will be answered."

The crowd began moving, gathering others as it progressed to the plaza before the temple. Nephi took Zannat's hand and followed. Destruction was evident on all sides: homes flattened, roofs caved in, roadways cracked and pitted.

"Wait here," he asked Zannat. "I will be right back." He dodged through the rubble as he ran quickly back to his house and gathered up bark paper and brushes. He was breathless when he returned to where Zannat waited. "I almost forgot my writing materials," he said. "Nephi and I must be prepared to record all that is said."

"By whom?" Zannat asked.

"By the Savior," Nephi said quietly.

A roar of voices rose from the crowded temple plaza. Survivors conversed about the voice and what it said. Some still wailed, lamenting loved ones. Nephi's ordained priests and the younger Nephi waited on the temple steps. Nephi climbed the steps and looked over the vast assemblage.

"There must be several thousand people here," he said to Zannat. A whisper reached him. It was a quiet voice, similar to that of three days before. He couldn't understand the words because of the noise from the crowd. He ran up the stairs and waved his arms to get attention, imploring the people to silence.

He could see that others heard the voice. Some cast their eyes about to see where it was coming from. Nephi fell to his knees on the steps, his bosum burning as the voice pierced him to his very heart. He glanced down, noting that Zannat and others in the crowd also knelt.

Again the voice came, but still Nephi could not understand the words.

A third time. This time Nephi understood.

"Behold My beloved Son, in whom I am well pleased, in whom I have glorified My name—hear ye Him!"

It was the voice of the Father!

Nephi looked up. High above him a light brighter than the morning sun illuminated the sky. His arm shook as he silently pointed. Eyes looked where he pointed. A hush as still as death settled over the crowd.

As the bright light came nearer, Nephi shielded his eyes from the glare. In the light was a Man! A Man dropping from heaven, clothed in a brilliant white robe, with light emanating from His being so He looked like the sun at midday.

"An angel," someone whispered.

No, Nephi thought. *This is no angel. His glory defies description. It is the Lord!*

The Man stopped His descent a few feet above the temple steps. He looked sadly over the silent crowd. Then he stretched forth his hands toward the people. *"Behold, I am Jesus Christ whom the prophets testified shall come into the world."*

A chill went up Nephi's spine. "Ohhs" and "Ahhhs" came from the people. Nephi could understand their feelings: though they believed the prophets and had attempted to live righteously in anticipation of this moment, they were awestruck. The time, prophesied for centuries, had finally come.

"I am the light and the life of the world. I have suffered the will of the Father in all things from the beginning. I have drunk out of that bitter cup which the Father has given me and have glorified the Father in taking upon me the sins of the world."

Struck with wonderment at what was happening, those in the temple plaza prostrated themselves upon the ground.

"Arise and come forth unto Me, that you may thrust your hands into My side, and also that you may feel the prints of the nails in My hands and in My feet, that you may know that I am the God of Israel, and the God of the whole earth, and have been slain for the sins of the world."

Cumorah, 387 A.D.

Tears filled Mormon's eyes and coursed down withered cheeks as he read again of the Savior's visit to the people of Nephi. His emotions were so high he could no longer read. He sighed as he set the plates on his lap and leaned back. "What a glorious occasion," he whispered to Moroni. "Every prophecy fulfilled from Isaiah down to Nephi: the Savior did come to His people."

Moroni, too, had tears in his eyes.

Mormon visualized the multitude coming forward, hesitantly touching the Savior's side, tenderly feeling the prints of the nails in His hands and feet, looking with awe at this being—this God. Mormon could almost hear the shout of joy as the crowd cried as one, "Hosanna! Blessed be the name of the Most High God!"

Bountiful, 34 A.D.

"Nephi."

Nephi looked up. The Savior beckoned him.

"Me?"

"Nephi, come forth."

Nephi rose shakily to his feet and climbed to where the Savior stood. He fell to his knees and kissed the Lord's feet.

"Rise, Nephi."

Nephi stood before the Savior of the world, looking into warm, kindly eyes—eyes filled with love and compassion.

"Nephi, I give you a special calling: the power to baptize this people when I am again ascended into heaven." He looked around at those before Him. *"Timothy and Jonas."* He singled out others, calling their names: *"Mathoni, Mathonihah, Kumen, Jumenonhi, Jeremiah, Shemnon, Jonas, Zedekiah, Isaiah."*

The eleven named, priests Nephi had ordained to teach the people, quietly and reverently joined him at the Savior's feet.

Jesus spoke directly to them, his eyes burning into their eyes. *"To each of you I give power to baptize. There shall be no disputations among you concerning the form of baptism. When a person repents of his sins and desires to be baptized in My name, this shall be your procedure."*

The Savior taught them the exact form of baptism, including the words to use. He sighed and looked over the vast crowd before the temple, then patiently continued, as if teaching small children. *"You shall baptize as I have commanded you. There shall be no disputations among you. Neither shall there be disputations among you concerning the points of My doctrine.*

"He that has a spirit of contention is not of Me but is of the devil. The father of contention stirs up men's hearts to contend with anger. Such things should be done away. I teach you the doctrine which the Father has given Me. I bear record of the Father; the Father bears record of Me; the Holy Ghost bears record of the Father and Me. The Father has commanded men everywhere to repent and believe in Me. Whoever believes in Me and is baptized, the same shall be saved and shall inherit the kingdom of God. Whoever does not believe in Me and is not baptized shall be damned."

Young Nephi, who had been recording the Savior's words on bark paper, shook his head in wonderment. His thoughts were so jumbled. *Was this day real? I ought to have someone poke me,* he thought. *The Savior of the world, here now. In the flesh, yet... Is he really flesh? A resurrected being. Walking. Talking. Teaching.* The whole day had an aura of unrealness—of awe. He breathed deeply to relieve the palpitations of his heart.

His father caught his eye and nodded. Nephi returned the nod and concentrated on his writing. He had probably missed a few of the Savior's words while he had been daydreaming. His father was just reminding him of his important task. He dipped his brush and painted quickly, catching each phrase as it fell from the Master's lips. But still he sometimes became so enthralled with what was spoken he forgot to write down the words.

The waiting crowd in the plaza was seemingly forgotten as Jesus focused on these who would be His disciples. *"Each must repent and become as a little child and be baptized in My name or you can not inherit the kingdom of God. Whoever builds upon this doctrine builds upon My rock and the gates of hell shall not prevail against them."* He looked at them sadly, as if seeing the future. *"Any who declare more or less than this will not be building upon My rock but upon a sandy foundation and the gates of hell stand open to receive such when the floods come and the winds beat upon them."* Again He paused and looked directly at each of those whom He had called. *"Go forth unto this people. Declare unto the ends of the earth the words I have spoken."*

Cumorah, 387 A.D.

Mormon could sit no longer. Emotion filled his being. He set the plates on the rock and walked to the cave's opening. The hillside dropped away before him.

"Father, there is danger in leaving the cave during daylight."

Mormon's voice quavered as he answered. "I know, but I must get away for a few moments." He paced down through the trees, looking out over the green hillside of Cumorah. Away from the cave he fell to his knees in the soft, red dirt. "Lord, I have also been Thy disciple. I have baptized in Your name all who came to me with a repentant heart. I have taught Thy people—declaring Thy words to all who would listen. Now I am ready to depart this life and join Thee in Thy Kingdom."

He plead with the Father to protect Moroni, then asked for strength for himself until he was taken home. He struggled to his feet and slowly returned to the cave.

Moroni, in the cave opening, seemed relieved at his return.

Mormon picked up the plate and read the Savior's words.

Bountiful, 34 A.D.

Jesus motioned for the twelve he had called to sit around him on the steps, then extended His hands towards the multitude. *"Give heed to the words of these twelve whom I have chosen from among you. I have given them power to baptize you with water. After you are baptized with water I will baptize you with fire and with the Holy Ghost. Blessed are you if you shall believe in Me and be baptized—especially after you have seen Me and know that I am.*

"Even more blessed are those who shall not see me but shall believe in your words when you testify that you have seen Me and know that I am. Blessed are they who shall believe your words and come down into the depths of humility and be baptized. They shall be visited with fire and with the Holy Ghost and shall receive a remission of their sins."

Nephi glanced at his son, watching how quickly the younger Nephi's brush traveled over the bark paper.

"Blessed are the poor in spirit who come unto me, for theirs is the kingdom of heaven.

"Blessed are all they that mourn, for they shall be comforted.

"Blessed are the meek, for they shall inherit the earth.

"Blessed are they who do hunger and thirst after righteousness, for they shall be filled with the Holy Ghost.

"Blessed are the merciful for they shall obtain mercy.

"Blessed are the pure in heart, for they shall see God.

"Blessed are the peacemakers, for they shall be called the children of God.

"Blessed are they who are persecuted for My name's sake, for theirs is the kingdom of heaven."

Jesus looked searchingly at each of the twelve, finally resting his eyes on Nephi.

Nephi felt as if the Savior were speaking directly to him.

"And, blessed are you when men shall revile you and persecute you, and shall say all manner of evil against you falsely, for my sake, for you shall have great joy and be exceeding glad, for great shall be your reward in heaven; for so persecuted they the prophets who were before you."

Jesus sat down on the temple step and motioned the people to gather closer. He taught them concerning His doctrine, telling them to be a light to the world, for *"a city that is set on a hill cannot be hid."* He challenged the people to let their lights so shine that others would see their good works and glorify their Heavenly Father.

Nephi listened attentively as the Savior taught them that He had come to fulfill the law, not to destroy it. *"All things which were of old time under the law are in Me fulfilled. Old things are done away and all things have become new. Therefore I would that you should be perfect, even as I, or your Father who is in heaven, is perfect."*

He taught them how to pray and how to forgive. *"If you cannot forgive men their trespasses neither will your Father forgive your trespasses."*

Nephi reviewed in his mind the people who had hurt him, tried to kill him or attempted to destroy his missionary work. *"I forgive each of you,"* he whispered.

Jesus instructed them in fasting, teaching them to fast privately in communication with God, not with a sad countenance to be noticed of others. He also taught them about wealth, cautioning them to *"lay not up for yourselves treasures upon earth but instead lay up for yourselves treasures in heaven. For where your treasure is, there will your heart be also."*

Jesus dropped his voice and spoke to the twelve. *"Remember the words I have spoken. I have chosen you to minister unto this people so take no thought for your life, what you shall eat or what you shall drink or what you shall put on your body. Is not the life more than meat and the body more than rainment? Behold the fowls of the air. They sow not, neither do they reap or gather into barns, yet your Heavenly Father feeds them. Are you not much better than they?*

"Which of you by taking thought can add one cubit to your stature? And why take thought of rainment? Consider the lilies of the field how they grow. They toil not, nor do they spin, and yet Solomon in all his glory was not arrayed like one of these. Therefore, if God clothes the grass of the field, which is here today and tomorrow is cast into the oven, even so will He clothe you if you have faith.

"Therefore, take no thought saying, 'What shall we eat? or what shall we drink? or with what shall we be clothed?' Your Heavenly Father knows your needs. Seek first the kingdom of God and His righteousness and all these things shall be added unto you. Therefore take no thought for the morrow, for the morrow shall take care of itself. Sufficient is the day unto the evil thereof."

Turning again to the multitude, which pressed even closer to the temple steps, the Savior taught them to not judge others or to cast pearls before swine. He taught how to receive:

"Ask and it shall be given unto you; seek and you shall find; knock and it shall be opened unto you. For every one that asks, receives; and he that seeks, finds; and to him that knocks, it shall be opened.

"What man is there of you, who, if his son ask for bread will give him a stone? Or, if he asks for a fish, will give him a serpent? If you, then, being evil, know how to give good gifts to your children, how much more shall your Father who is in heaven give good things to them that ask Him?"

There was so much to learn!

Jesus talked about the strait gate which leads to eternal life and the broad path which leads to destruction. Nephi nodded in approval as Jesus reiterated that people needed to be doers of the word, not hearers only. "He who hears these sayings of mine and does them I will liken unto a wise man who built his house upon a rock, and the rain descended and the floods came and the winds blew and beat upon that house, and it fell not, for it was founded upon a rock.

"Everyone who hears these sayings and does them not shall be likened unto a foolish man who built his house upon the sand, and the rain descended and the floods came and the winds blew and beat upon that house, and it fell, and great was the fall of it."

Jesus stood and stretched his arms towards those crowding the plaza. "Now you have heard what I taught the people of Jerusalem before I ascended to My Father. Remember these sayings of mine and do them so you will be raised up at the last day."

Jesus looked silently over the crowd of believers.

Nephi took his eyes off the Savior long enough to look at his wife, Zannat. She gazed earnestly at the Savior, transfixed, tears streaming down her cheeks. His own eyes misted and he could not see clearly. He looked at the multitude. They, too, seemed enthralled.

The Savior continued, answering their unspoken question. "The law is now fulfilled which was given to Moses. I am He who gave the law to Moses, and I am He who covenanted with My people Israel. Therefore, the law in me is fulfilled for I came to fulfill the law. That law is now ended."

He sighed audibly. "I do not destroy the prophets. Their prophecies which have not yet been fulfilled in Me will all be *fulfilled. I do not destroy those things which have been spoken concerning things which are yet to come. The covenant I made with My people is not all fulfilled, but the law which was given to Moses has an end in Me. I am the law and the light. Look to Me and endure to the end and you shall live. To him that endures to the end will I give eternal life."*

He paused and looked around the entire congregation. *"I have given you the commandments,"* he said. *"Now keep them, for this is the law and the prophets, for they truly testified of me."*

Jesus sat down again in the midst of the twelve. Nephi felt as if the Savior dismissed the crowd and concentrated entirely upon those He had chosen.

"You are My disciples," He said. *"You shall be a light to this people who are a remnant of the house of Joseph."* He spread his arms wide to encompass their surroundings. *"This land is the land of your inheritance. The Father has given it to you and did not command Me to tell those in Jerusalem about it."* He smiled. *"Neither did I tell them about the other tribes of the house of Israel whom the Father led away out of the land."*

Nephi, feeling less than bold, asked the Savior, *"The people of Jerusalem know nothing of us?"*

Jesus nodded and smiled at him. *"The Father commanded me to tell them, 'Other sheep I have which are not of this fold. Them also I must bring and they must hear My voice and there shall be one fold and one shepherd.'"* He sighed. *"But they were so stiffnecked and disbelieving that they did not understand Me."*

Again He looked around the circle of the twelve, gazing into each man's eyes. *"The Father commanded me to tell you that you were separated from the people at Jerusalem because of their iniquity. Because of their iniquity they don't know about you or the other tribes which the Father has separated from them.*

"You are the other sheep of whom I said, 'Other sheep I have which are not of this fold,' but they didn't understand Me, supposing I was speaking of the Gentiles. They didn't understand that the Gentiles would be converted through their preaching, and not by Me. The Gentiles will not hear My voice unless I manifest Myself unto them by the Holy Ghost."

He smiled, *"I also have other sheep which are not of this land, nor of the land of Jerusalem. They have not yet heard My voice or seen Me. The Father has commanded Me to go to them*

*so they shall hear My voice and shall be numbered among My
sheep that there may be one fold and one shepherd."*
        Jesus looked directly at Nephi. *"Write these sayings that
they may be kept and given to the gentiles. Through the Gentiles
the remnant of the people in Jerusalem, and the other tribes,
who shall be scattered forth upon the face of the earth because of
their unbelief, may be brought to a knowledge of Me, their
Redeemer."*
        Nephi wrote quickly as the Savior talked about the
Gospel going to the gentiles because the House of Israel did not
believe, and how the gentiles, if they repented and turned to
Him, would be numbered among His people, along with the
house of Israel. After talking at length about the gentiles and
the House of Israel, and what would befall them, the Savior
stood up. Nephi and the twelve stood with him.
        The Savior stretched His hand toward the people before
the temple, *"Behold, My time is at hand. I can see that you are
weak and cannot understand all My words which the Father
has commanded Me to speak. Go to your homes and ponder
what I have said. Ask the Father in My name that you may be
given understanding. Prepare your minds for tomorrow, for I
shall come to you again. Now I go to the Father and to show
Myself to the lost tribes of Israel. They are not lost to the
Father. He knows where He has taken them."*
        Nephi looked around. Zannat and the multitude still
knelt in silent awe of the Savior. Tears glistened in people's
eyes as they looked steadfastly at the Savior. It was as if they
pleaded for Him to tarry a little longer. Nephi turned back to the
Savior. Jesus stood with head bowed.
        He sighed audibly. *"My bowels are filled with
compassion towards you,"* He said. *"Have you any sick or lame
or blind among you? Bring them and I will heal them, for I have
compassion upon you. My bowels are filled with mercy for I can
feel your desire that I show you what I did unto your brethren at
Jerusalem, and I see that your faith is sufficient that I should
heal you."*
        As the people moved forward with their sick, Nephi
quickly organized the twelve to hold back the crowd, bringing
up each person, one at a time, for the Savior to heal. He watched
with awe as the Savior laid his hands on those who were blind,
or dumb, or afflicted in any manner and healed them. What joy
he felt as he saw the renewed joy and hope and faith in the eyes
of those healed, as well as those who stood in the congregation
and watched their loved ones become whole once again. When

all were healed, Jesus commanded, *"Bring your little children to me."*

Mothers and fathers carried or led their children to the temple steps. The crowd pulled back, clearing a space, as more and more children came forward. Jesus stood in the midst of the children, touching them, holding little ones.

Once more He looked at the congregation beyond the children. Many were parents, wondering what would happen to their children. He knelt and motioned to the children. When all had knelt upon the ground, He sighed. Nephi could barely hear His whispered words: *"Father, I am troubled because of the wickedness of the people of the house of Israel."* Then He prayed, His voice soft but commanding as He called upon the Father in behalf of the children. Nephi tried to write the words of the prayer, but the Spirit constrained Him not to write them. The prayer, softly spoken, penetrated to the entire congregation.

Nephi wrote, *"Eye has never seen, nor ear heard, such great and marvelous things as we saw and heard Jesus speak unto the Father. No tongue can speak, neither can there be written by man, neither can the hearts of men comprehend the great and marvelous things we saw and heard Jesus speak. No one can conceive of the joy which filled our souls as He prayed for us unto the Father."*

When Jesus finished praying, he rose to his feet and looked with compassion upon the congregation who remained bowed to the earth. They seemed overcome. Nephi could understand, for he, himself, felt drained of energy.

"Rise," Jesus said, motioning with his arms. Slowly, the people rose to their feet.

"Blessed are you because of your faith," he said to them. *"And now, behold, My joy is full."*

Nephi could see the Savior was crying. Tears ran from His eyes and coursed down His cheeks. He walked to the temple steps and sat down, beckoning children to come to Him. He set them on his lap and blessed them. Mothers brought tiny babies and laid them on His lap, and He blessed them and prayed to the Father for them. When the last infant was blessed he stood once again and looked at the congregation. Again, Nephi noticed the tears on His cheeks.

"Behold your little ones."

Nephi and the others looked. At first they saw nothing, then they heard singing and looked up. Directly over their heads, angels—bodies bright as if in the midst of fire—descended from Heaven. Angels mingled with children, ministering to them. Brightness surrounding them seemed like glowing fire. Suddenly, all was still. The angels were gone. A murmur rose from the multitude as they questioned each other as to what they had seen.

Nephi looked up. The Savior again stood before him. He beckoned.

"Nephi, bring bread and wine. Enough for the entire people."

Nephi swallowed and stood up. He motioned to the other disciples, who followed him from the temple steps.

"The Savior wants bread and wine for the whole multitude."

"Where shall we get that much bread?"

"Or wine?"

"For three days we have been unable to bake."

Nephi shook his head. "Today you have seen so many miracles and yet you question? Go home and get all you have. It should be sufficient." He took his son and headed for his own home.

Minutes later the disciples were back with vases of wine and baskets of bread.

The Savior smiled at them, then commanded the multitude to sit upon the ground. He took the bread and broke it into small pieces, blessed it and handed a piece to each of the disciples. *"Eat,"* he said.

"Now, give of the bread to each person in the multitude."

When all in the congregation had been served, the disciples stood once again before the Master.

"I shall ordain one among you with power to break bread and bless it and give it to the people of My church who believe and are baptized in My name. This you shall always do, even as I have done. Do this in remembrance of My body which I have shown you as a testimony to the Father that you do always remember Me. If you do always remember Me you shall have My Spirit to be with you."

Jesus knelt and blessed the flagons of wine. He handed a cup to Nephi. *"Drink of it, then let all partake."*

Nephi did so and passed the cup to Timothy. When all the disciples had drunk of the cup they poured and passed to the entire multitude, until all had partaken.

Jesus sat on the temple step and watched them. When they were finished they returned and sat down around him, waiting for his words. He leaned forward and addressed them intimately, looking with kindness and love on each of them.

"Blessed are you for what you have just done, for this fulfills My commandments and witnesses to the Father that you are willing to do that which I have commanded you. Always do this for those who repent and are baptized in My name. Do it in remembrance of My blood which I have shed for you, that you may witness unto the Father that you do always remember Me. If you do always remember Me you shall have My Spirit to be with you."

He paused and gazed into the heavens for a few moments, a dreamy look in His eyes. *"I give you a commandment to do these things. If you do so, you will be blessed for you are built upon My rock. But anyone among you who does more or less than these is not built upon My rock but is built upon a sandy foundation; and when the rain descends and the floods come and the winds blow and beat upon them they shall fall and the gates of hell will be open and ready to receive them. Therefore, blessed are you if you shall keep My commandments which the Father has commanded Me that I should give unto you.*

"Watch and pray always lest you be tempted by the devil and be led away captive by him. Pray in My church as I have prayed among you. Pray among My people who repent and are baptized in My name. I am the light; I have set the example for you."

He stood and gazed at the silent multitude. Nephi and the disciples circled behind Him on the steps.

"My people," He said in that clear yet quiet voice which carried to all parts of the plaza. *"Pray always lest you enter into temptation, for Satan desires to have you that he may sift you as wheat. Always pray to the Father in My name, and whatever you ask the Father in My name, which is right, believing that you shall receive, behold it shall be given to you.*

"Pray with your families that your wives and children may be blessed. Meet together often. Forbid no person from meeting with you but pray for them and do not cast them out. Hold up your light that it may shine unto the world. I am the light which you should hold up. Do that which you have seen Me do. You have all seen Me pray to the Father, and I have commanded none of you to go away, but rather have commanded you to come unto Me that you might feel and see. Do the same for all people. Remember that whoever breaks this commandment shall be led into temptation."

Jesus turned from the congregation and thoughtfully faced the disciples. *"I give you one more commandment. Do not let anyone who is unworthy knowingly partake of My flesh and blood when you administer it. Whoever eats and drinks of My flesh and blood unworthily eats and drinks damnation to his soul. So, if you know that a man is unworthy to eat and drink of My flesh and blood, forbid him. However, do not cast him out from among you, but teach him and pray for him to the Father in My name. If he repents and is baptized in My name, then receive him and minister to him of My flesh and blood."*

He sighed and shook his head sadly. *"But if he doesn't repent he shall not be numbered among My people, for I know My sheep and they are numbered unto Me. Do not cast anyone out from your meeting places or synagogues, even though unworthy, but continue to teach them. They may return and repent and come unto Me with full purpose of heart and I shall heal them. You shall be the means of bringing salvation to them."*

He gazed deeply into the eyes of each of the disciples. *"Keep these sayings which I have commanded you that you may not come under condemnation. Wo unto him whom the Father condemns. I have given you these commandments because of the disputes which have been among you concerning My doctrine. Blessed are you if you have no more disputes among you. Now I go to the Father for it is expedient that I should go unto the Father for your sakes."*

He stepped to Nephi and laid his hands on him. *"Nephi,"* He said, looking deeply into his eyes, *"I give you power to give the Holy Ghost to all who are worthy to receive it."* He moved from disciple to disciple, laying His hands on them and blessing them.

When finished He looked one more time at those He had chosen, then a cloud filled the plaza, completely covering the multitude who still knelt there. Nephi and the disciples watched as the Savior ascended again into heaven. When his radiance was no longer visible, the cloud lifted. People looked around for Him in vain. Jesus was gone.

Cumorah, 387 A.D.

Mormon cupped his hands behind his head and looked outside at the long shadows. The excitement of writing of the Savior's coming to Bountiful had wearied him. He ate the meager supper Moroni prepared for him and lay on his pallet, thinking of the Savior's visit, especially his compassion and love for the little children. As his eyes closed in sleep, a smile remained on his lips.

CHAPTER EIGHT

THE SAVIOR'S RETURN

34 A.D.

Nephi stared into the sky, shading his eyes with his hand, until the brilliance of the heavens returned to normal. Blue sky paled by comparison. He realized he had been holding his breath and slowly exhaled. What a day this had been. All his senses had focused so totally on the Savior he hadn't noticed how quickly the day had passed. Smell of the sea came to him, soft and salty. For the first time he noticed seagulls circling overhead and the croaking of parrots. The sun, a huge bronze ball, hung over the western horizon, casting long shadows across the plaza.

The crowd—noisily discussing what had transpired—slowly dispersed as people returned to their homes.

Nephi sighed again, still awed by all that had happened. He motioned for the other disciples to come close. "Brethren, before the Savior left us and returned to heaven He promised to return tomorrow to this same place."

Several nodded in affirmation.

"Many people will be here in the morning who did not hear the Savior's message," Nephi continued, "They must be taught His words—and they must be taught without variation."

"Is that possible?," Kumen asked.

"We won't have to rely on memory. My son, Nephi, took extensive notes of the Savior's words. We will make copies for each of you." He turned to his son. "Nephi."

"Yes, father."

"I want each disciple to have a copy of the Savior's words."

"Yes, father."

Nephi, thankful for such an obedient son, watched him as he hurried down the steps and through the remaining crowd.

"What about those who heard the Savior today?" Jonas asked.

"Repetition will be good for all of us. If people hear the message two or three times they might remember how to live it."

"Shouldn't we notify others of the Savior's visit tomorrow?" Timothy asked.

"A good idea," Nephi said. "Those here today will hopefully spread the word to relatives and friends who still live. Timothy, would you and Jonas send runners to Mulek, Moroni, Nephihah and all the villages in between."

"We will take care of it immediately."

"Thank you. Instruct all to come here... and early."

Nephi snapped his eyes open. Heavy, oily smell of smoke filled the small room. Flicker of candle flame reminded him of the urgency of what he was doing. He looked at his son. The younger Nephi sat across the table, his head supported by his arm slanted across the bark paper upon which he had been writing. His hand, brush still clasped loosely between his fingers, lay limp on the table. Nephi shut his eyes and dozed again, his breathing deep and regular. Again he shook himself awake, unsure of how much time had passed—how long he had slept. His eyes were sore from rubbing. The candle was burned to a stub. Night lay black outside the small room. Its silence, broken only by the usual night sounds—throaty croaking frogs, trilling of thousands of cicadas—lay heavy over the city.

The cocks will soon be crowing, Nephi thought. The sun will once again fill the earth with its warmth and light. Today will be the second most special day of my life. The Savior will come again to teach us. I must hurry with the scrolls. He picked up his brush and dipped into the now-drying paint. Figures flowed onto the paper—words and phrases which Jesus had taught.

He finished one copy and set it aside, looked anxiously at his dozing son, and quickly started another. *I could certainly use Nephi's help,* he thought, *but he is so tired I hate to wake him.*

Zannat opened the door, interrupting his thoughts. She glanced at her son, slipped into the room, and carefully moved his papers and set some fruit on the table before him.

"Eat. It's almost morning," she said.

"Thank you." He leaned back and wrapped his arms around her waist, burying his face in her bosom. He loved the smell of her—the woman smell of earth and maguey soap and smoke from the cooking fire. He felt her stir and released his hold. She leaned down and kissed his forehead, then walked over to the younger Nephi. Nephi watched as she gently stroked their son's neck.

The younger Nephi sat up with a start, gazed around wild-eyed until he saw his father—then looking guilty, lowered his eyes to the unfinished manuscript. "I'm sorry, Father," he said softly. "I must have fallen asleep."

Nephi chuckled. "That's all right, son. You were exhausted after a very exciting day."

"But I have disappointed you."

"We can still finish if we both write fast," Nephi said.

Morning came quickly. Nephi looked with pride at the twelve bark paper rolls lying on the table. "One for each disciple," he said to his son. "Now we will all be able to teach exactly what the Master taught." He clapped his hand on his son's shoulder. "Thank you again, not only for your help in copying, but in taking such complete notes of what Jesus said."

"The Spirit certainly helped," the younger Nephi responded.

The Second Day

As dawn brightened the east the square began to fill. The disciples, already in place on the temple steps, looked as haggard as Nephi felt. Apparently none had slept. Nephi climbed to the top of the temple pyramid to get a better view of the sunrise. As the sun peeped above the horizon, a broad sheet of gold spread like a fan across the sea, flaming toward the city. Buildings, those still standing, glowed tawny in the reflected rays. Clouds picked up the reflection, evolving from white to bronze against the blueness of the sky.

Nephi stood atop the pyramid for long moments, his mind immersed in what he had both seen and heard. *The Savior, like the sun, brings light to the world—a light predicted for over six hundred years. A light which lights everything in its path; everything it touches. I have been touched by that light*

*and will nevermore be the same. I am a changed person. I have a
new heart, a new being, a new destiny, a new calling: Disciple to
the Savior. How blessed am I.*

He slowly climbed down to the where the disciples stood.

"When do you think He will return?" Isaiah asked.

"I don't know," Nephi said, "but the crowd is restless. We
should start teaching them—using what He taught us yesterday."

"Agreed," Kumen said.

"But how?" asked Zedekiah. "They are so many. The
crowd has overfilled the plaza and fills the incoming streets."

"There are twelve of us," Nephi said. "We will divide the
crowd into twelve groups. Each of us will teach a group."

"That sounds simple enough," growled Shemnon.

"Six streets enter the temple plaza," Nephi continued.
"Timothy, Jonas, Mathoni, Mathonihah, Kumen and I will
each take a street and teach the people who are in it. The rest of
you go to the center of the plaza and get the people's attention.
Divide those in the plaza into six groups—one for each of you."

"How do we begin?" Jonas asked.

Nephi handed each a scroll and smiled. "I think the first
thing we should do is to have the people pray." He motioned to
his son who was sitting on a lower step. "Nephi, come with me."

"Brothers and sisters," Nephi said. "Let us kneel and
pray to the Father in the name of Jesus. Pour out your hearts to
Him. Exercise your faith. Pray for His Spirit to be with us."

He knelt on the hard-packed earth and the people knelt
with him. Following their prayer he taught them—everything
his notes contained of the Savior's words. When finished, he
knelt again, praying that the Holy Ghost should be given unto
them.

A voice whispered in his consciousness: *"Baptize My
people."*

Nephi rose and moved among the people, clasping
forearms, patting heads, showing concern for each person.
When all had finished praying he said, "The Savior
commissioned the disciples to baptize. Many of you have been
baptized and are members of the church. That makes no
difference; each must be rebaptized, according to the words and
pattern the Savior gave us."

He led the way to the sea. On the beach his brother,
Timothy, caught up with him. "We are to be baptized again?"

"Yes," Nephi said. "In order to fulfill all righteousness."

"But how?"

"Jesus gave us authority to baptize. He even taught us the words to use," Nephi said. "Timothy, you baptize me. Then I will baptize you and together we can baptize the rest of the twelve." Not waiting for Timothy's response, he slipped off his sandals and waded into the water until he was waist deep.

Cumorah, 387 A.D.

Moroni stirred the fire as Mormon read aloud the words he had written.

"And it came to pass when they were all baptized and had come up out of the water, the Holy Ghost did fall upon them, and they were filled with the Holy Ghost. Fire came from heaven and encircled them; angels came from heaven and ministered to them."

"And then the Savior returned," Mormon whispered.

Bountiful, 34 A.D.

Young Nephi couldn't keep his eyes off the scene on the beach before Bountiful. The twelve whom the Savior had called were all there, including his father, uncle Timothy, and cousin Jonas. Dozens of heavenly beings, clothed in white and radiant as the sun, surrounded the twelve. While he watched, another dazzling being suddenly appeared in the midst of the angels and disciples. "It's the Savior," he whispered. The crowd buzzed with excitement as they passed the word. "The Savior has returned."

Jesus turned to the multitude and raised His arms above His head. He lowered them. *"Kneel on the earth,"* he said quietly. He motioned to the disciples. *"Now you must also kneel and pray."*

Each began to pray, some hesitant, some fluent, voices rising and falling in cadence, the sounds picked up by the slight breeze blowing in from the sea.

Jesus walked away from the disciples—directly towards young Nephi.

Nephi noticed the brightness of the Savior's eyes, the love and compassion which seemed to reach out and encompass all those in the multitude.

Jesus glanced back at the disciples, then dropped on His knees in the damp sand. As the Savior prayed, young Nephi pulled out his brushes and paints and wrote the words of His prayer:

"Father, I thank thee that thou has given the Holy Ghost to these whom I have chosen. Because of their belief in me I have chosen them out of the world. Father, I pray that thou wilt give the Holy Ghost to all who shall believe in their words. Father, I pray unto thee for them and for all who shall believe on their words, that they may believe in Me, that I may be in them as thou, Father, are in Me, that we may be one."

The Savior stood, his countenance glorious, and walked to where the disciples prayed. He looked down on the praying disciples, smiled and raised his hands over them—apparently blessing them. Young Nephi was astonished. The faces and clothing of the disciples were as white as the Savior's—the whiteness exceeding any whiteness that he had ever seen. There can be nothing on earth as white as this, he thought.

The Savior left the twelve and knelt again and prayed.

"Father, I thank thee that thou hast purified those whom I have chosen, because of their faith. I pray for them, and also for them who shall believe on their words, that they may be purified in Me, through faith on their words, even as they are purified in Me."

Nephi listened, then watched as Jesus again stood and walked to where the twelve prayed. Sun-like brightness emanated from the Savior and the twelve—so bright Nephi squinted his eyes to see. Jesus seemed to listen to the twelve for a moment then once more knelt a little ways off and prayed. His prayer was filled with power. Nephi tried, but this time could not write the words.

Again Jesus stood and walked to the disciples. He gently raised them to their feet. *"Stop praying now so I may teach you,"* He said, *"but never cease to pray in your hearts."*

When they were all standing He said, *"I never saw such faith among the Jews. Because of their unbelief I could not show them so great miracles. None saw as great of things as you have seen, nor heard so great things as you have heard."*

He walked with the twelve to the temple steps, then climbed above them, commanding the attention of the multitude. A whisper went through the crowd like a mountain breeze through pine trees. Prayers stopped and everyone looked expectantly at the brilliant figure before them. He motioned upward with outstretched arms and the people raised themselves from their knees. He gestured to young Nephi. *"Bring me a basket,"* he whispered.

Nephi did so.

Jesus broke bread into the basket, blessed it and passed the basket to each of the twelve. *"Give to the multitude,"* He said, *"that all may eat in remembrance of My body."*

The twelve passed through the crowd, giving bread to each person. Young Nephi couldn't take his eyes off the Savior. Where did the bread come from? There's enough to feed the entire crowd—thousands of people. It's another miracle.

The twelve returned to the steps. "Everyone has partaken, my Savior," Nephi whispered.

The young Nephi could not help but notice that the basket was still filled.

Jesus passed a goatskin to Nephi. *"Now, drink of this wine in remembrance of My blood, which was shed for you."*

Nephi drank and passed the skin to each of the twelve.

"Now, let the people also drink in remembrance of My blood, which I shed for them," the Savior commanded. *"He that eats this bread eats of My body to his soul; and he that drinks of this wine drinks of My blood to his soul; and his soul shall never hunger nor thirst, but shall be filled."*

Nephi poured wine into earthen jugs. The twelve again dispersed, giving each person a swallow of the sanctified wine.

Young Nephi was even more amazed. Taste of the sweet wine lingered in his mouth. Bread was one thing to create out of thin air, but wine! Enough wine to let thousands of people have a sip. He watched his father and the other disciples as they filtered through the throng of people, tilting up the jugs.

When all had sipped of the wine, a mighty shout went up from the entire throng. Young Nephi found himself joining in, feeling the joy of knowing the Savior, loudly praising Him, giving Him the glory that was His.

Jesus sat on the step facing the multitude. His disciples quickly clustered below him. He spoke and the crowd quieted until the only sound was his soft voice. *"Behold,"* he said, *"now I finish the commandment which the Father has commanded Me concerning this people who are a remnant of the house of Israel."*

The youthful Nephi wrote as Jesus talked of the words of Isaiah concerning the scattering and gathering of God's chosen people and when they would be fulfilled. He spoke of the Gentiles and the enemies which would attempt to destroy this remnant.

"The Father commanded Me to give you this land for your inheritance, fulfilling the covenant which I made with your father Jacob. This land shall be a New Jerusalem and I,

along with the powers of heaven, shall be in the midst of this people."

He continued. *"I am He of whom Moses spake: 'A prophet shall the Lord your God raise up unto you of your brethren, like unto me. Him shall you hear in all things whatsoever He shall say unto you. And it shall come to pass that every soul who will not hear that prophet shall be cut off from among the people!'"*

Nephi didn't miss a word as the Savior spoke of Abraham's blessing and told those assembled they were children of the covenant. He talked of how the Father would gather His covenant people and give them Jerusalem as the land of their inheritance. He quoted Isaiah and spoke of signs that would signal when these things would come to pass. Jesus told them He would gather in His people from their dispersion and establish them again in Zion.

Young Nephi wrote as the Savior spoke, faithfully brushing His words onto the paper.

"Search these things diligently, for great are the words of Isaiah. He spoke as touching all things concerning My people who are of the house of Israel. All things that he prophesied have been and shall be, even according to the words which he spake. Give heed to My words. Write the things I have told you."

Young Nephi smiled. *That's one commandment I am keeping.*

"These words shall go forth unto the Gentiles. Whoever will hearken unto My words and repent and be baptized, the same shall be saved. Search the prophets, for many there be that testify of these things."

Jesus looked with compassion on the twelve He had chosen, as if He knew what the future would hold for them. Then He spoke again, this time expounding to the people the scriptures which had been written by Lehi and Nephi and every Nephite prophet down to young Nephi's father, Nephi. It was as if the Savior had memorized the words of Jacob, Benjamin, Mosiah, and the two Alma's. *No,* young Nephi thought, *the words are really His.*

"There are other scriptures you should write that you have not. Nephi," He called. *"Bring Me the records."*

Nephi hurried to obey. His son, Nephi, ran to catch up with him. At least he could help carry the records.

Heads turned as the two Nephis entered the temple plaza, their arms loaded with scrolls. The Savior smiled at them as they climbed the steps to where he stood. He glanced through the scrolls until He found the one He wanted.

"*I commanded My servant, Samuel, the Lamanite, to testify unto this people that at the day the Father should glorify His name in Me many saints should arise from the dead, and should appear unto many, and should minister unto them.*" He looked at Nephi and the others. "*Was this not so?*"

Timothy answered. "Yes, Lord, Samuel did prophesy according to Thy words, and they were all fulfilled."

"*How is it that you have not written it—that many saints did arise and appear unto many and did minister unto them?*"

Nephi shook his head. "I don't know, my Lord."

"*Write it,*" Jesus said, "*that the records may be complete.*"

Nephi beckoned to his son. Young Nephi brought brushes and ink and Nephi added the words to the record. While he wrote, Jesus taught from the scriptures. "Teach the things I have taught you. I now teach you the words which the Father gave to Malachi. These, too, you should write and teach to the people."

Young Nephi wrote quickly so as not to miss a word. Phrases rang in his ears:

"*... who may abide the day of His coming?*

"*... who shall stand when He appears?*

"*... will a man rob God? Yet you have robbed Me. But you say: Wherein have we robbed Thee? In tithes and offerings.*

"*Bring all the tithes into the storehouse, that there may be meat in my house; and prove me now herewith...*

"*The day comes that shall burn as an oven; and all the proud, yes, and all that do wickedly, shall be stubble...*

"*I will send you Elijah, the prophet, before the coming of the great and dreadful day of the Lord...*"

After the Savior taught the twelve, He turned to the multitude and gave the same words to them. Young Nephi followed what he had written, checking his accuracy, making changes when necessary so the record was correct. When Jesus finished the words of Malachi, He said, "*The Father commanded Me that I should give these scriptures to you for it is wisdom that they should be given to future generations who will read your records.*"

Then He began at the creation of the world and taught them all that had transpired, and all that would transpire down to the time He would come in His glory—when the elements would melt with fervent heat and the earth would be wrapped together as a scroll and the heavens and the earth would pass

away. He talked of that last day when all people should stand
before God to be judged of their works—whether they be good or
evil, and of that judgment when the righteous would be
resurrected into everlasting life, and the evil would be
resurrected into damnation.

He stopped talking and moved into the crowd, touching
and speaking to people. When completed, He paused before
young Nephi and his mother, smiled at them, stretched His
arms to the heavens, and quickly disappeared from view into
the sky.

There was silence for several moments, then a large
sigh, like wind through the treetops, passed through the
multitude. Chattering erupted, sounding like a forest full of
monkeys, as people discussed what they had seen and heard.

Young Nephi looked at his father. The elder Nephi's face
was flushed as if he had put forth great effort.

His mother, Zannat, stood and took his fathers's hand.
"What is it?" she asked.

Nephi shook his head as if still filled with wonder.
"Jesus blessed the children, healed the sick, the lame, the blind
and the deaf. He raised one man from the dead." He shook his
head. "We have seen and heard miraculous things." Tears filled
his eyes. "Come. Let us go to our house." He smiled. "I just
realized how hungry I am. We have not eaten today."

"Wait," Timothy cried. "What about tomorrow?"

"Yes," Jonas continued. "What do we tell the people?"

Nephi had one arm around Zannat and the other around
his son. "We will meet here again tomorrow and review the
words the Savior has taught us. Those who are ready will be
baptized."

Cumorah, 387 A.D.

Mormon, leaving the gold plates on the rock, stood
stiffly and stretched.

"Where are you going?" Moroni asked.

"Nowhere," his father answered. "I was just thinking of
all the wonderful things the Savior said, and yet I did not write
a hundredth part of what He taught the people."

"Why not? Nephi wrote all His words, didn't he?"

"Yes, but when I attempted to inscribe them on the plates
of gold the Lord told me not to write everything. He said, 'I will
try the faith of my people.' So I included only a part of the words
He taught during the three days He was with the Nephites."

"Now what will happen to what you have written?"

Mormon's eyes had a dreamy quality about them, as if a vision of the future opened to him. "These words will go to the gentiles and will be a test for them. If they believe these few things then greater things will be given them. If they do not believe, then the greater things will be withheld—to their condemnation. From the gentiles these words will then come back to the remnants of this people."

Bountiful, The Third Day; 34 A.D.

Nephi watched as the multitude again filled the plaza to overflowing. Many looked tired and drawn. And yet each person has experienced enough joy to last a lifetime. His eyes followed Mathoni and Mathonihah as they came up the steps, their heads together as they talked seriously. When they arrived at where he stood, Mathoni asked, "Nephi, we desire to go to Zarahemla as soon as possible to teach any survivors."

"A good idea. Do you want to take others with you?"

Mathoni shrugged. "Doesn't matter. We are just anxious to teach and baptize in the name of Jesus."

Kumen and Kumenonhi climbed the steps with a request. "We desire to go into the land northward and teach and baptize."

Timothy and his son, Jonas, requested the land of Nephi and the land southward. They agreed to take Zedekiah with them.

"Brethren," Nephi said. "Jeremiah, Shemnon, Jonas, Isaiah and I will remain in Bountiful. For the next two months teach, baptize and confer upon people the Gift of the Holy Ghost. We will meet here on the first night of the second full moon and report our missions."

He was interrupted by shouts of astonishment from the plaza.

Young Nephi ran panting up the steps. "Come quickly," he said. "Another miracle."

"What...?" Nephi cried.

His son grabbed his arm. "Come," he said.

Nephi and the disciples followed down the steps. They stopped short. The adults were on their knees, surrounding their children. The children, even babies hardly old enough to stand, taught the words of the Savior. They prophecied and told great and marvelous things that would happen to the people of Nephi. The twelve fell to their knees in reverence, listening to what the children said. Young Nephi tried to write, but couldn't.

Nephi, noticing, whispered, "These things are too sacred, too wonderful to inscribe on paper." Just one more experience that I will treasure all of my life. Who would have thought that babes would be used to teach us such truths? Who could have even imagined a crowd such as this kneeling and listening to children?

The two months passed quickly. Nephi was so busy teaching he hardly took time to eat. Zannat had to practically beg him to stay at home. Often, young Nephi accompanied his father as he visited the villages surrounding Bountiful.

"Father," young Nephi said.

"What is it, son," Nephi asked without looking up from inscribing the Savior's words from bark paper rolls to thin plates of gold. Drops of sweat beaded on his forehead and rolled down his cheeks as he concentrated on the intricate task.

"It is the time of the second full moon."

"So it is," Nephi put down his stylus. "There is so little time to get done all that needs doing; time passes so quickly!"

A full moon lighted the night sky as the twelve gathered in Nephi's garden. Smells of hydrangea and bougainvillaea filled the air. Tangy sea breezes brought smells of salt and fish. Birds chittered evening melodies. Zannat carried trays of fruit, nuts, cooked squash and sweet potatoes to set before them. During dinner the twelve shared stories of teaching the Savior's words and of baptisms and of giving the gift of the Holy Ghost.

"Let this meal be the last we eat until we pray as a group to the Lord," Nephi suggested. "Through fasting and prayer we may prove worthy to have Him visit us once more."

Nephi was so excited to have the twelve together he couldn't sleep. He walked to the temple before daybreak, thinking he would be the first to arrive. Morning dawned warm and clear, but before the sun had fully appeared all twelve disciples stood before the steps where the Savior taught just two short months before.

"Let's go into the temple on top of the pyramid where we can have privacy," Nephi said.

"The space is quite small," countered Timothy.

"Just right for the twelve," Nephi said.

They climbed the steps. Timothy was puffing by the time they reached the top. Nephi smiled. Timothy had always had a big appetite. He could usually out-eat any two men. Now it was catching up with him. The breadth of his paunch was immense.

"What now?" Zedekiah asked as they assembled on top.

"We must pray for God's counsel—all day and all night, if necessary."

As one they knelt on the stone of the temple. The sun arched its way up the heavens and started its long descent down to the western mountains. Still the disciples prayed. Air was hot and humid but they seemed not to notice. Growls of hunger came from flattened stomachs, but were ignored.

Prayers were interrupted by quiet words. The disciples looked around in the stillness. Jesus stood in their midst. On His face was the most beautiful smile Nephi had ever seen.

The Savior asked, *"What do you desire that I give unto you?"*

Nephi and his brethren looked at each other. Faces showed concern but no one spoke. Finally Nephi asked. "Lord, tell us the name we shall call Your church. Already we have had disputations concerning this matter."

Jesus looked at them, kindly concern showing in his eyes and demeanor. *"Why do people dispute? Have they not read the scriptures which say you must take upon you the name of Christ, which is My name? Whoever takes upon him My name and endures to the end shall be saved at the last day. Therefore, whatever you do you shall do in My name; you shall call the Church in My name; you shall call upon the Father in My name and He will bless the church for My sake. How can it be My church if it is not called by My name? If a church be called in Moses' name then it is Moses' church. Or, if it be called in the name of a man then it is the church of that man; but if it be called in My name then it is My church—if it is built upon My gospel."*

Jonas, his voice trembling, quietly asked, "Lord, from my youth I have been taught to follow the Gospel, but I am still not sure what all the Gospel entails."

Jesus smiled at Jonas. *"The Gospel is that I came into the world to do My Father's will. My Father sent Me that I might be lifted up on the cross; that after I had been lifted upon the cross I might draw all men to Me; that as I have been lifted up by men, even so should men be lifted up by the Father to stand before Me to be judged of their works, whether they be good or whether they be evil."* He looked around at the sober-faced twelve. *"This is My Gospel. If the Church is built upon My Gospel then will the Father show forth His works in it."*

"Who will be members of Your church," Zedekiah asked.

"Whoever repents and is baptized in My name. When I stand to judge the world I will hold guiltless those who endure to

the end. He that endures not to the end shall be hewn down and cast into the fire. No unclean thing can enter into God's kingdom. Therefore, no one enters into His rest except those who have repented and are faithful."

The Savior continued speaking, defining His gospel and how to enter into His kingdom. He turned to Nephi. *"Write the things which you have seen and heard. Write the works of this people. Out of the books shall this people be judged and by them shall their works be known unto men."*

He spread His arms to encompass the disciples. *"You shall be judges of this people according to the judgment which I shall give you, which shall be just. What manner of men ought you to be? I say unto you, even as I am."*

He looked around at the group of quiet men, fixing each of them with his direct stare. *"Now I go to the Father. Whatsoever things you shall ask the Father in My name shall be given unto you. Therefore, ask, and you shall receive; knock and it shall be opened unto you; for he that asks, receives; and unto him that knocks, it shall be opened."*

His eyes glistened with unshed tears. *"My joy is great because of you and this generation. The Father and the holy angels also rejoice, for none of them are lost."*

Timothy was astonished. "None shall be lost?" he exclaimed.

"None who are now alive of this generation are lost. In them I have a fullness of joy." Jesus rose from where he had been sitting and stared over the edge of the pyramid across the land Bountiful. He turned back to the disciples. Nephi noted the look of sadness on His face.

"I sorrow because of the fourth generation from this generation. They are led away captive by satan even as was the son of perdition. They will sell Me for silver and gold, and for that which moth does corrupt and which thieves can break through and steal. In that day will I visit them, even in turning their works upon their own heads."

Cumorah, 387 A.D.

Mormon shook his head sadly. "That's our generation," he whispered to Moroni. "And it has happened just as the Lord predicted. Now my only desire is to depart this life and rejoin my loved ones in the heavens."

"No, Father," Moroni said. "There is still much you must teach me."

Bountiful, 34 A.D.

Jesus taught the twelve. *"Enter in at the strait gate; for strait is the gate and narrow is the way that leads to life, and few there be that find it. But wide is the gate and broad the way which leads to death, and many there be that travel therein, until the night comes wherein no man can work."*

Nephi sensed that the Savior was about to depart again from them. He stood, followed by the rest of the twelve. They stood in a semi-circle around Jesus.

The Savior, eyes filled with compassion, gazed at each of them. *"After I have gone to My Father, what do you desire of Me?"*

Most of the disciples spoke at once, expressing their desires. He smiled and raised his hands. The babble ceased as suddenly as it had begun. *"Zedekiah,"* he said, *"speak for them."*

Zedekiah looked at the ground for a moment. He looked up. "Lord, we desire that after we have lived as long as an average man, that our ministry, to which You have called us, may end, so we can speedily come to Thee in Thy kingdom."

Jesus smiled. *"Blessed are you because you desire this thing of Me. Therefore, after you are seventy-two years of age you shall come unto Me in My kingdom. With Me you shall find rest."* He turned to Nephi. *"Three of you did not desire this. What do you desire when I am gone unto the Father?"*

Nephi, one of the three, couldn't answer. His heart felt in his throat, choking off all speech.

Jesus rested a hand on his arm. *"Never mind. I know your thoughts. You desire that which John, My beloved, who was with Me in My ministry, before I was lifted up by the Jews, desired of Me. More blessed are you. Like John you shall never taste of death but shall live to behold all the doings of the Father unto the children of men, even until all things shall be fulfilled according to the will of the Father. You shall never endure the pains of death, but when I come in My glory you shall be changed in the twinkling of an eye from mortality to immortality. Then shall you be blessed in the kingdom of My Father. You shall have no pain while you dwell in the flesh, neither sorrow save it be for the sins of the world; and all this will I do because of the thing which you have desired of Me, for you have desired that you might bring the souls of men unto Me, while the world shall stand. You shall have fullness of joy, even*

*as the Father has given Me fullness of joy, and you shall be even
as I am..."*

Jesus touched each of the nine with His finger as he
talked. They bowed their heads and shut their eyes at His touch,
and when they looked up, Jesus was no longer with them.
Neither were the three who had elected to stay on the earth until
his coming.

Cumorah, 387 A.D.

Mormon leaned against the cave wall near the entrance
and looked up at the stars which glinted brightly in the heavens
outside the cave. "And the three!" he exulted aloud to Moroni,
"were caught up into heaven and saw and heard unspeakable
things. They were transfigured—changed from this body of flesh
to an immortal state—that they could behold the things of God.
For over three hundred years they have ministered upon the
face of the earth, uniting as many to the Church as would
believe in their preaching, baptizing them, and giving the Holy
Ghost to them. They were cast into prison but the prisons could
not hold them. They were cast into pits in the earth but were
delivered by the power of God. Three times they were cast into a
furnace and received no harm. Twice they were cast into dens of
wild beasts. They played with the beasts as a child plays with a
suckling lamb and received no harm."

"Both of us have seen them," Moroni said.

Mormon seemed not to hear. His eyes, focused far away,
looked into the future. "They will be among the Gentiles and the
Gentiles will not know them. They will also be among the Jews
and the Jews will not know them. They will even minister to the
scattered tribes of Israel."

Moroni helped him to his pallet. He lay down, his eyes
closed, ready for sleep.

"Ah," he whispered. "Great shall be their works before
that great and coming day when all people must surely stand
before the judgment seat of Christ."

Moroni knelt beside his father until he heard his
breathing slow as he drifted into a quiet sleep.

CHAPTER NINE

MORMON

Cumorah, 387 A.D.

"I have finished my abridgement of Nephi's record of the Savior's visit." Mormon rose with a sigh of relief. "Only one more group of plates to abridge—from the time of the Savior until Ammoron commissioned me to keep the records of the Nephite people. When that is done my abridgement will be finished, leaving only my record of the Nephites down to the present."

"Father," Moroni said. "I am proud of your accomplishment."

"Of all the things I have done in my life, my most important calling has been abridging the records. Truly it has been a labor of love," Mormon responded. "I have learned so much by reading, studying and pondering the writings of these great prophets and then putting their thoughts into my own words." He flexed his cramped fingers. "We must finish the plates. After I am gone you will have the responsibility to complete the history of this people and preserve the plates to the Lord."

"I will do what I can," Moroni said. "But you are almost finished."

"The account I must now write was inscribed by Nephi on the plates—the fourth Nephi to serve as a scribe since Lehi and his sons left Jerusalem. You can be very proud, Moroni, that you are a literal descendant of Lehi." He sat down tiredly.

Moroni stood at the cave's entrance, looking into the distance beyond Cumorah. He turned to Mormon. "Father, fresh fish and clams would taste mighty good. I can go to the east sea, dig some clams and catch some fish, and be back within two days."

"Food to me at this time means nothing, but if you want to go, do so. I will be all right."

"We both need a change of diet." Moroni smiled. "I can almost smell the aroma of fresh fish roasting on the rocks."

"The change would be nice," Mormon mumbled. *But I hate to see you leave me,* he thought. He watched as Moroni gathered a few supplies. "Be very careful."

"Tonight will be a good night to go. There will be a full moon. By sticking to the trail I can be at the seashore by morning." He looked at Mormon. "I am concerned about you, though. Will you be all right for a few days?"

Mormon smiled. "Who would want to disturb a helpless old man? I believe I can look after myself. I want to finish this writing and get the plates secure once again." He stood and walked to Moroni. Placing his hand on his son's shoulder, he said, "My only concern is, if anything happens to me, will you finish the record?"

"I will complete any writing that you don't do, Father," he said, an impish grin on his face, "but knowing your tenacity I won't have to worry."

Father and son clasped arms. Mormon impulsively wrapped his arms around his son's shoulders. They stood for a few moments savoring their closeness. Tears glistened in Mormon's eyes and on his cheeks as he watched from the cave's entrance until Moroni faded from sight in the darkness. "My son," he whispered aloud, "I have a feeling I may never see you again in mortality."

Mormon spat out the bitter-tasting berries. He wasn't sure the berries were that bitter or that things just didn't taste good since Moroni left. Moroni had been his constant companion since the great battle and now he was gone.

Moroni is gone. My wife, children and all my people are dead. What is there to live for? He glanced at the stack of plates on the rock beside the cave's entrance. He answered his own question. *These are what I have to live for. Until I finish the records the Lord will not let me die.*

He glanced at the top plate on which he had just reviewed the Savior's visit. *I would like to tell of the three disciples who chose to remain on the earth. I grew quite well acquainted with them. There is much I could write,* he thought. *Several times they visited me and talked of their lives. I learned their names but the Lord prohibits me from writing them.*

He wrote: The three went forth upon the face of the land and preached the gospel of Christ unto all the people of Nephi. Many believed, were baptized and received the Holy Ghost. Thus the people of that generation were united into the church of Christ and blessed according to the word of Jesus.

Sighing, he thought of man's natural—or Satan-induced—inclination to slip back; to return to sinful ways. With ease of experience he wrote of the work of the three disciples, of their trials as well as successes. He paused in his writing, still nervous about Moroni. He walked back into the cave and stirred the small fire. *Perhaps some sage tea will help me relax,* he thought. He minced sage between his fingers into the pottery bowl. *I could have written how the three disciples ministered to me and taught me.*

Mormon sipped his tea, appreciating the warmth and fragrance of it. He pondered about the three—how they would visit the scattered tribes of Israel and minister to all peoples on the earth. *They truly serve as angels of God and can show themselves to any man. They will bring many souls to Jesus and will complete many great and marvelous works before the great day when all people must surely stand before the judgment seat of Christ.*

"I'm getting ahead of my story," he muttered. "After the time of the Savior there was almost two hundred years of peace; more peace than existed at any other time in the promised land." He yawned. "That was the time of the fourth Nephi—Nephi, the son of Nephi—who served as scribe during the time of the Savior."

Mormon had been careful to write only during daylight hours. He didn't want light from candle or fire to give away the location of the cave to any watching Lamanites. Now he felt a sense of urgency to complete the record. He added wood to the fire until it brightened the cave. He picked up the plate and wrote, stopping only to stoke the fire. Gray of morning lighted the cave's entrance when he finished his abridgement.

He was tired, but before he retired to his pallet he read over what he had written which chronicled the Nephite history from the time of the Savior until Ammoron set him apart as scribe and record-keeper:

The disciples of Jesus formed a church of Christ in every city. Within two years of the Savior's visit, everyone—Nephites and Lamanites—had joined the Church. Peace existed throughout the land. There were no contentions or disputes. All things were held in common and every man dealt justly with his neighbor. No one discriminated between rich or poor, bond or free. All were made free as partakers of the heavenly gift. They obeyed the commandments which the Savior had given, continuing in fasting and prayer and in meeting together often to pray and to hear the word of the Lord. Because of this the Lord blessed and prospered them. They became an exceedingly fair and delightsome people.

The disciples worked many miracles: healed the sick, raised the dead, caused the lame to walk, made the blind to see and the deaf to hear. Envy, strife, tumult, whoredoms, lyings, murders, and lasciviousness found no place among the covenant people. There were no robbers nor murderers; no Lamanites nor any manner of "ites." They were one, children and heirs of Christ.

Mormon sighed. What a time in which to live. What a contrast with his own time, when the people had become so wicked the Lord finally let them be exterminated by the Lamanites.

But that peace didn't last. As time passed some became lifted up in pride, wearing costly apparel and fine jewelry. People no longer had goods and substance in common. They divided into classes and built up churches to get gain. Some rebelled and took upon themselves the name of Lamanites so once again there were Lamanites in the land. Apostate churches, many of which professed to know the Christ yet denied the more important parts of His gospel, multiplied.

The wicked hardened their hearts and delighted in iniquity. They chose priests and false prophets to lead their churches. They persecuted the members of the true church of Christ because of their humility and belief in the Savior. The faithful performed many miracles but non-members despised them even more. The wicked tried many times to kill the three disciples. They adorned themselves with all manner of precious things and willfully rebelled against the gospel of Christ. They became more numerous than the people of God—waxing strong in their parts of the land. Once again the secret combinations of Satan—those which the Gadianton robbers had hidden in the earth—came forth.

In the two hundred and thirty-first year the people divided into opposing camps: Believers in Christ were called Nephites, Jacobites, Josephites and Zoramites. Unbelievers were called Lamanites, Lemuelites and Ishmaelites. Within a few years even those called Nephites became proud and drifted from the church—becoming vain like the Lamanites. By the time three hundred years had passed, the entire people, with few exceptions, had become very wicked. The robbers of Gadianton spread over all the face of the land. Gold and silver became their Gods—hoarded and traded back and forth to all areas of the country.

The righteous few, along with the disciples, carefully preserved the records. As disciples died, new disciples were ordained. The chroniclers—the record keepers—wrote what happened to the people. They guarded the sacred records with their lives—records which had been handed down from generation to generation—hiding them up unto the Lord that they might come again to the remnant of the house of Jacob according to the prophecies and promises of the Lord.

Mormon leaned back and looked into the starry heavens. *I am one of those record keepers. I have preserved the records. My last years have been spent abridging the records. My son will be the last of the chroniclers.* He put down the plate. All of the writings of the fourth Nephi to Ammoron he had condensed into a small portion of one plate. He munched on some fruit as he prepared for bed. Tiredly he lay on his pallet. He pillowed his head on his hands and watched the fire burn itself out. *Less than four-hundred years since the time of Christ, he mused. Peace only lasted two-hundred years. As a result of increasing wickedness—the Nephites are now exterminated from the face of the earth.*

Frustrated, he sat up and slammed his fist onto his knee, grimacing in pain as a result. *Oh, that the people could have foretold what their wickedness would bring. Yet they were told. Prophets from the beginning told them what would happen if they continued in their wicked ways. During my lifetime the church of Christ was a small minority of the people—persecuted, often meeting in secret, but faithful and loyal to the commandments which Jesus taught them. Now, here I am, the sole survivor of the Nephite people, with the exception of Moroni, whom the Lord has promised He would preserve as a valiant witness of the Savior and his dealings with this people.*

He lay down and finally slept.

When he awakened the sun was high in the heavens. Mormon looked around through the trees. No sign of Moroni.

He knew his son would only barely be at the seashore, but he already missed him. It was noon and time to eat but he had no hunger. His appetite and ambition for making a fire and cooking had gone with Moroni. He absently retrieved some dried fruit from the cave and munched while he pored over the records. The plates were now complete—the abridgment of all the records up to the beginning of his own life. He smiled. All that was left to do was to abridge his own writings. He picked up his stylus.

And now I, Mormon, make a record of the things which I have both seen and heard, and call it the Book of Mormon. He leaned back, the stylus tapping a rhythm on the rock as his thoughts went back to his own earliest memories. Uncle Ammoron had been a recluse—a hermit living far off in a cave. I really didn't know Uncle Ammoron very well, but...

Chapter Ten

Mormon's Youth

Land of Desolation, 321 A.D.

"Mormon, from my observations I believe you to be a serious lad and quick to observe."

Mormon looked up from the sand temple he was making. A few feet away, waves eased themselves onto the beach, depositing shells and sticks on the white, grainy sand.

His uncle Ammoron leaned on a knotty staff and looked kindly at him. A man of medium height, Ammoron towered over the young Mormon. Dark-skin, from being out in the sun so much, contrasted with hair as white as cresting foam on the waves which rolled onto the beach. Hands were bony but his face was full with harmonious strong lines. Mormon admired his uncle, the keeper of the records for the Nephite people. He waited respectfully.

"Mormon, I was already an old man when my brother, Amos, set me apart as scribe and record keeper. For fifteen years I have recorded those things which have happened." He sighed audibly, leaning hard on his staff. "Now that I am about to die someone must be appointed to take my place. I have no children. Like me, you are of the lineage of Nephi, Alma and Helaman. The Lord has inspired me to call you to this important calling."

Nephi stood and brushed the sand from his body. "But, uncle, I am only ten years old."

Ammoron lifted his hand for silence, ignoring Mormon's interruption. "You must receive scribe training and training in metalwork. As you grow to manhood, observe and record the things which happen to our people. Knowing I would soon die, I hid the sacred writings in my cave. Your father knows the place. Go to the hill Shim when you are twenty-four years of age. The Lord will show you the spot. Take out the first stack of plates, the plates of Nephi, and record on them the things you have observed. Leave the other records in the cave."

He turned slowly and started to leave.

"Wait, uncle. I..."

Ammoron turned to look at the lad. "My son," he said, "this is a great responsibility. Many covet the gold plates for their own wicked use. Protect the plates with your life. Let no one have the records until you turn them over to your successor." He paused and frowned as he seemed to contemplate the future. "Go tell your father what I told you." He shuffled off through the sand and up a tree-shaded path which led to the village.

Mormon ran to his father's workroom and tugged at his father's hand. "Father, come quickly. Find Uncle Ammoron."

The senior Mormon was planing a board, ready to attach legs which would make it a bench. Curls of shavings lay around his legs and on his hairy arms. "What is it, son?" He knelt beside him. "Why do we need to find Ammoron?"

Words gushed out. "He told me I was to be the scribe of the Nephite people and when I was twenty-four I would find the plates he hid and write everything that happened to the people."

Mormon lay the plane on its side on the bench. "You are to be the scribe?" He wiped sweat from his forehead, sat down and hoisted the young Mormon to his lap. "I should have suspected it. I am too old to learn to write and you are the closest relative. What else did he say?"

Young Mormon looked at his father. The elder Mormon was a large man, with aquiline nose towered over by a broad forehead. Eyebrows were full and without break, giving an impression of energy. Beneath the heavy eyebrows deep-set, kindly eyes glowed blackly. His hands were big, bony and long and when he talked his gestures were eloquent.

"He said he hid the plates in a cave on the Hill Shim. He said you would know where."

The elder Mormon soberly took his son's hands in his work-roughened ones. "Son, this is a great honor for you. You will be a chronicler like Nephi and Helaman." He called. "Ileea!"

Mormon's mother, her hands white from making the flour cakes which Mormon loved, entered the archway which led from the shop to their home. "What is it?" she answered.

"It's our son, Mormon," Mormon said proudly. "Ammoron has called him to be the scribe and keeper of records."

Ileea leaned against the door jamb, shock written on her comely face.

In his deep voice Mormon continued. "He must learn to be a scribe and work with metal plates. The best school of the scribes is in Zarahemla. I must take him there."

Ileea put a flour-covered hand to her mouth. "My son? Leave Desolation? But..."

Mormon pushed his son to his feet, dusted his hands on his rough leather pants and walked to his wife. He held her at arm's length. "Our son must go to Zarahemla. It is the Lord's will."

Preparations for the journey took several weeks. Provisions were bought and packed securely. Friends and relatives came to say their goodbyes. Whenever Mormon looked at his mother, tears filled her eyes and she would look away. She tried to hide her grief but her tears and anxiety were constant.

Young Mormon, a heavy pack on his back, turned with his father on the foothills above Desolation. He looked back over the city and picked out his house. It was the only home he had ever known. He could see his mother standing in the front doorway and could imagine her tear-stained eyes and cheeks. He would never forget how she cried as she fiercely held him to her. It was as if she would never let him go. He waved.

Far down in the city, his mother, a scarf in her hand, waved sadly in return.

His father put a hand on his shoulder and turned him up the path. He was on the way to Zarahemla. He didn't look back.

The first part of the journey, over gently-hilled terrain, was easy. Grass was knee-high and trees were loaded with fruit of all kinds. Brightly-colored birds chattered and scolded them from bushes and trees. Small animals scooted across the trail or stood on mounds watching them pass. Sun was hot overhead and soon Mormon's shoulders were rubbed raw from the straps of his pack. His father set a strong pace and seldom stopped to rest.

As they approached Bountiful, rolling hills leveled to coastal plain, extending as far as Mormon could see. Rivers were obstacles to be met and crossed. The trail crossed smaller

streams at shallow fords, but larger rivers presented problems.
With their packs they could not swim and the water was too deep
to wade across. The elder Mormon searched out dry logs and,
using lianas, lashed them together as rafts.

After a week's travel they reached the largest river of all.
Mormon collapsed on the river bank and slipped the pack off
his shoulders. Boats moved up and down the river—boats
different from the hollowed out canoes that plied the waterways
around Desolation. They were large, with sails and oarsmen.

"This is the Sidon," his father said. He patted the
younger Mormon's head. "Across the river is the city of Moroni,
named after Captain Moroni who saved the land from the
Lamanites."

Mormon looked across the broad river. A city with
temples and pyramids rose from the jungle. Huge walls abutted
the river. From that distance he could barely make out small
figures of warriors on top the wall. "How do we cross?" he asked
wearily.

"By boat," Mormon answered. "Boats cross the river
regularly from upstream. We stay tonight in the city."

Mormon was glad. He was tired of walking.

His father must have understood his feelings. He reached
down and squeezed his hand. "You will really enjoy the rest of
the journey. From here we go by boat to Zarahemla. The Sidon
will be our pathway."

The boat trip up the Sidon was an adventure for the
young Mormon. Jungle grew to the edge of the river, some trees
actually standing in the water. Wildlife lived and cavorted in
the trees: monkeys leapt from tree to tree, sloths hung upside
down, young ones lined up beside the adults, gaily-colored
parrots scolded them as they passed. An occasional jaguar stood
on the bank, tail lashing nervously. Ducks swam in calm lees in
the river, diving when boats came too close.

The broad river was a regular highway. Boats bounced
along, with rowers fighting the sluggish current going upstream,
as they were, or moving swiftly downstream towards Moroni
and the sea. Most contained trade goods and a few passengers.
The twelve rowers in Mormon's boat strained to force their boat
upstream. Muscles bulged on huge arms in rhythm. Mormon
vowed that someday his muscles would be large like the
oarsmen.

They entered a dark canyon. Black rock cliffs and green
forest reached high to the blue sky on both sides. Cliff and
sunlight formed a delightful contrast of light and shadow.

Never had Mormon seen such beauty. A day later when they emerged from the canyon, it was to discover a gleaming city stretched out along the grassy bank, heat-wavering under the midday sun.

"Sidom," Father Mormon said.

"We stop here to leave part of our load of fruit," an oarsmen said.

Mormon smiled at his son. "Perhaps we can explore the city while they unload."

Father and son hiked up the ridge north of the city until they could look at the river far below them. Mormon looked to the south into the valley where Zarahemla lay. "It's beautiful," he said in a hushed voice.

His father smiled. "The few times I have been here I had the same reaction."

The Sidon dominated the long valley. Mormon traced the ribbon of water to where it disappeared from sight. The river, like a many-hued ribbon of blue and green, weaved its sinuous way through the long valley. Below him it disappeared into the black canyon, towering mountains making it look puny. East and west, hazy mountains formed a backdrop for the valley's stage.

"It's a different world," he breathed.

"That it is," his father answered. "The Nephites have lived in this valley for eight hundred years, and before they came the Mulekites had already built the city of Zarahemla."

"Who were the Mulekites?" Mormon asked.

"Israelites who came directly from Jerusalem about the time it was destroyed. One of their group was Mulek, son of Zedekiah, king of Jerusalem. That is why they were called Mulekites."

"Oh."

"Come. We must reach the valley before dark."

That night, for the second time since they left Desolation, they slept in an inn.

Zarahemla was bigger than Sidom or Moroni, or any city young Mormon had seen. Stepped-up pyramids with temples on top dominated the city center. Stucco buildings and houses radiated from the temples in a broad arc, forming concentric circles. Further out, extending to river and mountains, mud and stick huts housed the poor. Temples, palaces and synagogues abounded. Fields of corn, squash, sweet potatoes and beans patterned hills and valleys. Young Mormon was amazed.

Mormon had never seen so many people. "People are as thick as the grains of sand on Desolation's beach," he commented.

His father frowned. "Yes, but sand is cleaner."

Day after day Mormon followed his father as they inquired concerning engravers. Each night, sore-footed, they returned to the inn. One day the young Mormon stayed at the inn. Father Mormon returned very excited. "I have found an engraver to teach you the fine art of engraving. Then you can fulfill God's calling. His name is Natschal."

"But I know so little about writing."

"You will learn. Natschal is expert in both Hebrew and Egyptian. There are few such tutors around these days. I was lucky to find him."

"Will I live with him?" Mormon asked timorously.

"Yes, for a time," Mormon answered. "It is part of the. apprenticeship."

"But..."

Mormon noticed the uncertainty on his son's face. "Don't worry, son," he said. "I will come each year to visit you. Besides, Natschal and his family are members of God's church." He smiled sadly. "One of the few faithful families in Zarahemla."

"Perhaps God guided us to him," Mormon said.

The elder Mormon nodded, pleased at Mormon's faith.

"How long must I be with this Natschal?" Mormon asked.

"Four years. After the first year you will only work with him half of each day. Then you will also attend warrior training and receive instruction in metalworking."

Mormon was frightened. He had never lived anywhere but in his father's home. Tears threatened to erupt as he followed the engraver inside a brownish-white, mud-plaster house. Wood doors pivoted in sockets at top and bottom. Windows, covered with rollable slat blinds to keep out the devastating sun, looked out over the city. It was much finer than their home in Desolation.

The first thing Mormon saw upon entering the house was Natschal's daughter. He guessed her to be about his own age. His breath caught as her large blue eyes locked with his. She shyly turned away and he noticed her long eyelashes which lightly brushed her cheeks as she lowered them. Her hair bubbled like boiling gold as she moved.

Mormon's father spoke first. "This is my son, Mormon."

The man wiped his hands on his apron, placed his hands on his hips, and gruffly responded. "I am Natschal." He pointed to the girl. "And this is Merena, my daughter."

Mormon's stomach churned nervously. He bowed formally. At that moment, though only eleven, he was convinced that someday Merena would be his wife.

Tiresome drill of painting tiny pictures and emblems on bark paper made days drag. Each character had to be painted many times until Natschal permitted him to proceed to the next character. Hands and eyes grew weary from the strain. Hebrew was hard enough, but Egyptian had thousands of characters to be memorized. Mormon wondered if he would ever learn it all. Natschal was hard to please, scolding him over every little mistake, cuffing his head until his ears rang. Hardest of all was when Natschal ridiculed him in front of Merena. Mormon could feel his face flush and his ears burn.

After Mormon learned the Hebrew and Egyptian symbols, Natschal brought out large rolls of Nephite scriptures. Though rough in his manners with Mormon, he handled the rolls gently, almost reverently, unrolling them carefully on the writing table. "Copy these to paper. When you become perfect on paper you will learn to inscribe on plates of brass."

One duty of his apprenticeship was to copy letters for people in Zarahemla to send to relatives in other cities. Most were fairly easy. Fearful of Natschal's temper, he wrote carefully and seldom made mistakes. Letters from his parents were rare. He treasured each one. Neither his father nor mother could read or write and had to hire a scribe like Natschal to write for them. Besides, the only mail service from Desolation to Zarahemla were travelers or traders who traveled between the cities.

He was rereading a letter from his father by candlelight when Merena burst into his room.

She was breathless. "Have you heard?"

He stiffened. "Heard what?"

"Lamanites have attacked Manti and march toward Zarahemla."

"But..."

"Father says every man is to take arms." She looked at him, her eyes wide with fright. "Will you have to go?"

Mormon rolled off his pallet. "I wish I could but they only take men who have had warrior training." He looked down at himself. "Not a skinny eleven-year-old."

Cumorah, 387 A.D.

Mormon stirred the fire in the cave. Night air chilled his old bones. He stared into the distance. Thirty thousand Nephites, Jacobites, Josephites and Zoramites had responded to the call to arms. He and Natschal were not among them. Natschal was too old and he was too young. The Nephites soundly defeated the Lamanites in a number of battles, forcing them back to their own lands. An uneasy peace lasted for the next four years. "But wait," mused Mormon. "I'm getting ahead of my story."

Zarahemla, 322 A.D.

Mormon's second year at Natschal's home was no better. He had looked forward to working with metal plates but he found the work even more difficult. Engraving tools were not flexible like the brush. Letters were difficult to inscribe and he made many mistakes. Natschal had little patience with him.

"Can't you do anything right?" he growled, cuffing his ear.

Mormon lowered his head, hiding his tears of shame, and continued inscribing.

Each evening he went to bed with muscles sore and aching, but his forearm soon became knotty and hard. The only thing which made his apprenticeship bearable was seeing Merena every day. Also he enjoyed the stories he inscribed from the rolls of scriptures. What really helped, though, was when he turned twelve, midway in his second year, he began mandatory warrior training. Every afternoon he reported to the warrior barracks next to the city wall. A large, battle-scarred warrior named Ezra taught beginning warriors the rudiments of weaponry. He had a shrunken mouth but his eyes were clear and gray and sly. Older warriors called him "old eagle" because of his battle experience. Neophyte warriors dubbed him "old buzzard." Regardless of the sobriquets, Mormon liked Ezra.

Leading Mormon and the other youths in war games occupied most of Ezra's time, but he often maundered around the drill field as he relived old battles. After a day of drill he would sit and tell stories of battles in which he had fought.

Sometimes his memories were unexpectedly poignant, as when he'd describe a warrior long dead. Mormon enjoyed the stories of heroism. In Natschal's scrolls he had read of General Moroni and his bravery in battle. I want to be just like him, Mormon thought.

For war games Mormon buckled on a wood shield covered with tough jaguar skin. Armor, quilted cotton and leather, covered him from neck to ankles. Mormon hated the hot and scratchy armor. He learned to string a bow and draw the gut to his cheek. Hour after hour he shot until he could notch, pull and release an arrow in seconds, with most of the arrows hitting the target. The sling was a more difficult weapon for him; whirl and release the stone at precisely the right moment. Mormon's favorite weapons were sword and spear. He was a large boy and liked the feeling of power when he held a man-sized sword in his big hands or hefted the smooth roundness of the balanced spear shaft. Weapons training came easy for him, and he excelled.

In Natschal's home he had eyes for little else but Merena. Whenever she passed his eyes followed her.

"Pay attention to your work," Natschal would shout if he saw Mormon's eyes straying. Several times Natschal whacked him with a stylus. "Concentrate on what you are doing."

Mormon set the goal to be an excellent scribe. With daily practice he quickly learned the basic fundamentals of engraving. But Natschal never praised him for his work. *Why doesn't he at least say I have done well?* Mormon wondered. *He is quick to point out my mistakes. I wonder if I can ever please him.*

Natschal one day came to Mormon. "Get your sandals and come with me," he said.

"Where are we going?" Mormon asked, somewhat fearfully.

"You are ready to learn how to make the plates upon which to write," Natschal said gruffly. "Your father commissioned me to not only teach you how to engrave but also to make plates."

They walked in silence across the city, dodging refuse piles, finally coming to a small shack in a dim alley. There was no chimney and smoke poured from open eaves, blacking what was once whitewashed stone. Coals glowed in an outside forge.

Natschal put his hands on his hips and shouted. "Alphus."

A man, his bare chest covered with black grime, pushed aside the curtain which served as a door. His face was round and cherubic under grimy beard, lighted by a ready smile which seemed to hover on his lips. He looked over Natschal and his companion.

"Well?" he grunted. His teeth, Mormon noticed, were mostly gone. The few he had were blackened, just like his body.

"This is the apprentice I spoke about," Natschal said.

The man walked around Mormon, eyeing him as if he were something to buy. "Has he ever worked with gold?"

"Only with an inscribing tool," Natschal said. "He must learn to make thin plates for record-keeping."

The man smiled—a broad, almost-toothless smile. "Thin plates. Those are better than the gold jewelry the women demand or shaving tools for the men." He motioned to Mormon, the smile still on his rough-blackened face. "Come in. My name is Alphus."

Mormon liked him immediately. Instead of the crossness of Natschal he was actually friendly. How could anyone dislike a man who smiled so easily?

Mormon still slept at Natschal's but spent each morning with Alphus, building the fire in the forge, pumping air over the glowing coals with the bellows, lifting and turning pots of molten metal, becoming as black as Alphus himself.

Afternoons were at the barracks, where swordplay, spear throwing, and archery kept him busy. His goals were apparent. Each time he picked up a weapon he said to himself, *I will be the best. I will be the best.*

CHAPTER ELEVEN

APPRENTICE AND WARRIOR

Cumorah, 387 A.D.

The sky over Cumorah, blue and cloudless an hour before, darkened with threatened rain as rolling clouds blotted out the sun. Mormon, a gold plate on the rock before him, sat in the cave mouth, watching as rain fell to the west in a wide, curving squall. Rain had always been a part of his life. Sun and rain. Rain and sun. Dusty ground or mud. A rainbow sprang from one gray corner as sun turned falling drops into glorious, curving colors. "My life, though filled with storms, has had an abundance of rainbows," he said softly to the air. "No one has been more blessed than I."

Rain softly pattered outside the cave as the squall line reached Cumorah. Mormon put down the stylus and rose stiffly. He walked out into the rain and held his palms up to the weeping sky. Sting of drops on his face refreshed him. He sniffed deeply of cleaned air; air purified by innumerable falling small drops.

The squall left almost as soon as it arrived. Mormon walked back into the cave, renewed by the damp interval. He resolutely picked up the stylus and continued writing, thinking of other storms, other renewals.

Zarahemla, 323 A.D.

Twelve-year-old Mormon needed someone to answer questions, someone to be a father-figure. He squatted on his heels before the forge, watching Alphus add gold ore to the kettle. The smith appeared rough and uncouth but Mormon liked him. He felt Alphus had a depth of character far beyond his menial tasks.

First raindrops fell into the fire, hissing and sizzling, interrupting his train of thought. Little wisps of steam rose into the air and disappeared.

"Pump," Alphus said.

Mormon pumped up and down on the rod, forcing air into the fire. Color changed from orange to whitish-blue as air fanned flames, seeming to almost consume the forging kettle.

Alphus hummed a tuneless song as he leaned over the fire to watch the kettle. Sweat sizzled like rain in the fire as it dripped from his round face. He took a long rod and stirred the lumpy mess in the kettle, dropped in a small amount of blue rock and stirred again.

He looked at Mormon, his face twisted in a crooked smile. "Stews almost done," he chuckled. "A little copper to harden the gold and we're about ready." He stirred once again, then seemed satisfied. "Tongs," he said.

Mormon handed him the tongs, handle first.

Alphus reached into the fire and slid the tongs under the kettle. With practiced air he pulled the kettle from the fire, balanced it on a plank, then poured the molten, golden metal into a shallow mold gouged into the wood. He worked his way down the plank, pouring a thin layer into each rectangular depression.

The metal cooled almost as soon as Alphus finished pouring. With a practiced, smooth motion, Mormon handed him the small tongs even before he asked for them.

Alphus tipped his head back and laughed, slapping his dirty tunic with his free hand. "You learn quickly, son. You'll be a fine goldsmith." He deftly picked up one of the sheets with the tong and laid it on a flat stone.

"Now, watch while I tool it," Alphus said. With a bronze hammer he carefully started at the outer edge, working his way around the unfinished plate. "Be careful with this or you'll punch right through the thin metal."

Mormon watched, open-mouthed, impressed by the ease with which Alphus made the metal paper thin. When the plate was large enough—and thin enough—Alphus took his knife and squared off the edges. The surplus gold he put back into the kettle. "Now you try it." He handed Mormon the small tongs.

Mormon pulled a gold sheet from the plank mold. He put it on the flat stone and picked up the hammer. Carefully he began pounding the metal. On his third blow the gold parted under the hammer and stone showed through. The plate was ruined.

"It takes a sure hand," Alphus said.

Mormon's eyes smarted as he held back tears. *Will I ever learn*, he wondered. He dropped the hammer and began pulling off his leather apron.

"Where are you going?" Alphus asked loudly.

"I can't do it," Mormon said angrily. "Besides its starting to rain. I'm going home."

"Pick up the hammer. You'll try another piece."

Mormon looked at Alphus in surprise. He refastened the apron and reached down and picked up the hammer. It was the first time Alphus had ever spoken sternly to him.

"You will persist until you succeed," Alphus said in a softer voice. He patted Mormon's back with huge, rough hands. "Anyone who is trying and learning will have failures. That's the way life is. A person cannot learn unless he tries. And, if he tries, he will make mistakes."

Mormon looked up at him, a knot in his throat.

"The thing is," the smith continued, "you must keep trying. The only person who doesn't make mistakes is the one who doesn't try." He put his hand over the smaller hand of Mormon, clasping hand and hammer handle. "Feel my rhythm." He gently hammered the plate, forcing it thinner as the edges expanded.

Alphus talked as he worked. "It took years of practice before I could do this without a mistake." He folded up the ruined plate and put it back into the kettle, then handed Mormon the tongs.

Mormon picked up another sheet of gold and put it on the stone. Calming his breathing he began pounding the plate, trying to be as smooth as the goldsmith. He felt Alphus' approval as he resolutely struck the metal, his blows falling in a soft rhythm. This time he didn't ruin the plate until it was almost finished.

"Well done. You pick it up more quickly than any apprentice I have had—even more quickly than I did in my youth."

Mormon's face glowed with the unexpected praise. He had worked with Natschal over a year and had never been praised even once. "Thank you," he said, wadding the plate up and putting it back into the kettle. Then with uncanny confidence, perhaps born of Alphus' expressed faith in his work, he took a third plate and worked it without error.

While working, both forgot the impending storm. They were quickly reminded when huge drops began falling into the fire, almost putting it out.

"That's enough for today," Alphus said as he placed a slab over the forge. "You'd better get on back to Natschal's before you get drenched."

But it was already too late. Rain fell in a fury, soaking everything around. "Stay," Alphus said. "We will stir up some sweet chocolate and wait out the storm."

Alphus' house was simply furnished. An indoor forge took up most of the one small room. Since there was no firepit or table, Mormon assumed that Alphus cooked and ate as well as worked at the forge. A filthy pallet lay along one wall.

Mormon sat with his back to the forge, sipped on the sweet chocolate and enjoyed the peacefulness of the grimy shack. "Don't you have any family?" he finally asked.

Alphus threw back his head and laughed. "Who would have such a one as me?" He held out his rough, calloused hands. "No woman would let me touch her with these." He sobered. "My wife is my fire and my forge. My children are the baubles I make."

"Don't you ever get lonesome?"

Alphus shook his head. "Neighborhood children come to watch me work. Also, I often have an apprentice such as yourself." His voice gruffened. "Besides, I am too busy to be lonely." He set his cup down and looked at his pupil. "But what of your family?"

Mormon swallowed. "My father and mother live in Desolation."

"Then what are you doing in Zarahemla?"

"I have been called as scribe to my people. I need to learn to be a scribe and goldsmith. Father felt the best teachers were in Zarahemla."

Alphus sipped his chocolate and nodded. "Probably true. Only the goldsmiths in the temple city compare to our craftsmanship—and few there are who teach inscribing." He looked at Mormon. "Are you sure you really want to be a scribe and goldsmith?"

Mormon hung his head. "No," he said, looking at the ground.

"What do you really want to be?"

Mormon looked up, his eyes shining. "A warrior."

Alphus slapped his knees in his mirth. "A warrior! Then why do you fuss with smithing and scribe work?"

"Because that is what I have been called to do."

"Called?"

"Yes. My uncle Ammoron was scribe for the Nephite people. He called me to take his place."

Alphus looked at him quizzically, seeing how serious he was. He shook his head and mused. "You want one thing, but are willing to give that up to do something else because you were 'called?'"

Mormon nodded.

Alphus looked out. "Still raining." He poured more warm chocolate in Mormon's cup. "So, do you have a plan?"

Mormon looked up at him. "A plan?"

"Yes," Alphus said almost impatiently. "How do you expect to accomplish your goals unless you have a plan?"

Mormon shrugged. "I will continue my apprenticeship with you and Natschal."

"And then?"

"Then I suppose I will return to Desolation."

"What about your desire to be a warrior?"

"I attend warrior training like all other boys my age."

Alphus exploded, warm chocolate frothing on his lips. "Is that all! You attend! Why don't you set goals of what you want to accomplish? Do what you want to do!" he shouted. "Be the best warrior in all of Zarahemla!"

Mormon was amazed at Alphus' reaction. "But how?" he asked. "I must still be an apprentice."

"Then be an apprentice, but also be a warrior. Give your best to all that you do. Be the best engraver, the best goldsmith, the best warrior, but whatever you do be what you want to be." Alphus sat down, his head cradled in his rough hands.

Mormon looked at him, still not understanding the reason for the outburst.

"Look at me," Alphus said softly. "I wanted to be a stone mason, a builder of temples and fine buildings." He looked at his gnarled hands spread open before him. "And I could have been one of the best." He shrugged. "But instead, I became a goldsmith because my father was a goldsmith and his father before him. I sacrificed my dream for the dream of others." He grabbed Mormon by the shoulders. "Hold to your dream," he said grimly. "No matter what it takes to make it come true."

"But I can't give up my responsibility to become a scribe!"

"Agreed! Do both things, but do both things well!" Alphus toyed with a stick, stirring the coals in the forge. "You

have decided to devote your life to service to God, to be a scribe.
That is commendable—especially at your young age. But you
must also earn a living; you must be able to support your family.
Become a great warrior. Become a leader of warriors!" He paced
back and forth in the narrow cubicle of his home. "The
opportunities of this world are all around us. We have to have
the ability to see them. We can't see them if we always keep our
eyes"—he waved his arm disdainfully at the forge—"on the
ground. If we don't look around we lose our opportunities. If we
run fast we catch opportunities that are left behind by the man
who moseys through life. Many people, because of their total
involvement with the mundane, try to start living after they
reach the age when most people have already died. Learn to live
now! Take advantage of opportunities as they come!"

Mormon still didn't know what to say. No one had ever
spoken to him like this.

Alphus stopped before Mormon. His voice was softer,
almost pleading. "You cannot say, 'Well, I'll try it tomorrow.'
You must have a goal and a plan—a plan of action." He suddenly
smiled. "What are two ways to get to the top of a palm tree?" he
asked, tilting his head in a quizzical way.

"Other than just climbing, I don't know," Mormon said.

Alphus slapped his leg as he roared in his laughter. "We
can either start climbing or we can sit on a coconut and wait for
the tree to grow."

Still not sure just how to take Alphus, Mormon asked,
"You think I can be a great warrior and still fulfill my calling as
scribe for the Nephite people?"

Alphus grasped Mormons cheeks between the palms of
his rough hands. "Yes," he hissed. "Just give it all you've got."
He sat down on a stool and sighed wearily as if the conversation
had taken something out of him. "The rain's easing up. Perhaps
you had better start for Natschal's."

Mormon looked forward to his talks with Alphus.
Though rough in hands and looks the smith's heart was
soft—always willing to listen and to offer sage advice.

For months Mormon heated gold, poured it into thin
molds, and hammered the sheets into fine plates. Each day he
became more adept. Each day Alphus praised him, seeming to
take pride in his skill. Soon he was engraving fine lines and
pictures, filling up a plate with his Egyptian and Hebrew
writing, melting it down and reforging it again for more
practice.

Days passed quickly as he drilled on weaponry at the warrior barracks or cast plates and engraved on them at Alphus' home. Each evening he returned to the house of Natschal where he paid for his apprenticeship by copying legal papers and writing letters on bark paper. He saw little of Merena. When he did see her, he shared his thoughts about Alphus.

"He takes more than a master's interest in me."

"Perhaps you have become to him the son he never had," Merena replied, wise beyond her years.

Mormon pondered that thought. Each day Alphus shared with him his knowledge and wisdom. Each night he warned him. "Be careful as you travel back to Natschal's house. There are many thieves in this city. They murder for no reason."

The decadent nature of Zarahemla's inhabitants was no secret to Mormon. Garbage and refuse littered the streets. Human waste stunk in main thoroughfares. It seemed as if people took no pride in themselves or their surroundings. Even worse to Mormon than foul garbage waste was human waste. Beggars vied for stoops in which to sit to pander those who passed. Painted ladies gestured provocatively from open windows. Drunks, arms and legs askew, slept in the streets. Thievery and pillaging were commonplace. People could not walk through the city, daylight or dark, without fear of being robbed or beaten. Toughs accosted people even in the temple plaza. Mormon always walked with hand on sword.

The wickedness of Zarahemla was one of Natschal's favorite subjects. "No longer are the people close to the Lord," the dour-faced man said. "Wickedness prevails upon the face of the whole land, even to the point that all miracles have ceased."

Mormon resolved that he would never let the wickedness affect him. He avoided fights as he walked through the streets, but several times had to draw his sword to clear passage. Only his size and his knowledge of weapons kept toughs from assaulting him directly. Most days he arrived at Natschal's before dark.

One night, in the beginning of his fourteenth year, he worked late at Alphus' home. He was finishing a plate, one he had carefully pounded into a perfect thinness. Even in his own critical eyes it was beautifully done. On it he carefully enscribed King Benjamin's sermon—a favorite scripture—from Natschal's scrolls.

"That is especially fine." Alphus' eyes were bright and shiny as he looked at Mormon.

Mormon looked up gratefully. "May I take it to show to Natschal?" he asked.

Alphus shrugged. "You may keep it, but remember there are those, who, if they knew you were carrying a gold plate, would attempt to wrest it from you."

"I will protect it well," Mormon said. He attempted to wrap the plate in a piece of tanned leather, but the thin plate was awkward to package.

"Here," Alphus said, a smile on his face. He carefully rolled it around Mormon's left forearm, up the sleeve of Mormon's loose tunic. He looked at it with satisfaction. "There. No one will know you have it."

Mormon swung his arm awkwardly. The plate was heavy. "At least it will not affect my sword arm," he said.

His journey through the city seemed twice as long as before. Maybe it's the night, he reasoned, or maybe it's the gold. Streets were dark and Mormon jumped at every imagined shadow. As he crossed the temple plaza, ruffians, recognizing him, scorned and taunted him. "Goody, goody Christian." They pelted him from a distance with garbage and rocks.

Mormon stuck to his path down the center of the street. A drunk bumped into him and was pushed roughly aside. The ruffians no longer shouted at him but Mormon couldn't shake the feeling of being followed. He walked faster, not wanting to get into a fight. He tried to plan ahead. If they attack me, where will it be? And where can I best defend myself? Wildly his eyes scanned the dark street ahead. Yes, up there. He increased his pace and turned quickly into a little niche between two buildings. He flattened himself against a wall, sword in hand. High walls around the little square created almost complete blackness.

He could feel his heart beating against his tunic. His hand holding the sword was sweaty. Shifting his sword he wiped it dry on his sleeve. He squinted at the street, every muscle tensed for the effort to come. His mouth felt dry and he licked his lips. He had never fought anyone except in mock battles at warrior training. Can I do it for real? he wondered.

Footsteps. He made out the deeper shadows of three men. They stopped, looking around. "He was right ahead of us," one growled.

"Looking for me?" he said and suddenly attacked.

"Get him!"

Mormon stabbed hard and felt the sword's tip bite into something soft. There was a low groan and a man fell forward. Mormon raised the sword and struck backhand, moving forward in the darkness. His blade struck something hard. He slashed again and felt the bronze blade bite into flesh. He gritted his teeth and pushed, feeling the pull on the sword as his assailant slipped to the ground. He crouched, feeling the presence of the third man across the little square.

"Come on," he said. "Let's get it over with."

The only answer was the slap of sandals on hard ground as the man scurried away from him.

Darkness prevented him from seeing the extent of the injuries to the two men. He hurried on toward Natschal's home, arriving depressed. He had hoped he would not have to fight. Now he had not only fought but had hurt someone.

"Oh," Merena cried as he entered. "You're hurt."

He looked down. A trickle of blood flowed down his bared thigh. He didn't know he had been nicked.

As he told his story, Natschal patched up the cut on his leg while Merena mended the torn tunic where someone's knife had barely missed crippling him. "Why did they attack you?" Natschal asked, suspicion in his voice.

"I don't know," Mormon said. "They couldn't have known I was carrying this." He pulled the plate from his sleeve and carefully unrolled it, smoothing out wrinkles. "Alphus wanted me to show you this," he said, almost shyly.

Natschal took the plate, peering at it in the lamplight. "The work of an amateur," He said gruffly. "One who thinks he can write like a master craftsman when still but an apprentice." He dropped the plate to his writing table. "Tell Alphus to send me a plate when it is done right," he said crossly as he stumped away.

Mormon angrily clenched his fists to his side, holding back his desire to shout at the old man's retreating back.

Merena placed a hand on his shoulder. The touch was magic to his soul. His anger quickly left him, replaced by a feeling he could not explain. He looked up at Merena.

"The plate is beautiful," she whispered into his ear. She bussed his cheek with her lips and then was gone.

Natschal's criticism was forgotten.

Chapter Twelve

Warrior Youth

Cumorah, 387 A.D.

Mormon subconsciously fingered the tiny scar on his thigh. He looked down and grinned. *So small—but my first battle scar.* He didn't have to look to see dozens of other scars on his torso; scars won in countless battles during sixty years of war.

He laced up his sandals, pulling the last loop tight over atrophied calf. He sighed. *Not much left of what used to be strong legs. But they served their purpose. They carried me across the land into hundreds of battles.* Suddenly he felt depressed. He looked up at the dark roof of the cave. *I must get out of here for awhile. I'll take a walk. Perhaps that will help.*

As he walked he thought of Merena.

Zarahemla, 326 A.D.

Natschal was ill. Pale cheeks and sweat on his forehead portended trouble.

I hope it is not the fevers, Mormon thought. He watched as Merena wrung out the cotton cloth, placing the damp rag on her father's forehead, cooling him while she crooned soft words in his ear. She looked so beautiful as she knelt beside the rough couch.

The sickness did not soften Natschal's tongue. "What do you stare at?" he growled at Mormon. "Have you never seen a sick man." He grasped Merena's wrist. "Get me some fruit, golden oranges from the farmer's stalls."

Merena stood up and looked at her father. Without a word she turned to Mormon. "Come."

Mormon was surprised as he walked beside Merena towards the outskirts of the city. She was a woman. *I am almost fifteen now, so she must be at least thirteen. She is old enough to marry.* He swallowed at his thought. *But I am not. I must complete my apprenticeship and serve in the army before I can marry.*

"Where are we going?" he asked.

"The fruit is fresher in the village market, outside the walls," she said. She looked up at him. "Besides, I need to walk. I am so tired of staying in the house."

That was all right with Mormon. He reached down and took her hand in his. She didn't resist. He was aware of the stares of the men they passed. Mormon was torn between feelings of pride to be walking with Merena and jealousy for the way the men ogled her.

They passed through the walls of the city—walls which long since had lost their ability to protect. Stones were broken out and big gaps marred the wall's continuity. Thatched huts greeted them as they passed into the small village. In the center was the village square dominated by a ceiba tree so huge it looked as if it had been growing for thousands of years. The village was literally built around the tree.

The tree sheltered the market place. Fruits and vegetables of all descriptions lay in small box-like patches in its shade: oranges, lemons, mangoes, papayas and fruits he didn't recognize. Beans, squash, sweet potatoes, and corn formed colorful patches under the huge tree. While Merena selected her fruit he walked around the ceiba tree. Flies resting on green moss in its shade rose in swarms at his approach. The gigantic tree was gnarled and fluted. He had never seen such a tree in Desolation.

Looking up at the interlocked limbs above him, Mormon almost stepped on a woman guarding her vegetables. "Excuse me," he mumbled and hurried back to where Merena waited.

"Are you ready?"

She nodded and started to pick up her basket.

"Here, let me," he said. He hefted the basket under one arm and hurried to catch Merena who was almost out of the square. She walked proudly, back straight and head erect. Afternoon sun was bright on her hair, highlighting red tints in the long, silken strands. He took long strides to keep up with her.

As they entered the old city a gang of ragged street urchins fell in behind, just out of Mormon's reach. "Ya, ya, ya," they chanted. Their teasing voices took on a sing-song as they chanted lewd rhymes.

Merena pretended to ignore them.

Mormon swung around angrily but before he took two long strides the boys were scattered. As soon as he turned back towards Merena they were again right behind him.

"Take this," he said, handing her the basket.

She leaned toward him and touched his arm with hesitant fingertips.

Mormon hoped he hadn't offended her.

She wrinkled her nose in an anxious way. "Be careful," she whispered.

Mormon pulled his sword and whirled, but behind him was an empty street. As soon as he turned the mocking chant began again. He was glad when he finally closed Natschal's door behind him and Merena. He stood there, leaning against the jamb.

"What's the matter?" Natschal asked irascibly.

"We were followed by a street mob who made fun of Merena."

"Curses on them," screeched Natschal. He lay his head back on the pillow.

Merena, kneeling beside her father, looked up at Mormon with a pleading look. "You need to rest, Father," she said. "I'll peel you an orange."

Mormon took the hint. "I need to work on some plates," he said. "I will be late for supper."

Merena stood and placed her hand on his. "Go with care," she said. She placed several oranges in his hand. "Here, take some fruit. Perhaps Alphus would like a fresh orange."

Mormon told Alphus about the gang and what they said.

Alphus smiled grimly as he carved on a gold ornament. "Ah," he sighed, "a very small problem." He waggled his carving tool at Mormon. "You will be beset with many larger ones. Although there are problems in the world we don't have to take them into our lives. Be bigger than the problem! It is overcoming problems which makes us strong."

"The people seem so...so bad!" exploded Mormon.

Alphus chewed on his tongue as he carved. "I understand your concern, son. Gangs roam our streets. There is constant threat of war with the Lamanites. Many people starve or are ill and unable to care for themselves." He laid down his shaper. "The question is, what can you do about any of these problems?" He picked up his tool and continued carving.

Tears of frustration filled Mormon's eyes. Embarrassed, he turned to the forge and blinked them away. For a moment he couldn't answer. When he found his voice, he said, "I don't know, but I intend to do something." He went back to his work but he couldn't keep his mind on what he was doing. Alphus' question nagged him. He would pick up the plate he was working on, then put it back down. Sometimes his eyes refused to focus. He couldn't even see the fine inscribing he had done on the plate.

Back at Natschal's home he prayed, "Can I do something about the unrighteousness of the people? What can I do about war with the Lamanites? What can I do about poverty and want and crime? Will being a scribe of the records fill the needs of the people? There is no longer a chief priest. How can I put myself into a position where I can help?"

There seemed to be no answer. Mormon threw himself into his warrior training with even more vigor and dedication. His instructors were amazed at his skill in weaponry. Even in practice he used the sword and javelin with such force his fellow trainees refused to joust with him.

Caleb, commander of his training company, called him to his side. "I have been watching you. You handle the sword well."

Mormon fidgeted under the stare of the commander.

"The Nephites need warriors like you. I am assigning you to a regular warrior patrol. You will spend the next month in the field." He saw the fleeting look of worry cross Mormon's face. "This will be your first real fighting, won't it?" he asked.

Mormon didn't tell him about the street fight. "Yes, sir."

"It's only the first few moments that are bad," Captain Caleb assured him. "Once you feel your sword bite the first time, you forget and then it comes natural."

"Yes, sir," Mormon saluted and left. Even with his dislike at the thought of killing, he was excited. Regular warrior duty! He didn't know whether to be happy or sad. He would have to tell Merena. And Alphus. He hurried to Natschal's home.

"Merena," he almost shouted. "Captain Caleb selected me for a warrior patrol."

Merena, who had been patting out corn cakes, looked at him, a question in her eyes. "Warrior patrol? What does that mean?"

"I will no longer be in training, but will be assigned to a patrol of experienced warriors. We will be away from Zarahemla..." His excitement died as he thought of being away from Merena for long periods of time.

Merena continued patting the corn dough into little flat cakes to bake in the beehive oven. She didn't look up. "What about your apprenticeship?"

"I...I didn't think about that," Mormon stammered.

"Sounds as if you didn't think of lots of things," Natschal commented irascibly as he entered the room. "Your father pledged your work to me for four years. You have been here little more than three, and most of that time your skill has been such that you were of no value. Now that you have finally become a little useful, you leave to go gallivanting around the country posing as a warrior. Paugh!" He turned on his heel and left the room.

A feeling of sadness swept over Mormon. He had been excited by Captain Caleb's appointment. Now? He looked at Merena to find her watching him. Her dark eyes were expressionless but he detected the beginnings of a smile on her full lips.

"Perhaps this is what the Lord wants you to do," she said.

"But to leave you; and leave my work?"

"You have learned all that father and Alphus can teach you."

It was a simple statement, but Mormon found himself thinking about it. Though Natschal never said so I feel the old man is secretly pleased with my work. Alphus is—he has said so many times. Can Merena be right? Perhaps this is the answer to my prayers. Maybe this is how the Lord wants me to help the people—by being a warrior. He wondered how Alphus would take the news. Like the stoic he is, Mormon thought. He will say this is where I can best serve my people and my country.

"It seems to me this gives you an opportunity to serve your people and your country," Alphus said when informed of the news. Mormon smiled.

Cumorah, 387 A.D.

Mormon, his back to the rough rock of the cave, was deeply enmeshed with his thoughts of Merena and that first experience of being a regular warrior. Recalling his youth was like trying to remember the details of a dream, with the same baffling mixture of familiar and strange. But some experiences really stood out. *How my life has changed. I was very lucky, both in love and in war. What if it weren't luck but God's means of helping me be a help to my people?*

Land of Zarahemla, 326 A.D.

For almost two months the patrol guarded the border between Manti and the east wilderness. Mormon was amazed at the lack of defenses. Manti was the only fortified city. Little villages lay along many streams. Any attacking force would wipe them out with little resistance. Farmers tended fields of corn and squash and herded flocks without apparent concern about the Lamanites. The warriors came across several destroyed villages: huts burned to the ground, fields trampled and villagers nowhere to be found.

"Probably taken into slavery," one warrior commented around the campfire.

Mormon leaned on the shaft of his javelin, staring into the fire. He heard the campfire talk but his mind was elsewhere. So much land to protect and so few warriors. People should live in cities where there is some protection. They could farm during the day and return to the city at night. He caught himself.The city offers protection from the Lamanites but no protection from the gangs and robbers. Maybe that's why the people moved out into the country—to avoid the criminals and robbers.

The squad leader was talking. "We must be the eyes and ears of Zarahemla," he said. "Our only purpose is to detect Lamanite incursions into our land."

"Shouldn't we follow them back into the land of Nephi and battle them?" one of the warriors asked.

"Ha!" the squad leader exclaimed. "Then what would you do? Fight the entire Lamanite army?" He took a stick and stirred the fire. "No, we will stay within the borders of the land of Zarahemla. If we surprise any Lamanites then we give battle."

After leaving the valleys of Zarahemla and Gideon their path led through dense, tropical rain forest. For days they saw little of the sun. It was like being in perpetual twilight. The path they followed was but a notch hemmed in on either side by giant trees, all draped in hungry, life-sucking parasites and saprophytes—a narrow tread not quite reclaimed by the jungle. Warriors used their swords to cut down intruding jungle growth. Bands of monkeys cursed them and chattered through the treetops. Brilliantly colored parrots mocked them obscenely. Insects swarmed around their heads with a perpetual high-pitched whine.

The path split as they entered the flat plains near the east sea. Ahmeron, the squad leader raised his hand. They stopped and looked for tracks in the mud of the trails. Footprints of sandaled, long-striding men showed on both trails. Mormon estimated the tracks had been made three or four days previously. Ahmeron divided his men into two patrols, eight men in each.

"Mormon," he called. "You lead one of the patrols." He motioned towards the left trail. "Take your warriors and scout out the trail."

Mormon was surprised. He was the youngest warrior in the patrol. But he had learned to obey. "Yes, sir," he said. There was little murmuring from the squad. They seemed to accept his leadership. He marched the patrol until nightfall, then had his men climb trees in which to sleep. He wormed his way off the trail, into the jungle, and climbed a tree, hoping it wasn't already occupied by a snake. He lashed himself to the trunk then tried to get some rest. It was not easy. Insects swarmed around him, probing with stingers. Night noises of the jungle—the jaguar's cough, the owl's cry, the scream of a monkey in the coils of a boa—made sleep seem even more impossible. The jungle seethed with life and death—an enormous battlefield in which the struggle was endless.

The first rays of dawn, leaking through the leafy canopy overhead, awoke Mormon. He blinked, stretched, yawned and almost fell out of the tree. Embarrassed, he climbed down, drank from a vine, and assembled his patrol. He hoped he did not look as bad as they. All were covered with bites and red welts from the rough bark of the trees. He was hungry and instructed his men to keep their eyes open for fruit or coconuts. He found a few mamei and sapodilla which only whetted his appetite.

Around a bend in the trail they spotted a large iguana sunning itself in a single ray of light that somehow pierced the foliage overhead. Mormon threw his javelin. The creature writhed on the forest floor, pinned to the dirt. Mormon pounced on it, skinned it, gutted it and directed his men to build a small fire. Pieces of obsidian soon yielded necessary sparks and a small fire cooked the white flesh to a state of doneness. Feeling somewhat better, the warriors continued onward.

The trail led to a river. Mormon sent warriors in both directions, but there was no ford. His only choice was a raft. Heavy bamboo, hard as iron, grew thick in the jungle. The warriors slammed and hacked with their swords, cutting tubes of bamboo as thick as their forearms, each tube a series of buoyant watertight compartments. They lashed them tightly together with vines and cut a pole for steering. Mormon allowed only three men at a time on the fragile craft, and even then their weight pressed it down until water sloshed around their insteps. One man brought back the flimsy raft and two more went across. Mormon waited until last. He breathed more easily when all were safely on the opposite bank. He didn't know what kind of creatures might be in the turbid water—he had heard of flesh-eating fish and dragon-like creatures that slept in the mud.

Mud of the riverbank was churned up by many feet, some in sandals and some barefoot. Mormon studied the footprints for long moments. "Many Lamanites have come this way," he said.

His men looked at him silently, waiting his command.

"The tracks are fresh. They are not far ahead of us," he continued. "I will lead down the trail. Follow single file without talking or noise."

The trail was easy to follow. Those who had preceded them had cleared away all brush. Mormon and his men moved forward with hardly a sound. Before the sun had reached its high point in the sky, Mormon stopped his men. "Shush," he said, his finger to his lips. He pointed ahead.

They strained their ears. Murmur of many voices came from the trail ahead: not alarmed voices, but rather the voices of men tired and complaining about being so far from home.

"How many?" whispered one of the warriors, a wiry man named Samuel.

Mormon held up both hands three times.

"Thirty?" Samuel raised his eyebrows. "We are outnumbered. Do we dare attack them?"

Mormon again put his finger to his lips. "Helam, take Ammon, Lehi and Samuel with you. Slip quietly through the jungle and get on the other side of them. We will give you plenty of time. When you are in position, chatter like a disturbed spider monkey."

"Then what?" Helam asked, his eyes intent on Mormon's.

"Then, with all the noise you can muster, charge down the trail at the Lamanites. They will be surprised and frightened. Hopefully, we should take most of them prisoners."

Helam nodded. Within moments he and his followers had disappeared into the jungle.

"Let's get off the trail in case some of the Lamanites come this way," Mormon said.

Waiting was hard. Mormon's stomach seemed tied in knots. His mouth was dry, though he was not thirsty. Beads of salty sweat ran down his forehead into his eyes, stinging and blinding. He kept wiping them with his forearm.

The sound of a monkey screeching. The signal!

He motioned to those following him and hit the trail on the run, yelling and screaming at the top of his lungs.

The Lamanites, caught by surprise, had little time to grab for weapons. A spear hissed past Mormon. He dodged and charged the thrower, his sword poised. He felt the blade grate on a rib and he swung it clear. He didn't have time to think about this being the first man he had ever killed. It was pure training and instinct. He stepped over the body and raised his sword against the next man, who dropped his weapons and stood with hands in the air. Fighting, what there was of it, was over in minutes. There were more Lamanites than he had estimated from the tracks. Five Lamanites were dead and several wounded. Thirty-four sat with hands on their heads as prisoners.

Samuel, of Mormon's men, was the only one wounded. A spear pierced his arm just below the elbow. After patching the wound, Mormon and his warriors herded the prisoners down the trail.

Ahmeron was pleased, and upon their return to Zarahemla, Mormon was called before Captain Caleb. "You have been cited for bravery," the Captain said. He chuckled. "Your first patrol and you wipe out an entire Lamanite company." He clapped Mormon on the back. "Congratulations, from now on you will be a regular patrol leader."

One patrol followed another. Hundreds of Lamanites had filtered across the loosely-drawn border. Mormon was cautious, not taking chances, but his successes continued to mount. Patrols were not all fighting the enemy, however. Every time Mormon left Zarahemla he carried with him a roll of bark paper, brushes and paints. Whenever he had time he pulled out writing materials and wrote letters to Merena and his parents. Sometimes he wrote poems. He was careful not to let the other warriors see what he wrote. They would really tease him—a tough warrior, a squad leader, writing mushy letters and poems for his sweetheart.

The limited time in Zarahemla was busy. He had nearly completed his scribe training. Even Natschal had seemed impressed with his last plate. When he asked Alphus what else he had to learn, the goldsmith shrugged. "I have taught you all I know."

Time with Merena was precious. They stood on the roof, amidst overhanging bougainvillea, celebrating the last rays of the evening sun. Her robe fluttered in the slight, evening breeze. He wanted to take her in his arms, but stood silent as the sun finally set.

Merena shivered despite the warmth of the air. When she spoke, her voice was low. "I dread the coming of war," she said. "I die a little inside every time you leave on patrol with your warriors." She turned to face him. He had never seen her more lovely. In the soft light of dusk her dark hair was muted. Her eyes flashed as she looked at him. Tears formed in the corners of her eyes, built to overflowing and rolled down her cheeks.

Gently he curled the fingers of one hand under her chin and tilted her head up so their eyes met.

"Is there no way for us to avoid war?" she cried.

"I don't know," Mormon said sadly. "The Nephites do not want war but when enemies come into our land, what are we to do?"

A sob escaped Merena and she turned to the parapet. "For my whole life I have known the grief of battle. Will it never end? Must you be a warrior?"

"There is nothing else to do," he said. "We must defeat the Lamanites or they will defeat us. We pray for God's help in defeating them, but there still must be warriors."

Merena turned hotly to him. "It is not God's will that men fight one another."

He smiled at her fervor, his white even teeth contrasting with tanned face in the fading light. "No, it is not. But God has to allow man his agency, and if that agency is to choose war..." He shrugged as if to say, "What can we do?"

Merena buried her cheek into his chest. She knew he was speaking the truth, but still the fear in her breast intensified the pounding of her heart.

Hesitantly, holding her close to him, he asked. "Merena, I desire very much that you be my wife." His voice faded as he wondered what to say next.

She turned her face up to his and met his lips with her own. He tasted the saltiness of her tears on her lips as he hungrily returned her kiss.

Breathlessly she broke away. "Oh, yes," she whispered.

Cumorah, 387 A.D.

A tear traced its path down Mormon's wrinkled cheeks as poignant memories overcame the inertia of time. So many years had passed and yet events were as clear as if they had happened yesterday. Cumorah seemed so far removed.

Zarahemla, 326 A.D.

As his fifteenth birthday approached, Mormon had never been so busy: finishing scribe training, completing his apprenticeship with Alphus, courting Merena in his few spare moments, and being gone for weeks at a time on the interminable patrols into the east wilderness.

More and more he found himself turning to the Lord. His life was totally frustrated. He was in love and couldn't marry Merena because of his warrior obligation. He was through with scribe and goldsmith training but there was no way he could use the training. Ammoron's instructions were that he wasn't even able to pick up the plates until he was twenty-four. In addition to all of that, he was concerned about the lack of faith in so many of the people—especially the warriors with whom he served; not only lack of faith, but outright wickedness. It seemed to him as if the entire Nephite nation had rejected God.

Every night, even while on patrol, he found a quiet place where he could plead with the Lord. Many nights he prayed fervently for hours. It seemed that the Heavens were completely closed to him. "Please answer me, God," he pleaded.

One beautiful starry night, in the hills high above Sidom, he prayed, then sat looking at the heavens. Stars seemed almost like friends, he had observed them so much. Each night they inexorably marched in their circle around the polar star, reliable and steady. *I want to be like that,* he thought. *I want to be as trustworthy as the stars in the heavens.*

He picked up a small pebble and skipped it down through the thick brush. "Father," he prayed aloud, "I have tried to do what you wanted me to do. Following Ammoron's call I set goals to be a scribe and goldsmith. Those goals have almost been met. I set the goal to become a warrior to help defend our people against the Lamanites. That goal is also met. Now Father, I need further direction in my life. What am I to do?"

He was startled by a voice. It was not a loud voice, but one that seemed to pierce his very heart. He looked around. Everything seemed just as before. The hillside was empty. The heavens, filled with thousands of stars, looked just the same. The voice continued. *"My son, I am pleased with what you have accomplished. I have watched your determination and have felt your anxiety over the decadent condition of my people."*

A bright light seemed to be materializing just above Mormon's head. He drew back. In the light a figure emerged. *"I am Jesus Christ. I created the heavens and the earth, and all things that in them are. I was with the Father from the beginning. You believed in Me so redemption is yours. I am the light and the life of the world. I came to redeem the people on this continent but they have rejected me."* The Lord paused and looked down upon Mormon with eyes brimming with compassion.

Mormon had never felt such a feeling of love emanating from another being. It was as if his whole person had been enfolded within the bosom of the Savior. A warmth raced through his body and he shivered. Fear left him and he found his voice. "Lord, I tried to preach to the people but it is as if my mouth is shut."

"Preach no more to this people. They choose to wilfully rebel against Me. I took the three beloved disciples out of the land because of the iniquity of this people. Because of the hardness of their hearts, I cursed the land and its inhabitants. Their treasures will become slippery and will be lost. The power of the evil one will remain throughout the face of the land, fulfilling the words of my servants, Abinadi and Samuel."

Mormon listened as the Lord told him things which He forbade him to write, then the Savior disappeared as quickly as He had come. Mormon was too shaken to move. He spent the rest of the night in that spot. The next day he wrote to Merena: *I was visited of the Lord and tasted and knew of the goodness of Jesus.*

★★★★★

Mormon's arm rose and fell almost in cadence with his heartbeat. Each mallet blow flattened the plate before him until he had it as thin as bark paper. He raised his arm to strike one more blow when Alphus called.

"Mormon!"

He struck the final blow and wiped his forehead with his forearm, which only served to smudge his face with charcoal.

"You are to report to the governor."

"The governor?"

"Yes, and you'd better be quick. The governor does not like to be kept waiting."

Alphus watched Mormon go. He was not surprised. Mormon, large for his age, was the model of a Nephite warrior. His arms were bulky, muscled heavily from pumping the forge and wielding the sword. Long, blond hair hung past his shoulders, framing his high-cheekboned face. Icy-blue eyes peered out from under heavy brows. *Yes,* Alphus thought. *The Nephites love a winner and Mormon has been an obvious winner from his earliest teens when his body shot upward and filled out so dramatically and his already striking features started to settle into comely manliness.*

He smiled. Natschal would be surprised at what had happened to his apprentice. He had not recognized Mormon as a man on the rise—but Alphus had, even before Mormon became a man.

CHAPTER THIRTEEN

GENERAL MORMON

Cumorah, 387 A.D.

Mormon stirred the little fire and wondered what Moroni was doing. *I have been alone much of life,* he thought, *and yet I have never been so lonely as I have since Moroni left.* His thoughts went again to his youth. *If I had known then what I know now would I have accepted the governor's appointment?*

Zarahemla, 327 A.D.

"But sir, I'm only sixteen."

"Age has nothing to do with this appointment," the chief judge remonstrated with a wave of his hand. "When someone demonstrates the necessary skills and maturity, age is of little matter. Your skill in weaponry is well known, as is your expertise in leading men much older than you. I am told that during the past year you have been responsible for the capture of several hundred Lamanites. Your instructors in warrior training highly recommend you." He fiddled with a dagger which lay on the table between them, then leaned toward Mormon in an intimate way. "Frankly, I have no one else I can trust with the responsibility. Members of the Gadianton band have infiltrated the officer corps. Besides, you are large for your age and show all the leadership necessary for this position."

"But..."

"No buts." The chief judge raised his hand to silence Mormon. "I need a loyal warrior who is skilled in the art of warfare. Within a short time I think the Lamanites will get brave enough to mount a massive offensive against us—no more little company size raids." He sighed. "Mormon, this is your calling. It is your destiny. Someone must save this people."

"Save the people?" Mormon recalled similar words Alphus had spoken a year before.

"Yes," the chief judge said. "Gadianton robbers infest the land, robbing, murdering, extorting. Our people are so fearful of the robbers and the Lamanites that they hide their treasures in the earth. Lamanite bands are at our borders, threatening to invade anytime." He shook his head. "As I said earlier, someone must save this people and I assign you that responsibility."

Mormon stood and saluted, his hand and arm thumping his chest as Captain Caleb had taught him. "Sir, I am at your service."

As he left the chief judge's chambers he was more than a little awed at his appointment. Only sixteen and the general over all the Nephite armies. He looked up into the blue of the sky. Lord, I will need Thy help. By the time he arrived at Alphus' door his awe had turned to sadness. At Natschal's house he had read the scriptures, copying the words of Helaman, Abinadi, and Samuel the Lamanite. They all predicted the time now present in the land when the power of the evil one would dominate. All predicted the people would hide up their treasures in the earth and they would be lost because God had cursed the land. But, as if the scriptures were not clear, the Lord, Himself, had verified those things personally to him.

God told him that he must do what he could to help the people, though their destruction was predicted. He sighed and entered Alphus' house. His friend must be first to hear the news.

Alphus was not surprised. His lack of surprise confused Mormon.

"It is only as I predicted," he said. "A man who knows where he is going always gets there."

Natschal's reaction was more expected. For the first time Mormon could actually see pride in the eyes of the old man.

Cumorah, 387 A.D.

Mormon again stirred the fire as he thought of that first commission as general of the Nephite armies. All was not easy in his new position. Older officers envied his appointment. Mormon thought specifically of Annobet. Annobet had been a strong leader in his time. His features were vigorous and stern, with eyes turned down at the corners—a suggestion that in some far-off age there was an infusion of Lamanite blood. His eyes flashed with hard intelligence and implied a capacity for ruthlessness and possible cruelty. The only weakness in the man's features was his mouth. Annobet's mouth was not the mouth of a determined leader, a man of action, but that of an indecisive, introversive man. His receding chin seemed to confirm the implications of weakness.

"I was too young to deal most effectively with the politics and jealousies of my command," he mused aloud, "so I relied heavily on my non-commissioned officers. They had years of experience and knew how to handle the officers, even Annobet. I also gained strength from the Lord." He leaned back against the cave wall. "And I had one other advantage: I knew my Nephite warriors—their needs, their wants, and their weaknesses. They were motivated to defend their land."

He remembered his challenge to them: "The Lamanites and robber Nephites are our enemies. Follow me into battle and we will destroy them. I will not expect you to face any danger I do not face, or suffer any hardships I do not suffer. I know you will do your duty for I believe in you. I hope you believe in me. Be proud to be Nephites fighting our nation's battles."

Mormon smiled as he remembered how his warriors rallied around him. Spies kept him informed of Lamanite preparations. He started his own preparations by building up the fortress at Manti where the main attack would undoubtedly come. When completed, Manti's defenses looked very impressive. Surrounding the city on three sides were steep hills whose unusual concentric pattern formed an immense natural fort. Mormon built up natural lines of defense along the ridges before the city, forming each defensive position like the glacis of a fort, sloping gently away towards the enemy, but with steep reverse slopes, so the defenders could lie in wait in these relatively protected ravines, then move up to sweep off with spears and arrows an enemy advancing up the long glacis.

Land of Manti, 327 A.D.

"What a hornet's nest they will come upon," Ahmeron said enthusiastically as he surveyed Manti's defenses. Mormon was less enthusiastic. He did not have time to build other defenses and it would be so easy for the Lamanites to bypass this one well-protected segment of the border to attack other cities.

The Lamanites, when they came, came with power. The bronzed warriors, ruthless and fearless, attacked his defenses in waves. His warriors were frightened as they saw the numbers of bodies piling up on the glacis. Behind the lines, confusion and alarm steadily mounted.

"Hold your positions," Mormon commanded. "Do not retreat."

He had all he could do to keep his men in their defensive positions. This was his first major battle and he was nervous.

Mormon saw that he could not hold Manti. He summoned Caleb who had commanded his warrior training company. Caleb was a striking officer. Mormon had always respected him for his neat and precise thoughts. There was no bluff in his speech. Good sense seemed to dominate his decisions. His face burned with determination and anyone listening always felt that whatever task he set was already accomplished.

"I feel I need to pull back, but wonder if I should attempt to hold our positions," he said. "What would you suggest?"

Captain Caleb's clear eyes looked Mormon right in the face. "Meeting an attack is like catching a coconut in your hands as it falls from the tree. Shock is dissipated by drawing back the hands. A little 'give,' a little suppleness, and the violence of the impact is vastly reduced."

Following Caleb's counsel, Mormon organized a fighting withdrawal, tenaciously holding to each piece of land until it could be held no longer, making the Lamanites pay dearly for each forward step they took. But his own losses were great. He admired the courage of his warriors. These were Nephite warriors fighting on Nephite soil—every inch of it hallowed.

He wrote Merena. *"Feelings of unity and patriotism created a courage which reason alone could not inspire. My army, though in retreat, fought off the attackers and became a fighting team."*

He didn't tell her of the months of unremitted, bloody, disheartening failures which his army had experienced. He, himself, didn't know how long he would be able to call on his warriors to continue fighting. Mormon really cared for his men, even suffered what they suffered. He knew what wounded men looked like and how they felt. He knew how much little things mattered to the fighting warrior. With natural insight, as he inspected the men in the various armies, he knew what to look for—where to give a word of praise and where to find slovenly work.

Their retreat took them to the city of Angola. Mormon put his entire army to work building fortifications, but Lamanites attacked before the fortifications were finished. Step by bloody step they retreated, from Angola to the land of David, and finally, with their backs against the west sea, Mormon set up his defenses in the land of Joshua.

Captain Annobet came to Mormon. He looked ill—his face feverish, his body inflamed. "We can retreat no farther," he said. "I can still save Zarahemla. I feel I have but a short time to live and victory must be mine before I die."

Mormon wondered if the captain was losing his sanity. "What do you suggest?" he asked coldly.

"To lead a counter-attack on the enemy."

"That would be suicide," Mormon said. "Lamanites outnumber us almost two-to-one. All you would do is kill more of our men."

Mormon watched as Annobet returned stiff-backed to his unit. The man worried him. He hoped Annobet would do nothing rash in his unstable condition. The captain was not popular with his warriors. Mormon had heard them call him the "butcher." He was a killer and he looked the part. His face, burned and blackened by the summer sun, made him as dark as any Lamanite. His mouth was wide, thin-lipped and cruel. His jaw seemed permanently set, like a crocodile with its teeth clamped onto a monkey it was vigorously worrying to death. His jet-black hair stood up fiercely in disarray. He walked with a quick nervous gait and had a habit of standing with his hands behind his back, his head thrust forward.

Mormon, in his letter to Merena, said, *He gives me the impression of an eagle searching for prey. But he is still one of my most competent captains. He is precise and nobody is better at planning an attack or a defense. His problem, though,* "Mormon wrote, *is that fear and death mean nothing to him. He is reckless of all lives and none more than his own. He charges at the head of his warriors, fighting sword in hand when he could escape; thundering implacable orders to his men and when necessary, defiance to his superiors.*

Mormon's men toiled through the night strengthening Joshua's defenses. Making the job even more difficult was the avalanche of rain which began at midnight. The city was filled with refugees from all the land before them. Any who stayed in the path of the Lamanite army would have been killed. At dawn Mormon was startled by the blast of a trumpet. He ran up the ladder to the wall. Before him Annobet's army marched towards the oncoming Lamanite force. There was nothing Mormon could do to stop them. He watched as the armies met. It was as if some evil, superhuman power from stygian regions wrested control out of Annobet's feeble hands. With terrible force his army was swept along at ever-mounting speed towards the waiting Lamanites. As the fighting started, Mormon sensed the presence of that evil being, marshalling events to his own pattern, working to destroy the Nephites.

Frustrated, filled with anxiety and dread, unable to help, he and his warriors watched the battle from the city walls. The Nephites seemed leaderless. Apparently Annobet had been killed in the initial thrust. The battle somehow continued through its own impetus. Mormon thought, There can be no end to it until the last Nephite hobbles out from behind the city wall and the last Lamanite limps out from the forest to exterminate each other with clubs or teeth and finger nails. He thought of the twenty-four gold plates which King Mosiah and Alma translated. The plates told of the battle of the last two survivors of the descendants of Jared: Coriantumr and Shiz. Perhaps that is what will happen here, he thought.

Shortly the battle was over. Light-skinned warriors fell back in disorder, Lamanites in close pursuit. Mormon ordered a covering force outside the wall to protect the wounded as they streamed back. The sight, like a vision of hell, reduced even the strongest nerves. The skeleton of Annobet's army, led by a wounded officer leaning on a stick, passed back through the gate. Men staggered with small steps, zigzagging as if drunk on palm wine. Mud covered everything. Mormon had difficulty telling the color of their faces from their tunics. Warriors said nothing. They had even lost the strength to complain. Those watching the sad parade became pensive—air of sadness like that which comes when a funeral passes by. Men wept in silence, like women.

Mormon turned away. "This is no longer an army. These are corpses," he said to his aide. That night he wrote a letter to Merena. *Annobet's disobedience to my orders killed most of his command, including himself. He has also weakened our defense and endangered the life of every warrior and refugee here. My heart broke as I saw our young men fighting such an uneven battle—knowing their enthusiasm would soon turn to suffering. When the survivors of the battle returned,* he continued, *their expressions were indescribable—frozen by visions of terror. Their postures showed total dejection as their spirits sagged beneath the weight of horrifying memories. They hardly even replied when I spoke to them.*

Lamanites laid siege, throwing their armies in a half-moon around the city—from the sea on one side to the sea on the other. They stayed well out of arrow range, and waited. Mormon had the frustrating feeling of striking out at empty air. The Lamanites had destroyed Annobet's army and now appeared to be waiting to destroy the rest of the Nephites.

Weeks passed. Hunger and thirst became regulars in the city. Warriors and refugees alike were reduced to scavenging any remnants they could find upon the dead. Water supplies dwindled. Mormon was sickened as he saw men drinking from a green, scum-covered pool of stagnant rain water. In the pool, his black face downward in the water, lay a dead man, swollen as if he had not stopped filling his stomach with water for days.

But even with all the horror and destruction, the people did not repent of their evil ways. Mormon seemed to be the only one who realized the enormity of what was happening. His anguish brought him even closer to God. He prayed fervently and continuously, imploring God to put an end to these indignities. Never had he prayed with so much heart.

Not a day went by but what the Lamanites attempted to cut through Mormon's defenses. Every day saw more men wounded; more men dead. These attacks flung the silent and gloomy defenders on the walls into acute depression. War, appalling war with blood and carnage raged on. Warriors developed a callousness towards wounded and dead alike. He wrote Merena, *Death used to be a cruel stranger, the visitor with soft footsteps. Today, death is a mad dog in the house. Our men drink beside the dead, sleep in the midst of the dying, laugh and sing in the company of corpses. The frequency of death, which makes life seem even more precious to me, has brought only lassitude to the men.*

In the beginning of the siege's third year, a Lamanite messenger bearing a white flag stood before the fortified city. Mormon, looking down from the wall, cried, "Let him in. I will see him here on the wall."

The Lamanite youth, no older than Mormon, silently handed him a message. "I weary of this siege," the note said in poorly written Hebrew. "I, Aaron, king of the Lamanites, desire to come to battle with you. If you are willing to come out from behind your fortifications and have battle with us, I will withdraw my army from before your city and give you three months to prepare."

Mormon showed Caleb the note. "What do you think?" he asked.

"I think this is the only way out of the siege," Caleb replied. "We should take Aaron's offer."

"We will lose many warriors," Mormon said, "And some of the officers will not agree. For them to continue to hold out week after week against the siege is a symbol of honor."

Caleb snorted. "They think nothing of men who are sick, wounded and dying. At least a battle will be decisive. Three months gives us time to rebuild strength into our warriors."

Mormon nodded his agreement. He walked to where the Lamanite youth still waited. "We agree to King Aaron's terms," he said.

Within an hour Lamanites poured from the forest like ants when one has kicked an antheap. Thousands of them lined up and marched away from the city. Then silence returned.

With Lamanite armies no longer surrounding the city, Mormon sent scavenging parties into the forest to find food. Lamanites had stripped everything. The forest was bare; there were no fruit or nuts left within miles. Mormon was forced to send to Zarahemla for provisions.

He sent a note to Merena. *I am three years older than when you saw me last. I imagine your beauty has matured and you are now even more beautiful. I can hardly wait until I see you once again.* He thought a moment, then wrote, *I'm afraid I have changed terribly. The long war has engendered a horrible lassitude in me. My nerves are strained. Sometimes I feel crushed and flattened.*

"How did the other officers feel about Aaron's offer to battle?" Caleb asked.

"Some officers groused about it," Mormon said, "but most approached it like a jaguar on a branch who sees opportunity approaching and about to pass below. They were optimistic about winning the battle and looked forward to fighting once again."

Caleb laughed. "Our men will be like an iron sword that has been tempered for just the right length of time—hard and tensile but not yet brittle."

Mormon wished he felt as confident as Caleb. He paced the wall, hoping the provisions would soon come. Clear moonlight lighted the tranquil landscape. Warriors stood on the wall with affected casualness, hands in tunics, gazing at the mysterious dark shapes of the forest to their front. No longer did they wonder who would emerge on the morrow. The Lamanites were gone. Among the shadows was an occasional cracking of twigs and murmuring of muffled voices as supply parties brought in whatever they scavenged. Otherwise, silence.

A month passed, then two. Mormon worried that his men were not strong enough for battle, but reinforcements came from Zarahemla. The city was filled with warriors. Constant supply parties brought necessary provisions. Noise of swords beating on swords as men trained and practiced their death-dealing arts filled the city. The noise was better than the silence.

A note came from Aaron, king of the Lamanites. "We will be in the valley before Joshua on the next night the moon is full."

Mormon consulted his astronomer. "Three weeks." Three weeks to make sure his army was prepared. Three weeks to eliminate all negative thoughts and feelings. Three weeks to pump his men with food and water to give strength to do battle. Three weeks to complete all necessary training so each man was at his very best.

He looked at his latest strength figures. "Forty-two thousand men," he whispered.

All day Mormon watched as dust clouds rose into the heavens. The night of the full moon had come. The armies of the Lamanites filled the valley. Mormon marched his men from the city, lining them up in rows, feather banners waving in the breeze, javelins piercing the sky. Swordsmen, slingers and bowmen stood shoulder to shoulder, bowmen in front. Slingers filled the rows between archers and swordsmen. Every man also carried a spear. They stood in stoic silence, watching the enemy forming across the valley.

Mormon stood in front of the ranks of Nephites. The rays of the morning sun caught him directly in the face. He turned away, looking in silence upon his men. Timing of this battle would be so important. He knew the men were keyed up—emotions at a high pitch of excitement.

The whooping and beating of hundreds of drums across the valley pulled him around. The Lamanite army, larger than his own, marched inexorably across the valley. His face became grim with purpose. He could not let the Lamanites have the initiative. "Forward," he cried, raising his arm and thrusting it towards the oncoming Lamanites. Feather banners dipped and reared again to the heavens as Nephite warriors stepped resolutely forward.

As Lamanites came within arrow range, Nephite bowmen dropped to one knee and without command loosed streams of deadly arrows. Nock and shoot, nock and shoot, until quivers were empty. Hundreds of Lamanites fell, but their comrades came on in waves. Bowmen fell back, their only arms now their spears. Slingers took their place. Air was filled with "Whrrrr, splat," as slings whirled around heads. Stones found their marks among the oncoming Lamanites.

Lamanite archers found their range and Nephites pitched forward to the earth. Mormon shouted, "Hold your ground," but his voice was lost in the crescendo of thousands of angry voices as Lamanites and Nephites met in the center of the valley. Spears arced through the air. First sounds of sword meeting sword began a clamor that would not end for hours.

Mormon glanced at Caleb. The huge captain stood erect, laughing and howling as he swung his sword in mighty sweeps. His stance exposed too large an area of his great chest but he appeared unmindful of danger.

To Mormon the battle was as appalling as it was breathtaking. Dark and light warriors died in violent profusion. Some lay inert, others struggled frantically to regain their feet but were trampled by the mad rush of warriors. Then he had no more time to look or to think. Dark bodies of Lamanites were all around him. Lift and thrust; swing the sword; chop and hack at the fierce faces. Sweat poured down his forehead and into his eyes, stinging and blinding. He had no time to wipe it out. "Keep swinging," he muttered fiercely.

He knew that Aaron would not permit this carnage to continue for long. When he realized the sheer strength of his numbers was not winning the battle, he would resort to more strategy. As he thrust, he felt and then saw the red stickiness which slid down his arm to his wrist. The shoulder of his tunic was soggy with blood. At first he felt no pain, then pain blossomed through his entire body. Someone's sword had cut him, but luckily he was still able to use his arm.

He put the pain from his mind, letting his sword beat a rhythm on the enemy's heads and bodies. All sense of time and numbers was lost. It was as if he were alone, fighting the battle all by himself.

Mormon saw that the Lamanites were slowly retreating and knew that Aaron had finished with this appalling sacrifice of lives. He and his men, better armed and armored, had won the first round of the battle. After a brief respite he knew the attack would renew and would be the beginning of the end. Retreating Lamanites brought out their bows. Mormon saw one raising his bow. He yelled, but his yell came too late.

Captain Caleb made no sound other than a surprised grunt that was half curse, half laugh. Then he turned and sat down, declining his head so he could see the tufted shaft of the arrow protruding from his left shoulder. He grasped the shaft with his left hand, gave a yank which drew the barbed obsidian point part way back through his flesh, and released his grip abruptly, his sigh coming through his teeth, his face whitening suddenly.

Mormon stepped over to Caleb. "Watch the Lamanites," he yelled over his shoulder. He leaned over the big captain—the man who had first assigned him as a warrior in a regular patrol.

Caleb looked up at Mormon, smiling disdainfully but panting in pain.

"This will hurt," Mormon said.

He stiffened as Mormon took hold of the shaft with one hand and braced the other against the huge chest. Before Caleb knew what he was doing, Mormon shoved the arrow through, breaking off the point as soon as it penetrated Caleb's back. He pulled out the shaft and examined the wounds in front and back. They were ragged and ugly but did not bleed much. That would come later. He called for someone to bind the wounds, then stood up.

Lamanites ringed the valley, caring for their wounded. In the valley floor itself, thousands lay dead or dying. The valley in places resembled a dump in which accumulated shreds of clothing, smashed weapons, battered armor, and bleeding flesh.

Behind him Caleb grunted. "An artery of Lamanite blood has been cut and it flows incessantly in large spurts."

For two days the fighting raged back and forth over the same narrow, corpse-saturated valley. In the blazing summer heat the screw of horror tightened. Where there had been thousands of men, there were now hundreds. The terrible odor of blood and gore and ripped intestines filled the air.

Mormon no longer had any sensation in his wounded shoulder. He felt a bond linking him with the others who were surviving the battle. It was more—much more—than the normal feeling of affinity that binds together men who have endured shared hardships. Whoever floundered through this morass full of the shrieking and the dying, whoever shivered in those nights, had passed the last frontier of life and would henceforth bear deep within him the leaden memory of a place that lies between life and death—or beyond either.

On the third day the battle ended. Mormon and his remaining Nephites occupied the battlefield along with the thousands of dead. The Lamanites had lost. The few who remained alive had deserted the field and returned to their own land. Mormon rested on his sword. "Is the battle—any battle really worth the price?"

CHAPTER FOURTEEN

COURTSHIP AND MARRIAGE

Cumorah, 387 A.D.

Mormon's loneliness was a pall upon him. The cave confined him. Food was tasteless. Cumorah itself contained too many bitter memories. Yet, *memories are all I have.* He lay on the pallet thinking of his life. *When we defeated the Lamanites in my first real battle as commander of the Nephite armies, my only desire was to return to Zarahemla, see my parents, and marry Merena. I was also concerned for the Nephite people. I wanted them to repent of their sins. When I heard their mourning I rejoiced. But I was wrong. They didn't sorrow for their sins; their sorrow was that God would not permit them to be happy in their sins.*

Zarahemla, A.D. 331

The familiar street brought feelings of both anguish and joy to Mormon. "Merena," he whispered. He shook his head. *I faced thousands of Lamanites without fear but now as I approach the home where lives the one I love I am suddenly fearful.*

He pushed past several beggars in the street. They sat cross-legged, eyes unfocused, waiting for coins to fall into outstretched palms. *Is it my imagination, or have the numbers of beggars in Zarahemla increased in my absence?*

One loped after Mormon. "Alms. Alms." He cried, thrusting his frail and crooked body into Mormon's path.

Mormon thrust past him.

Wagh!" cursed the man.

Mormon turned to gaze at him, then continued thoughtfully to Natschal's door. Not only were there more beggars, but the beggars were more aggressive. He straightened his shoulders and knocked, softly at first then with an insistence born of four absent years. The door opened a crack, then swung wide on its leather hinges. Standing before him was all and more than he had imagined in those four long years. "Merena," he whispered.

Tears sprang to her eyes. She smiled and stepped to him. He grasped her tiny hands in his sword-calloused palms.

"Merena," he said again.

She pulled him into the cool interior of the house and shut the door. Then she threw her arms around him. "Oh, Mormon," she moaned. "I have missed you so very much."

Long moments passed as they silently embraced. Mormon held her to arm's length. "Your father?"

"I'm still here," a raspy voice announced from the dark shadows at the far end of the room.

Merena squeezed his hand and pulled back from him. She looked up sadly into Mormon's eyes. "Father is worse," she whispered. "Nothing seems to please him." Aloud she said, "Mormon has returned."

Supper was delicious: fresh-baked sweet potatoes and corn cooked in its husks; much different than warrior food. Mormon talked little, only tersely answering Merena's questions about the wars. His thoughts focused on Merena and his future with her. Natschal ate silently, his eyes filled with pain.

With supper over, Mormon ran out of words.

"Weather is lovely," Merena tried to break the lengthy pause with small talk.

Mormon put his fingers to her lips, too serious for small talk. He faced Natschal and cleared his throat. The words he had mentally practiced tumbled out. "I completed my apprenticeship to you and Alphus. Now I am willing to pledge my continued service to you as scribe and engraver in return for Merena's hand in marriage. For her, I will work as many years as you desire."

"Bah!" Natschal growled. "How can you be of service? You will just get started on a project and war will again break out and you will be gone."

Gorge in his throat almost choked him in his anger, but Mormon swallowed and continued calmly. "We have beat the Lamanites so badly that it will be many years before they dare attack us again."

"And what of the robbers and murderers who follow the Gadianton band?" growled Natschal.

Mormon spread his hands in a gesture of helplessness. "Until the people themselves desire to do away with that element, there is little the army can do."

"Then we will continue living in fear of our lives and homes," Natschal said, his eyes glinting under heavy, gray brows. "Have you not noticed the mourning and lamentation of the people since your return?"

"Yes," Mormon said sadly. "I hoped the sorrow I saw was sorrow for their iniquities; that they were truly repentant and were turning to God." He sighed and took Merena's hand in his. "My heart rejoiced when I heard their mourning. I wanted them to again become righteous so the Lord would forgive them."

Natschal laughed derisively. "And?"

"They mourned because they could not hold their riches. As Samuel prophesied their wealth became slippery and they lost it."

"Their sorrow was not unto repentance?" Merena asked.

"Far from it," Mormon said. "They curse God and wish to die because they do not have happiness in sin." He laughed without humor. "Those with wealth say they wish to die because they can not hold their wealth, but when it comes down to it they struggle with the sword for their very lives." He mustered his courage before the still irascible Natschal and returned to his plea. "You have not answered me concerning Merena," he said. "I have pledged my work to you for Merena's hand in marriage."

"Marry her," Natschal grumbled, "but she is not to leave me." His eyes became crafty. "It will cost you five years of service."

Mormon squeezed Merena's hands. "Five years is a small price to pay for such a lovely wife," he said softly, looking into Merena's dark eyes.

The wedding was a small one. Natschal had few friends in the valley. Mormon's father came from Desolation but his mother was too sick to travel. Alphus, looking old and haggard, was there. Several warriors, Samuel, Caleb and several others, attended.

Cumorah, 387 A.D.

I was barely twenty years of age, Mormon thought. *That was fifty-six years ago. We had fourteen years of comparative peace before I had to return again to war. And Merena loved me.* An involuntary shudder shook his body. *And oh, how I loved her. Just a few more records to abridge and I will join her once again.*

Zarahemla, 332 A.D.

"My dear, I never thought I could be so happy," Mormon said as he kissed her throat.

"Shh. Father will hear you," she said.

"I don't care. We must live in his house but I will not sacrifice our precious time together for any man—even your father."

She chuckled quietly and turned her back to him.

Mormon cuddled up to her on the pallet, laying his arm across her shoulders. "Besides," he whispered, "I have already served more than a year of my indenture; less than four more years and we will be free."

Merena turned and put her fingers on his lips. "Even then I will not be able to leave this house."

"It doesn't matter. I love you and will always love you. Where we live is of little consequence as long as we are together."

"Mormon," she said hesitantly.

"What is it my love?"

She was silent.

Mormon reached over and was surprised to feel the wetness of tears on her cheeks. "Why do you sorrow?" he asked.

Merena giggled. "I do not sorrow. I just did not know how to tell you that we are going to have a baby."

"A baby?"

"Shhh!."

Mormon's life seemed a whirlwind as he waited expectantly for their baby to be born. Natschal's joints were swollen and useless. Mormon not only did all of his copying and enscribing, but also cared for Natschal's every need. The old man greeted each service rendered with grumbling and carping but Mormon accepted Natschal's demeaning ways without complaint.

Every day he walked to the barracks where he observed the training of new warriors. He desired continued peace but knew the Lamanites. They would come again in battle—as soon as they felt they were strong enough to win.

With the few senines he saved from his military pay he hired several maids to care for his now-obviously pregnant wife—against Natschal's grumblings and Merena's protestations.

Whenever time permitted he visited Alphus. His friend no longer was able to work his forge. Mormon, saddened by how his friend had aged, tried to do the work for him, but Alphus shook his head.

"No," he said. "I will live until I die, and I would rather use my time talking with you."

"Then talk," Mormon smiled, brightened by Alphus' courage and positive outlook. His friend was still the philosopher.

"Your short life has proven a basic law," Alphus began in his scratchy voice. "That which we desire we usually get."

"I did get Merena," Mormon quipped.

"The law involves more than that," Alphus said seriously. "For those who desire wealth above all else, wealth comes. For those who want friends, friendships form. If a person loves honesty he gets honesty."

"And if we want righteousness..."

"We get righteousness," finished Alphus.

"Like attracts like?"

Alphus nodded wisely. "The law never fails. For instance, when you were a youth working at my forge you desired courage. You have been blessed with abundant courage."

"Though I desired it, I worked hard to obtain it," Mormon observed.

"That's part of the law," Alphus said crisply. "If we desire something strongly enough we do what it takes to obtain it."

Mormon thought of all the things he had wanted in life, most already accomplished. "I guess I have been influenced by this law, though I didn't realize it," he mused.

"The laws of man's success are just as inviolable as the laws of nature," Alphus said wisely. "They can either work for or against us. We might as well take advantage of them and have them work for us."

Mormon thought often of Alphus' words. His friend had taught him goal setting and now had opened his perspectives on having a successful life.

"But what is success?" he asked Alphus. "Isn't it being in tune with God? Marrying the mate you love? Having a family?"

The old man was silent for some time. Then he responded. "It is all of those, but much more. Success is life itself. It is not the end but the journey. It is not only the marriage, but the courtship. It is not the accomplishment of the task but the doing of it. It is not the winning of the battle, but the fighting and accomplishing. You have talked to me about faith. Isn't faith only the vision of what is to come? Isn't faith part of doing what is necessary to complete the task? Faith and hope become the plans and strategy for winning the battle."

Each time Mormon visited Alphus his concept of life was broadened. Alphus was his mentor, his teacher and counselor. One day, after a particular trying time with Natschal, Mormon was less than cheerful.

"What troubles you?" Alphus asked.

"Natschal," Mormon growled. "I wish he were like you. All day he sits around and complains. I have never heard him say a word of praise."

"What does it matter how someone else acts or what someone else says?" Alphus said. "No one determines your attitude but you. Otherwise, every time someone was happy would it make you happy? When someone around you is sad, does that make you sad? When someone is a complainer, carper and condemner, should that make you react and become one also?"

Mormon laughed out loud. "You have made your point, my friend," he said. "I will not complain again—no matter what provocation I might have."

Even with Mormon's care and nursing by Merena's maids, Natschal's health continued to deteriorate. He sat glumly in the darkened house hours on end and never talked or did anything useful. When spoken to he replied with crossness. The day finally came when he no longer responded, even crossly. He had died in his sleep. Mormon's only sorrow was that Natschal did not at least live long enough to see his first grandson.

Mormon nervously kicked the gravel in the path as he paced before his house. He had paced since early morning, and with each step he became more distraught. "Why can't I be as

calm now as when lying in wait for Lamanites to attack my
armies?" he muttered. He paid no attention to the sweet
smelling red and yellow flowers Merena had planted on both
sides of the path.

He resented Leera, the bossy midwife. She dominated his
home. She would not even let him inside—pushing him away
from the door with the words, "You go do something. I will take
care of Merena and tell you when the baby is delivered."

A maid-servant ran from the house, went to the well,
and returned with a basin filled with water. Mormon jumped as
Merena screamed. He ran to the house and attempted to push
inside.

"The pains have begun," Leera said as she pushed him
back, "but it may still be a long time. Merena is young and
small. Have patience, Mormon."

"Patience!" scoffed Mormon as he turned and continued
his pacing. "That is not one of my virtues."

He paced and thought, paced and thought, almost
tempted to go visit Alphus while waiting for the baby to come.
Finally, his limited patience disappeared. "That is my wife in
there," he muttered, "and I must be with her." He pushed open
the door and stepped inside, ignoring Leera's objections. The
room, hot and oppressive, smelled of wood smoke and pinesap.
His nose wrinkled involuntarily at the acrid smell. Red-hot
coals glowed in a brazier standing on the stone floor.
Dominating the room was the huge wooden bed which he
impulsively had made for Merena—over her objections that it
was too extravagant.

She lay in the bed, propped up by pillows. Mormon
quickly moved to her side and took her small limp hand in his
large one. She lay quietly, but he could sense her pain. Beads of
sweat stood out on her knotted forehead. Her fine brown hair
was matted and plastered to her face.

She wrenched in agony as a pain hit her, fingernails
biting deeply into Mormon's calloused palm. She moaned, then
sank back into the blankets. New drops of perspiration formed
on her pallid cheeks. She smiled wanly at him, seeming to feel
his tender concern and helplessness. How frustrating it was to
be there but to be unable to help.

"It will soon be over, my dear," he soothed. Merena
didn't answer but he felt the gentle squeeze of her hand.

Pains came regular and close together. Mormon's hand
again seemed almost crushed by the small hand within it.

"The time is here," Leera said.

A servant girl quickly brought a basin of hot water from the brazier. Mormon was hustled out of the way.

His first child, as Leera had predicted, was a boy, born in the 337th year after the sign of the Savior's birth. Mormon sent word to his father, a widower now living in Zarahemla and to Alphus. He picked a name for the infant: Moroni, the name of the Nephite general he admired so much.

Grandfather Mormon christened the eight-day-old boy while family and friends stood around. He blessed the baby: "Moroni, you will be a leader of men. Just as that first Moroni raised the Title of Liberty for his people, you will be God's instrument in proclaiming to the world the message that liberty comes only through obedience to the Gospel of Jesus Christ."

The elder Mormon continued his blessing on the baby while the new father pondered his words. *How wonderful it is to bring such a child to this earth. Thank you, Lord, for letting us be creators with Thee.*

After the blessing, Mormon proudly took little Moroni into his arms. He held him close, smelling the soft, sweet baby smell of him. He whispered into the tiny ear, "Moroni, you will be a champion. You and I, no matter what adversity may befall us, will spend our lives in service to the Master."

*****

"I'm, sorry I don't have more time to be with you," Mormon apologized.

Merena merely smiled and continued rocking the baby.

"Between my commitments to the army and the scribe business I took over from your father I seem to keep busy all the time. I haven't even had time to write a history of my people as Ammoron commanded me." He spread his hands in frustration.

"My darling, it is all right," Merena said.

"No, it isn't all right," he almost shouted. "I married you to spend time with you—not with the army, not even with my brush, stylus and paper or plates. It is my family I am most concerned about." He choked on his words.

"Please don't disturb the baby," Merena said. "You are becoming too upset. Why not take some time from your army duties and be at home with us?"

"Because my spies report the Lamanites are organizing again for war," Mormon said miserably. "We must be prepared to defend our lands once more against them."

*****

"It's a girl," the midwife said.

Mormon held up the two-year-old Moroni to see the baby. She was a beautiful little girl. Dark hair, contrasting with clear-white skin, hung in natural ringlets onto her neck. Eyes, large and luminous, gazed around unfocused. "She seems awfully pale."

Merena smiled contentedly at the baby lying on the bed beside her. "It is her natural baby color," she said. She cradled the baby in her arms. "What shall we name her?"

"I named Moroni," Mormon said. "You name the girls."

"Then I name her Sophrista," Merena said firmly.

Sophrista, unlike Moroni, was very frail. Immediately after birth she contracted some disease. Mormon prayed over her until she finally got well. Though she never gained her strength, she was a happy child. She brought real joy into Mormon's life. He often held her on his lap, tracing her blue blood vessels with his finger. Her skin remained waxy and parchment-like, almost transparent.

"You seem restless," Merena said as she nursed Sophrista.

"Not restless—excitement!" Mormon chuckled.

"Excitement?"

"It's hard to explain. I have just been visited by three of the Savior's disciples." His words rushed out.

"The three disciples who didn't taste of death?" Merena seemed anxious.

He nodded.

"Tell me what they said. Why did they come to see you?"

"One question at a time, my dear. In the first place, they reminded me that Ammoron commissioned me to get the plates of Nephi and write the history of my people."

"Your twenty-fourth birthday is next week."

"I know."

"What else?"

Mormon could tell her curiosity was getting the better of her. "They ordained me a disciple?"

"What?"

"They ordained me one of the Savior's disciples."

Merena lay the baby down and walked to Mormon. She took his hand. "A disciple? One of the twelve?"

He nodded. "There aren't twelve now, but selected men have been ordained to carry on the work of the Gospel." He shrugged. "The three remaining disciples of the Master chose me as one to carry on the work."

Merena breathed out heavily. "What a responsibility. And what an honor."

Mormom pulled her tight against him, holding her close. Words were not necessary. Finally he released her and asked, "Where is little Moroni. I must tell him."

"Now that I am twenty-four I must go to Antum and get the plates," Mormon said.

"Where is Antum?" Merena asked thoughtfully.

"Near Bountiful," Mormon said. "Even by boat the trip will take me several weeks."

Merena paused before saying anything. "We will miss you. Since you accepted Ammoron's appointment to be the scribe you must get the plates and begin writing the history of our people."

"I know," he said. "It is what I have been training for most of my life. I must ask Father for directions."

Mormon found the hill Shim, as his father had described it. The hill was not large but he searched for two days before he located the cave within which were cached the plates. He pulled back brush and sticks and carefully rolled away the stone which covered the cave's entrance. No one had prepared him for the sight which greeted him: plates of gold and brass stacked almost to the roof of the cave; a large sword, which he knew must be the sword of Laban; two clear stones in a breastplate of bronze—the interpreters—all covered with layers of dust.

Before he touched anything he knelt at the cave's entrance. "Thank you, God," he prayed. "I will be your scribe and record custodian."

The small plates of Nephi were near the cave's entrance, just as Ammoron had told him fourteen years before. He picked them up and wiped off the dust. A tingle went through his body. "These are the plates my ancestors kept the records on," he whispered. "Now I must complete that record." He backed out of the cave, leaving the rest of the plates undisturbed. Carefully he replaced the stone in the cave's entrance and camouflaged it as best he could. With the plates of Nephi tucked under his arm, he started his journey home.

Moroni and Sophrista grew and developed as the uneasy peace between Lamanite and Nephite lengthened into more than ten years. Peace gave him some freedom from his army duties, but Mormon kept busy with his scribe business and writing the history of his people. Mormon felt a great loss when Alphus, who had been mentor and friend, died. No longer would he have the talks which meant so much to him. His father also died. Now, outside of his immediate family, there was no one close to him in Zarahemla.

Mormon's greatest family concern was Sophrista. She was a darling girl, happy to a fault, pleasant to have around, but weak and sickly. Mormon longed to take her to Desolation, to the beach, where ocean and sun would put color into her cheeks.

"The time has come," he told Merena, "when we can leave this wicked city and return to Desolation. The climate there will be much better for Sophrista."

"But, Mormon," Merena said. "Zarahemla has always been my home. And what about your army duties?"

"I can fulfill my duties as well in Desolation as in Zarahemla. Our parents no longer live. We have no really close friends. Besides, my father left me a home in Desolation which you will love.

In Desolation Mormon had more time to spend with young Moroni. He took him hunting and fishing in the nearby forest and river. He taught him the lessons of life he had learned from Alphus. He also taught Moroni of God and His willingness to be part of our lives. "Son, whenever you need help, your Father in Heaven is there. All you have to do is pray. Live worthily to receive His help and He will help you."

Moroni was a typical boy. He loved to be out with Mormon or his friends. Now that he approached twelve years of age, warrior training took much of his time. Mormon, remembering his own warrior training, did not worry about Moroni. He knew his son was learning to use various weapons and practicing unit tactics and maneuvers.

"Where is Moroni?"

"He went on warrior training with the other boys." Merena looked up at the sun's position. "They should be back soon."

"Mormon. Merena." The shout came from up the street.

Mormon stepped from his house onto the street. A weird parade threaded its way toward him. In front was Moroni. Following him were the other boys, singing and chanting. Two of the larger boys carried a dead jaguar on a pole between them.

They stopped in front of him and set the pole down. One of the older boys—Mormon thought his name was Ammah—stepped forward. "Moroni killed the jaguar," he said.

Mormon didn't hear the rest of what was said. He saw the bloody bandage on Moroni's arm. "You are injured." Against his son's protestations he bodily lifted him and carried him into the house.

Merena cried as she bandaged the arm.

Mormon, once he determined that Moroni was all right, was content to be the proud father. Again and again he asked Moroni to tell the story of killing the jaguar.

Dinner was a special occasion. Merena fixed some of Moroni's favorite foods: honey on corn cake, roast fish, and fresh beans from the garden. Sophrista said little, just adored her older brother with her eyes across the table. Filled to the brim, happy with the attention from his family, Moroni retold the story, not elaborating on his feelings. He told of praying and of God's apparent answer.

Mormon cleared his throat. "Son, you have done today what few adults have done. Because of your faithfulness the Lord has blessed you. Now, with your permission, I would also like to give you a blessing."

Moroni choked up. With tears in his eyes, unable to speak, he nodded.

Mormon laid his hands on Moroni's head. "Dear son, Moroni, as a disciple of our Lord and Savior, Jesus Christ, and in His holy name, I give you a father's blessing." The words of the blessing fell from his lips. As he spoke the Spirit seemed to enter him. It was as if he were ten feet tall with long arms reaching down to Moroni's head. Words came: "The Lord has a special mission for you to perform here on the earth. He will take a special interest in you because of that mission. Live worthy of His blessings. When you have completed your mission, Jesus Christ himself will call you home to live with Him." He ended the blessing and stood there, depleted of his strength. He slowly removed his hands from Moroni's head. Moroni stood, clasped his forearms, then threw himself into his arms.

Nine-year-old Sophrista would not be left out. She ran and threw her arms around Moroni's waist.

As soon as Mormon could speak, he announced, "Tomorrow I travel to check out the defenses in our outlying cities. Since Moroni has demonstrated his manhood so well, I will take him along as one of my warrior escorts." He looked down to see what effect his words had on Moroni. Sophrista jumped with excitement and she and Moroni danced around the room.

"Watch your arm," Merena warned nervously.

Next morning she fixed breakfast, worried about her young son making the long journey with Mormon. She packed dried fruits and nuts and bid them a tearful goodbye. When they left she stood in the doorway and watched until they turned the corner and waved. Crying softly she turned back into the house.

Mormon had his son walk beside him as they traveled from Desolation. He told him of battles which had taken place. He pointed out where Teancum had defeated Morianton. When they arrived in Bountiful, he showed his son remains of the fortifications which General Moroni and Teancum had built almost four-hundred years before. In Bountiful he met with the commander of the fortifications, and went on an inspection tour. He was saddened to see the disrepair. If the Lamanites attacked, there was little to hold them from capturing Bountiful.

In the barracks that night, he noted Moroni's apparent agitation. "What troubles you, son?" he asked.

"Father, today I saw someone sacrificed at the temple." His son shuddered as he remembered. "The priest cut out a man's heart and held it up for the people to see."

Mormon listened intently to Moroni. He shook his head in revulsion, saddened by the degradation of his people. "Cultists," he hissed. "Sacrificers! My son," he said gravely, "my heart is saddened by what you describe. The Lord condemns those things which you have witnessed. He cannot look upon sin with the least degree of allowance." As he said this, he noticed a look of horror on Moroni's face. "Son," he said. "It's all right. The robbers and priests will have to pay for their sins. The main thing is to keep ourselves from sin."

Tears formed in Moroni's eyes and ran down his cheeks. Mormon leaned over to comfort his son. Moroni buried his head in his father's shoulder and sobbed. Mormon was perplexed. This was the first time Moroni had cried like this since he was an infant.

Moroni stopped crying and looked up. "Father, I have also sinned. I took a loaf of bread from the baker's stall in the market place."

Mormon was relieved. This was a problem easily solved, as long as Moroni had contrition for what had been done. "My son," he said, "you have done right in telling me. The Lord has provided a way to repent and be fully forgiven." He explained to Moroni. "When Alma was so wicked, the Lord told him that if a person confesses his sins and repents of them with the sincerity of his heart that he would be forgiven. I can feel your regret for what you have done, but there is one more thing which must be done to have full repentance."

"What, Father?" Moroni cried.

"It is necessary that you make restitution for that which you have done and then forever forsake those sins."

"What is restitution?" Moroni asked.

"In this case it is paying the merchant for the bread which was taken."

Father and son walked back to the plaza before the temple. Moroni led the way to the baker's stall, then went in and told the baker what he had done. Mormon listened proudly as his son said, "I have brought the money to pay for what I took."

Mormon smiled at the surprised look on the baker's face. Apparently no one had ever done such a thing before. The walk back to the barracks was in silence. Mormon put his arm around his son's shoulders. Today Moroni had learned a great lesson and Mormon was proud of him.

The rest of the inspection tour was without incident. They traveled from Bountiful to the West Sea where they built boats and paddled northward to the city of Joshua. In each city Mormon inspected fortifications and talked to warrior commanders. From Joshua they traveled east to Teancum, past the Hill Cumorah, and then back to Desolation.

Mormon, saddened by what he saw, wrote: *The Spirit of the Lord has ceased to strive with this people. They are without Christ and God in the world and are driven about as chaff before the wind. They were once a delightsome people and had Christ for their shepherd. Now Satan leads them and they are tossed about as a vessel is tossed on the waves, without sail or anchor, or anything with which to steer. My heart is filled with sorrow because of their wickedness. Three hundred and forty-five years have passed since the time of the Savior. Our people are without defenses. Cities lie unprotected. I pray the Lamanites will not attack, but I know they will. And when they do...*

CHAPTER FIFTEEN

WARS, WARS, WARS

Cumorah, 387 A.D.

The cave was empty and dark. Mormon sat away, his back against a tree. Gnarled hands toyed with a rounded stone, as if rubbing its smooth surface would create a miracle. He yawned, making eyes water—eyes that gazed into the darkness without seeing. He spit, then wiped the back of his hand across his mouth. "Wars!" he muttered.

Desolation, 349 A.D.

Mormon, accompanied by Lamah, his aide, stood by the edge of the road, watching his warriors return. He had sent out forty-thousand men. Fewer returned. The warriors of Gilgal's ten thousand tramped through the dust. The commander, Captain Gilgal, left the ranks and approached through the mist.

"What happened?" called Mormon.

"The Lamanites counterattacked, destroying our initial success. Hundreds of my men were killed."

Gilgal's report only confirmed what Mormon had learned from the early arrivals. While his warriors straggled back into Desolation, Mormon reviewed his situation. No-man's land—swampy lowland thickly overgrown with brush, dotted with ponds and tiny lakes and quicksand—extended southward down to the river. Along his front towards Bountiful, hilly terrain gashed by ravines provided avenues for attack and escape for thousands of Lamanite swordsman and archers. Here and there the Lamanites had broken through, forcing Nephites back. Now a deathly silence hung over the battlefield.

When all his warriors were back within Desolation's fortifications, Mormon returned to the barracks. Through the night he sat huddled on his pallet, prayerful and tense. Only the uneven breathing of Gilgal who lay next to him disturbed his concentration. He stood up, crossed the room and stood for a moment looking down at the youthful face of Ammoni, another commander. He walked through the door. Outside nothing—vaporous sky, dampness in the air, black earth below—nothing indicated that two armies were engaged in a life and death struggle; a dark, sleeping landscape. Mormon was uneasy. He drew his sword and picked his way along the wall through watching warriors. He knew they also felt the unusual silence.

He stopped at another sleeping area. Though sky had poured rain all afternoon he could have counted the drops of water which fell on him from the tree limbs above. With sword in hand he stood like a gloomy statue, blocking the entrance. He felt the silence, keenly, like a man who suddenly becomes aware that someone in the room is no longer breathing. He looked down at the row of stretched-out sleepers. Nearly fifty lay hunched up in their wretchedness. Almost underfoot lay Lamah, sleeping with open mouth.

He returned to his own pallet, then lay awake until dawn lighted the eastern sky. Before the sun rose above the horizon he and Lamah bolted a breakfast of ash cakes and fruit and set out along the wall. He looked around uneasily. To the south, where the Lamanites were camped, and toward the swamplands where for weeks the clatter and noise of battle had been heard—silence now lurked like an omnivorous maw.

He sighed. *I am too old to be effective as commander of the army. I need to be home caring for Merena, Moroni and Sophrista.* With the rising sun, noise of battle rose into glistening sky. Screams and yells, clash of swords and phhht of arrows burst on his consciousness. He tried to shut the sounds out, but his inner self cried in anguish over what was happening to his people. His commanders, who at one time felt the emotions of sympathy, love and fear, could hardly be reached by anything any longer. Most warriors seemed to actually enjoy killing and maiming the enemy.

Along the whole battlefront death stalked the Nephite positions. Yet, Mormon reflected, even during the battle he could enjoy the beauty of earth and sky. His eyes were still clear and his hearing keen. It was mechanical, automatic, but he saw and heard. From the wall he watched as human figures bounded out of a gully and moved over the ground like dry leaves swept before the wind. They stumbled over one another, fell and remained on the ground or stood up again, struggled on a little farther, only to fall again and run again—these figures were no longer members of a warrior unit.

A tall captain emerged from the battle staggering and gesticulating like a drunkard, suddenly breaking out into peals of laughter. This was no longer a commander; it was a madman. A figure crawled over the grass like a worm, leaving a trail of blood behind him, and finally tumbled into a hollow.

The trickle of warriors turned into a rout. Soon the entrance to the village was jammed by thousands of Nephites. On flowed the stream: swordsmen, bowmen and those who had been slingers. Most abandoned their swords and slings and bows as they ran. Others dragged their weapons with them. Mormon could not stop the retreat. Scattered remnants of his armies straggled down the road. Others had been left behind.

Mormon tried to stem the tide, calling on warriors to stand and fight. As well might he stand in the midst of the mighty Sidon and try to turn it upstream. Looking into the gray warriors' faces he could almost read their questions: "For what are we dying, general?" "Will our wives and children dry their tears on the banners of victory or must they weep forever?"

Mormon had to ask himself, *What will I answer the mothers when they ask: where is my son? Where is the father of my children?*

Men walked silently and watched as Mormon strode past. The sky hung low over the land. The wind whipped mist across the surface of the river. The endless procession moved on. Many were wounded, hobbling along on legs which had been cut or pierced.

Mormon stood on the road until twilight. By that time the column of retreating warriors reached into Desolation.

It was the beginning of the end. The Nephite army was defeated.

Lamah stood silently at attention before his commander. Mormon gave him a piercing, frozen glance. He was pale; his eyes glistened with ill-concealed rage as he reported to Mormon.

"Ammonihah's ten thousand are not holding. Dan's ten thousand held on so desperately to its dugouts that now it is too late and they are in a real fix. Zoram's ten thousand was almost destroyed in the first Lamanite thrust."

Mormon's saw his task as preserving those who could be saved. "Fast retreat is our only chance," Mormon said. "Dan's ten thousand must be pulled out before every man is destroyed. The breaches in the line in front of Ammonihah's army must be cleared again and held."

"And Desolation?"

"The city must be held. We must retake the ground before the city. Adjustments with the line between our army and the Lamanite army will have to be drawn in blood." He resumed his pacing.

A mud-coated figure entered. Layers of dirt and dried sweat made Gilgal almost unrecognizable.

"Thank God you are here," Mormon exclaimed, grasping forearms with him. "What is your situation?"

"My troops are demoralized. Our food is gone."

"You must take over Zoram's location and hold it so Captain Dan and his men can pull back."

"Very well, sir. I'll have the hill occupied tonight."

"The hill must be held until new positions have been taken up closer to Desolation. Captain Ammonihah and his men are already falling back."

Captain Gilgal rose.

"The hill," were Mormon's parting words. He turned to Lamah. "What about the evacuation of the women and children and the shifting to the rear of Desolation?"

Lamah looked at him blankly, then shook his head.

The sky clouded over, but a gap remained where stars gleamed brightly. The gap of clear sky touched the horizon near Desolation. Mormon wondered whether his wife and children, who had been in the city, were still safe. Followed by Lamah, he left the wall. Up front his men were dying, there he might also die, but perhaps he could save what was salvageable. Dotted in a long line were Nephite warriors. It was not yet dawn. Mormon moved on into the hollow that led into a ravine. In the ravine were a group of men, waiting for the dawn and the resumption of battle. He heard them talking.

"Where will it end?"

"Have we been abandoned?"

"The city cannot be held."

"But Mormon will do everything in his power."

Half a dozen bows, a few slings and tired men, but the village had to be held. Men lay in the dirt like rabbits and like rabbits they slept with wide-open eyes. Perhaps they were dreaming; perhaps this very minute they were being tormented by sights and sounds of yesterday, recorded without their knowledge by stunned ears and dulled eyes, so that every horrible detail might later be reviewed. Some groaned and cursed, swore at others who refused to fight.

Mormon found Captains Gilgal and Dan near the head of the ravine. They tiredly leaned on their spears, waiting for first light. He gave them directions for the battle, feeling helpless and inept. A star set and the sky turned gray. Mormon's eyes turned away from the dawn, toward the west. Toward the west—God's will—was this God's will.

He said as he left, "God protect you." They looked at him blankly. He shook his head as he walked. No, he thought, *God no longer protects this army. The men have forgotten God so why should he remember them?*

Battle lines before Desolation were overrun. Mormon's headquarters evacuated in panic as dark-skinned warriors pressed ever closer.

"Stand and fight," Mormon shouted. In vain he tried to slow the exodus of warriors. Even seasoned warriors, men trained in war, ran at the first sighting of Lamanites. The road leading northward from Desolation boiled over with frightened warriors fleeing northward towards Jashon. Officers attempted to restore discipline. Warriors marched, some in orderly fashion, some in disorder. They broke up, they reassembled. The stragglers and dispersed warriors were easy prey for the Lamanites who followed.

Mormon sent Lamah ahead and hurried to his home in Desolation. Would Merena and Sophrista still be there? Moroni, young as he was, had fought in the battle. Was he one of the faceless Nephite warriors lying in the dust, cut down by fierce Lamanites?

Merena and Sophrista had not evacuated. They were waiting anxiously for his return. He held them close, trembling in his anxiety.

"Have you evacuated the city?" Merena asked.

"It is impossible to stop the retreat," he said. "We must flee. That is the only way you will be safe."

"But where will we go?" Merena asked. She held her daughter to her, cradling her head against her shoulder. "And what will happen if the Lamanites catch up to us?"

Mormon refused to think of that possibility. He had seen what Lamanites did to their prisoners. They were worse than the Gadianton robbers who had turned to sacrificers. "Hurry and pack what you will need," he said brusquely. "We will travel with others towards Jashon. Perhaps there our people will be safe." But in his mind he knew that the safest place would be for the warriors to stay and defend Desolation. Here they at least had fortifications.

Warriors mingled with other refugees on the road leading north from Desolation. Mormon grabbed warrior after warrior, attempting to turn them back to defending their city. "Think of your wives and children, your homes!" he shouted in vain. Men looked at him, fear in their expression, eyes dilated, then turned and hurried up the well-used trail.

He shrugged. "At least in Jashon we will be near where Ammaron deposited the records," he said.

Merena acted as if she did not hear him. She trudged onward, a small pack on her back carrying all the earthly possessions she could save.

Mormon helped the frail Sophrista. He knew the journey would be hard on her.

Cumorah, 387 A.D.

Upon the plates of Nephi I made a full account of all the wickedness and abominations that has been before my eyes since I have been old enough to understand the ways of man. All my days my heart has been filled with sorrow because of their wickedness. Nevertheless, I know I shall be lifted up at the last day.

Mormon, stylus in hand, read what he had written. A tear ran from the corner of his eye, down over wrinkled cheek, and hung on his jaw, refusing to fall. His eyes were blank as he remembered again the exodus from Desolation.

Land of Desolation, 349 A.D.

The column made slow progress. There was no rest on the trail. Those who lingered were killed by the Lamanites. Mormon knew there was no one to stop them. His only concern was to protect his little family, now just part of the hurrying mob. Lamanites were not the only danger. Robbers plagued the trail, taking advantage of people's fear, stealing from the helpless. Mormon, sword in hand, walked beside Merena and Sophrista.

Lamanites pressed the hunted and driven Nephite refugees until they came to the land Shem. They could go no further. Mormon finally convinced the warriors to stand and fight. Discipline overrode confusion; pride overcame discouragement; courage controlled fear.

"Fortify the city the best you can," he instructed his officers. "Lamah, bring all the people inside the walls." He watched, still with a feeling of pride in his people, as order came from chaos. They had little time. Some Nephites did not succeed in getting inside the walls. The Lamanites surrounded Shem, destroying everything outside the walls, setting siege to the city.

The land was waste and void. Traces of human beings who had lived here and set up their mud homes had been wiped out. Roads were no longer roads. Villages had been shattered by armies—Nephite and Lamanite—which had passed through in the frenzy of battle. Nephite and Lamanite warriors who had come in place of the inhabitants found no shelter left. Never before had such huge masses of men occupied the land surrounding Shem. Never before had men died here in such numbers.

In a dugout on a slope of the Shem hills, his face gray with weariness, Mormon bent over another face that also showed the traces of exhaustion. "Gilgal, are you asleep?"

"Yes."

"It is imperative that we rouse the men, prepare them to defend the city. I have surveyed the defenses. Food and water supplies will be exhausted in mere days. People will starve." He looked at Gilgal and wondered, *Will this be the site of the final battle between Lamanites and Nephites?*

The two men found Lamah and went into the city, prepared to make a last effort to rouse the men from their defeatism.

Into this atmosphere of extreme dejection burst a mud-stained figure from another world. It was young Moroni. The warriors crowded around him, fatigue and thirst temporarily forgotten. He had achieved the impossible: crept through the Lamanite lines to bring news to the city.

"There is dissension in the Lamanite camps," he told his father. "Leaders are fighting to take control. Now is the time to defeat them."

Mormon needed no urging. With Moroni and Gilgal beside him, he went from group to group, challenging warriors to stand boldly before the Lamanites, shaming them to fight for their wives and children, their houses and their homes. His words had the desired effect. Warriors responded with vigor. For the first time in months they did not flee but stood their ground with boldness.

Cumorah, 387 A.D.

Mormon recalled the battle. Thirty thousand Nephites against fifty thousands Lamanites and dissenters. The Lamanites, torn with internal strife, were beaten and fled back the way they had come. Mormon led his Nephite armies in pursuit of the fleeing Lamanites; came against them in battle again, and again did beat them. It was not a victory in which Mormon took much pride.

Land of Shem, 349 A.D.

Captain Gilgal said, "We beat them soundly, didn't we?"
"But the strength of the Lord was not with us."
"What do you mean?"
"We beat them this time but we were left to ourselves. The Spirit of the Lord did not abide in us." Mormon looked Gilgal in the eye. "We have become weak just like the Lamanites."
"We beat them, regardless. That is nothing to sorrow about."
"My heart sorrows because of the calamity of my people, their wickedness and abominations."

Cumorah, 387 A.D.

Mormon recalled how they continued to pursue the Lamanites and Gadianton robbers until they had completely won back the lands of their inheritance. Then in the 350th year he negotiated a treaty with Lamanites and Gadianton robbers in which they divided the lands of their inheritance. The Nephites received the land north of the narrow passage in the land of Bountiful. The land of Zarahemla and all the other lands south of the narrow passage became the land of the Lamanites.

Desolation, 350 A.D.

Desolation was almost deserted. Mormon and his little family, with others returned to reestablish their lives, walked through rubble-strewn streets. Some houses still stood. Others were without roofs or walls. For a while they went on across an open field—a field which had once been filled with growing squash and sweet potatoes. The land had gone back to what it was before the Nephites colonized it. From east sea to west sea was wasteland. Villages were destroyed: homes desecrated, furniture smashed; crops of corn and sweet potatoes and squash trodden underfoot by thousands of warriors. It was dark when they reached their home.

Mormon left his family in what had been their house. He would have liked to stay and help clean up and make the house once again livable, but duty called. There was still an army to maintain, warriors to train, a land to defend. He knew that, even with a treaty, he could not relax his vigilance.

Cumorah, 387 A.D.

"My words are all of war and fighting," Mormon mused. He stood and stretched. Sitting in one place for any length of time made his joints stiff. "But this was also the time of my children growing and maturing. When the treaty was signed Moroni was eighteen, a successful warrior. Sophrista, though sickly and weak, was really a joy for us. And me—I was almost forty years of age." He looked at the plate on which he had been writing. "How do you put that information into the record of a people?"

CHAPTER SIXTEEN

SCRIBE AND ABRIDGER

Cumorah, 387 A.D.

Mormon stirred restlessly. War, killing, death—the memories haunted him: dreams, recurrent dreams, horrible dreams. He turned on his side but bony hip on hard floor waked him. Rubbing sleep from his eyes he sat up and looked around the now familiar cave—the cave which had been his home for two years. Acrid smoke of last night's small cooking fire permeated the sleeping area.

Outside, first light of morning turned darkness to gray. He hobbled to the cave entrance and stood without moving, just watching. Damp morning dew formed a fine mist over rocks and shrubs. Trees were still indistinct shapes. He could not see the valley where his people had died by the thousands; he could not even see the saddles leading to the ridge over which Moroni had trudged such a short time before. But he began to see the outlines of the ground: a tree here and there, a hint of the trail leading to the saddle.

The last stars faded from sight. He smelled the newness of morning. Birds, silent during the darkness, greeted the arriving day with merry chatter. Dew glistened on grass and leaves as gray sky lightened to soft pastels. A smile appeared on Mormon's stubbled face. He watched in silence as slowly the golden morning sun appeared. It was a moment he knew and loved. "Another beautiful day," he whispered, "and Moroni should return today." He busied himself with morning chores, watching as rays of sunlight shafted through leaves and branches.

In the cave, he picked up the plate on which he had been writing. He sat, stylus poised, as he recalled the continuation of the history of his people and his own life. He wrote: *Ten years passed before the Lamanites again came to battle. During this time of peace I employed my people in preparing their lands and arms against the time of battle.*

He smiled as memories flooded his mind. The ten years were used for more than preparing for war. During that time, his son, Moroni married Armora and they had their first children: my first grandchildren. The time was also a time of sadness; a time of death and dying. Isn't it always the case that births and deaths usually compensate.

Land of Desolation, 350 A.D.

"Mormon!" Merena's cry was frantic—almost hysterical.

He dropped his hoe and ran quickly from the field. Merena stood by the house, her shawl clutched to her lips. She pointed.

Mormon looked down the rain-puddled trail. Two young men, one a gangling youth with blond hair and short beard, trotted toward him. "It's Moroni!" he shouted.

"He's come home." There was a note of disbelief in Merena's voice. "He's really come home. I thought I would never see him again."

The youth waved.

Mormon ran to meet them. He grabbed Moroni in his arms and spun him around, hugging him tightly, unconcerned about any embarrassment the young man might feel. He pushed the breathless youth away and looked at him. "You're back!" he cried.

"I'm not sure I will survive the homecoming," Moroni said jokingly. "Father, I want you to meet my team-mate, Bilnor."

Mormon grasped Bilnor's arm, his huge hand completely circling the youth's forearm near the elbow. "Welcome, Bilnor," he said. "While you are in Desolation, our home is your home."

Dinner was more lavish than Mormon remembered Merena ever serving: fresh-baked ocean fish, clams, yams, squash, corn-on-the-cob and all the hot, sweet chocolate they could drink. Moroni, prompted by Bilnor, told of their journey to the temple city to play pok-a-tok, and how they beat the nobles' blue team.

Moroni self-consciously attempted to skip his part in the victory, but Bilnor filled in the details of his own injury and how he watched the game from the sidelines. He told of the big opponent who devoted himself to elbowing and beating on Moroni. His eyes shone as he told of the wondrous play: of Moroni receiving the ball on his knee, bouncing it into the air, and then with his elbow sending it true to the goal high on the wall.

Mormon visualized—could almost hear—the roar of the crowd, the fury of the blue team, the relief of the victors. "What happened to the blue team?" he asked. He was aware that in the temple city members of losing teams were often sacrificed to the pagan gods, which recalled his own anxiety as he thought of the possibility of Moroni's team losing the match.

"We congratulated them on the fine game they played, gave them their lives, then went to dress." Moroni spoke matter-of-factly. He looked at his friend. "Then in the dressing room we thanked God for the victory."

Merena bustled around the table, setting more food before the young warriors.

"Something else exciting happened on the way home," Bilnor said, awkwardly clearing his throat.

Mormon looked expectantly at Moroni.

"I met a girl," Moroni blushed.

Merena smiled knowingly. "A girl?"

"I met her on our way home," Moroni said. "She was being held captive by some robbers. We rescued her and..."

"And he fell in love," Bilnor finished.

"And so," Moroni said, blushing again under Mormon's glance, "we plan to get married."

"Whew!" Mormon said. "You certainly move quickly. When you left Desolation for the Temple City you didn't even know any girls. Now, when you return, you are betrothed."

Moroni started to speak but Mormon held up his hand. "We need to know about this girl before we can approve a wedding."

"But, Father."

"No buts," Mormon said. "First, where is her home?"

"Moroni."

"A clean city. Does she have a family?"

"She lives with her parents."

"Are they Christians? Do they believe in Christ and His church?"

Moroni toed the ground before answering. "I taught Armora about the Savior and baptized her," he said. "But her parents have no interest."

"No interest? No interest in their salvation? No interest in the God of our fathers?"

Moroni shrugged. "They have been exposed too long to the myths of Quetzalcoatl."

Mormon shook his head sadly. "As have most of the Nephites. That's one reason why the Lord has refused to let me preach to the people."

The journey to Moroni was without incident. Merena, unable to make the trip because of Sophrista's weakened condition, sent her blessings. Mormon, Moroni and Bilnor walked down the coast to Bountiful, then traveled by boat to Moroni for the wedding.

Mormon approved of Armora at first look. She was not the prettiest girl he had ever seen, but vibrant skin and rosy cheeks gave her a healthy robustness. She had an impertinent saucy tilt of her head. Eyes, pale gray, reminded him of Merena. Her jaw showed strength beneath a button nose and dimpled cheeks. "Welcome to my family," he said, as he gave her one of his bear hugs. In a quiet ceremony he married Moroni and Armora.

A year later Armora blessed Mormon and Merena with their first grandchild, a boy whom Moroni named Gidgiddonah.

Land of Desolation, 358 A.D.

Mormon, grim-faced and dressed in full armor, followed a group of warriors through the streets of Desolation. Prostitutes flaunted themselves from openings on both sides of the street. Warriors shouted bawdy jests as they reached out to touch exposed skin in the narrow street. *Mormon looked on the scurrilous scene and asked himself, How is it possible that a people could degenerate so fast—so much in such a short period of time. He shook his head to clear it of the welter and odium.*

On top of Desolation's wall, he breathed deeply to rid his senses of the turpitude he had just witnessed. "Lord," he whispered. "My people are lost. How could they drift so far from Thee?" He walked along the top of the wall, for the hundredth time inspecting Desolation's defenses.

A whisper: "Mormon." He stopped. The familiar voice came again. This time he recognized the Lord's voice. *Mormon, my son, the time has come to cry repentance once again to this people. Call upon them to repent. Tell them to be baptized and again build up my Church and they shall be spared.*

Mormon knelt, tears glistening in his eyes. "Lord, it shall be done."

He hurried home, surprised but gladdened when he saw Moroni in the garden with Merena. He kissed Merena warmly, then put an arm around each of them. "The Lord has spoken to me," he said softly, his voice trembling with emotion. "For the first time since my fifteenth year He commanded me to preach repentance to this people."

Moroni looked at him with awe. "What did the Lord say?"

Mormon carefully repeated the words. "Cry to this people to repent and come unto Me. Be baptized and again build up My church and you shall be spared." His heart was so full he could not speak for a moment. Then he put his hand on Moroni's shoulder. "Son, I call you as the first missionary to assist me in this work. The Lord gave me the distinct feeling that you would serve a mission in the cities north of Desolation."

Moroni looked up at his father. Mormon was still taller than he, thick as a tree, with a mane of white hair and bushy eyebrows and a face the color of old wood, seamed and scored by the weather. "Father, that is a great honor. What shall I do with my family? Shall I take Armora and Gidgiddonah with me?"

"I understand your concerns, son, but the time is short. This may be the last chance to save our people. The Lord has promised that if they do not repent they will be totally destroyed." He put his hand back on Moroni's shoulder. "You will be hated and ridiculed, perhaps even beaten. If Armora and the baby went with you, they would be in constant danger. They can stay here with your mother where they will be safe."

Moroni didn't speak for a moment, apparently contemplating what Mormon had just said. He sighed. "Thank you Father. I accept but must tell Armora." He turned and hurried from the yard.

Mormon gathered Merena into his arms. "My dear," he said, "I am almost fifty years of age. I had almost given up hope of ever again calling this people to repentance. Thank God He has given them one more chance."

Merena said nothing, but he could feel her trembling. He knew of her anxiety—the worry about dangers faced, both for himself and for Moroni. He squeezed her, trying to give her an assurance he himself did not fully feel.

Moroni preached in the vicinity of Desolation for several months while waiting the birth of his second child. He had a difficult time leaving Armora. The child was another son. He named him Moronihah and was soon on his way northward.

For two years Mormon preached with limited success to the people of Bountiful and Desolation. A few stalwarts, like Ammonihah in Bountiful, listened to his words. Most laughed at his message. Moroni's letters from Boaz, Teancum, Jordan and Joshua indicated a similar lack of success. There was a long period of time without letters, then a letter came from the fabled temple city of the high plateau to the north. Moroni had established a church and baptized many people. Mormon rejoiced in his son's success.

His own mission was interrupted.

Desolation, 360 A.D.

The letter from the Lamanite king was poorly written, but it took no scholar to interpret its intent. *Our people thirst for your blood. Once again we prepare to come against you in battle. Your land will be ours and you will yet be our slaves.*

"I know you don't want to leave your village. But if you stay the Lamanites will surely destroy you. Come to Desolation. After we have defeated the Lamanites you may return to your homes and farms." The message, repeated over and over by Mormon and his officers, finally had an effect. Thousands of refugees crammed into the walled city of Desolation. Mormon knew that feeding such a population would be a problem, but what could he do? To leave them outside the walls would mean certain death or enslavement.

Near the narrow neck of land, just west of Bountiful, running parallel to the river and sloping down to it was a line of rolling hills. Between these hills, like a gleaming plate cracked by ravines and fissures, was the narrow neck, Mormon's most natural defensive position. The bend of the Sidon and Moroni formed the southern edge of this big plate. A low plateau sloped all the way to the Sidon. It was a land savaged by frequent storms. Here, on the high plain, Mormon's army took positions.

Mormon wrote quickly, his stylus cleanly cutting the symbols into the soft gold.

My Dear Son, Moroni. In the three-hundred-sixty-first year the Lamanites came down to battle against us. We defended our cities and drove them back to their own lands. They came again to battle the next year, and again we beat them. We killed a great number of them, throwing their dead into the rivers.

My people, filled with pride in their victory over the Lamanite armies, boasted in their own strength. They swore by the heavens and also by the throne of God that they would go to battle against their enemies to avenge themselves of the blood of their brethren who had been slain.

I loved the Nephites. Many times have I led them to battle. I prayed continually for them, but because of the hardness of their hearts my prayers were without faith. I delivered them out of the hands of their enemies three different times. Even then they did not repent of their sins. When I could not talk them out of this foolishness I refused to continue as their leader. In their wickedness they decided they would avenge themselves but the Lord felt differently. His words came to me: 'Because this people did not repent after I delivered them they shall be cut off from the face of the earth.'

Desolation, 362 A.D.

"I know all your arguments," Mormon said. "My decision is made. I utterly refuse to lead this army against the Lamanites."

"But why?" Gilgal exploded.

"The Lord has told us that we can go to war to protect our land and families, but that does not include going after the Lamanites into their own land. 'Vengeance is mine!' He said."

Gilgal and Lamah walked away, shaking their heads.

I can imagine what they are saying, Mormon thought as he watched their retreating backs. *They are saying that Mormon has finally lost his nerve.* He smiled. *What they say doesn't matter. I am the only one who can control my destiny. I will do as the Lord commands. Right now that means standing as a silent witness to testify to the world what I see and hear, according to the manifestations of the Spirit which testified of things to come.*

Lamah and Gilgal's visit left him despondent. He knew he would miss the army. Though he detested the wickedness of the men, the army had been his life for over thirty years. *My life has reached the age of a complete cycle of fifty-two years and now it is time to leave fighting to younger men.* That thought reminded him that Moroni, returned from his mission, was now with the Nephite army into which he had been drafted.

His resignation was not all that made him despondent. He moved his family to Boaz to get away from the fighting, but he was afraid the move came too late for Sophrista. She was unable to get up from her pallet. There she lay, closer to death than life. He went in to her, knelt beside her and took her hand. It was dry and creped, her skin so pale it was almost transparent. Only her smile was the same: luminous, cheerful, self-effacing.

"How are you, Father?" she asked quietly.

He kissed her gently. "I am excited to be home with you and your mother," he said. "Now if only Moroni could be with us."

"I feel he will be home soon."

"I'm afraid not until the fighting is over," Mormon said. "And who knows when that will be."

"You miss it, don't you?"

"Miss it?"

"You miss the leadership of your armies and the excitement of battle."

"Aren't you the perceptive one?" he chuckled. Though he laughed, he knew she was right. "Rest now, my pretty."

Sophrista closed her eyes—with eyelids so transparent the veins stood out like purple strings.

Merena looked up as he entered the living area of the house. She didn't need to ask "how is she" because she already knew. Instead, she motioned Mormon to her side. She was holding little Bilnor, Moroni's third son. He was a beautiful boy, sweet and loving. Mormon had enjoyed him much more than the older boys—mainly because he had more time to play with this youngster.

He wandered around the house, listless, not knowing what to do. The garden needed weeding, but he had no desire to do that. Repairs were needed on the house, but they could also wait. He really didn't feel like doing anything around the house.

Merena knew his mood.

He paced back and forth across the hard-packed earth floor, then stopped before Merena. "I must go see Ammonihah and determine how the Church is doing in Bountiful."

"Is it safe to travel?" Merena asked, gently rocking Bilnor in her ample lap.

"The Lamanites have been driven back into their own lands and the Gadianton robbers are hiding in the hills."

"How long will you be gone?"

"Several weeks." He picked up Bilnor and hugged him. "I will miss you and the children," he said, "but my stewardship is to make sure the remnants of the Church remain strong."

He left Boaz before first light. Bountiful was but a few days' journey. Several days of hiking and several nights of sleeping beside the trail brought him there. Ammonihah, the local church president, greeted him warmly. The members, though few in numbers, were pleased to see him. From Bountiful he visited Lehi, Morianton and Mulek, calling the people to repent; preaching to them of faith, hope and charity. In Moroni, he preached his strongest sermon to the assembled priesthood holders. Ammonihah had a scribe write his words:

"I, Mormon, speak to you through the calling Jesus Christ has given me. I speak to you church members who are the peaceable followers of Christ, who have obtained a sufficient hope by which you can enter into the rest of the Lord.

"God says you shall know men by their works, for if their works are good, then they are good also. He said an evil man cannot do that which is good, for if he offers a gift, or prays unto God, except he shall do it with real intent, it profits him nothing and is not counted unto him for righteousness. If an evil man gives a gift, he does it grudgingly, so it is counted unto him the same as if he had retained the gift. It is also counted evil for a man to pray without real intent—it profits him nothing—for God does not receive such a prayer."

Mormon drew an analogy between fountains and men, stating that a bitter fountain could not bring forth good water or a good fountain bring forth bitter water. "Likewise," he said, "a man being a servant of the devil cannot follow Christ and if he does follow Christ he cannot be a servant of the devil."

He preached that all good things come from God and all evil things come from the devil. "The devil is an enemy to God and fights against Him continually. He invites and entices men to sin and to do that which is evil. On the other hand, God invites and entices us to do good and to love Him and to serve Him."

Mormon cautioned the members to not credit God with evil things or to believe that any good things came from the devil. "The Spirit of Christ is given to every man, that he may know good from evil, and you can know with a perfect knowledge—as clear as daylight is from the dark night. Do not judge wrongfully, for with the same judgment which you judge you shall also be judged. Search diligently in the light of Christ that you may know good from evil. Lay hold upon every good thing and condemn it not and you certainly will be a child of Christ."

Mormon talked of the years preceding the coming of the Savior: a time when God sent angels to prophets who declared that Christ should come. Mormon's voice became husky as he continued his sermon. "Men began to exercise faith in Christ, and by faith they laid hold upon every good thing up to the time of His coming. Even after the Savior came men were saved by faith in His name. By faith they became the sons of God."

He looked around the synagogue at the priesthood holders. Then he challenged them. "My brothers, have miracles ceased because Christ has ascended into heaven?" He answered his own question. "No. Angels still minister to those of strong faith. They call men to repentance and declare the word of Christ unto the children of men that they may bear testimony of Him. By so doing, God prepares the way that men may have faith in Christ, that the Holy Ghost may have place in their hearts."

Mormon paused in his sermon and gazed over the congregation. He quietly asked, "My beloved brethren, have miracles ceased? Have angels ceased to appear unto the children of men? Has God withheld the power of the Holy Ghost from them? Or will He, so long as time shall last, or the earth shall stand, or there shall be one man upon the face thereof to be saved?"

"No!" He answered. "It is by faith that miracles are wrought. It is by faith that angels appear and minister unto men. No man can be saved unless he has faith in the name of Christ. So if these things have ceased then faith has ceased also and awful is the state of man for it is as though there had been no redemption made." Mormon sighed. "But my brethren, I judge better things of you, for I know that you have faith in Christ because of your meekness. But those who do not have faith in Him are not fit to be numbered among the people of His church."

He wiped his brow. It was hot in the synagogue. "Let me speak to you concerning hope. How can you have faith unless you have hope? And what shall you hope for? Because of your faith you shall have hope through Christ's atonement and the power of His resurrection to be raised to life eternal. If a man has faith he must also have hope, for without faith there cannot be any hope.

"But you cannot have faith and hope unless you are also meek and lowly of heart. If so, faith and hope are vain for none are acceptable before God save the meek and lowly in heart."

Mormon listed the characteristics of those who had charity, such as suffering long without complaint, being kind and not puffed up with pride. "That person who has charity," he said, "seeks not her own, is not easily provoked, thinks no evil, and rejoices not in iniquity but rejoices in the truth, bears all things, believes all things, hopes all things, and endures all things. My beloved brothers, if you have not charity you are nothing, for charity never fails. Cleave unto charity, the greatest of all, for charity is the pure love of Christ."

Mormon challenged the members to pray to the Father with all the energy of their hearts so they would be filled with Christ's love and be purified through Him.

As he journeyed home towards Desolation, he thought of his sermon. It was probably the best he had ever given. He rested beside a stream as he reflected on his words.

A voice whispered to him, *"Mormon."*

Even after the many times he had heard the whispering of the Spirit, Mormon still looked around to see where the voice came from. He smiled as he realized that it really came from within himself—that the Spirit was speaking directly to his spirit.

"Mormon, return quickly to your home. You are needed there."

CHAPTER SEVENTEEN

THE END COMES TO THE NEPHITES

Desolation, 364 A.D.

Mormon, face haggard from exertion, staggered through the door. "I don't know why," he gasped as he embraced a surprised Merena, "but the Spirit whispered to me to return home quickly. Is it Sophrista?" He didn't wait for Merena's answer but for the first time noticed they were not alone. Three men stood just inside the door—as if they had barely arrived. Moroni, his son, stood before them. Mormon recognized the men at once. "Praise God." He whispered hoarsely. He embraced each of the men.

"Moroni, do you know these men?"

Moroni shook his head.

"These are the three Disciples, those who elected to stay upon the earth to continue teaching the people. I haven't seen them since my youth." Tears of joy filled his eyes.

Moroni looked at the three with awe. He stepped forward and clasped forearms with the Lord's servants, surprised that translated beings would have such solid bodies.

Mormon, recovered from his exertion, took Merena's hand and watched as the leader of the three addressed Moroni.

"Moroni," the disciple said. "The Lord has observed your faithfulness. Your commitment to Him and His work is beyond question. We have been commanded by Him to ordain you as a disciple and special witness."

Mormon sucked in his breath. These same disciples laid their hands on his head and ordained him more than thirty years before. Now Moroni had been chosen to serve as a disciple.

An exuberance of joy made him want to shout. Merena leaned against him. He enclosed her in one of his arms as he listened. The other arm he rested on Moroni's shoulder.

The disciple continued. "With great faith Mormon magnified his calling as a disciple of Jesus Christ. Yours will be the opportunity to continue the work he began. The task will not be easy. Satan would love nothing more than to detract you from your mission. He will use his awesome arsenal to destroy you."

Mormon watched his son's face as the disciple talked. He knew the arsenal of which the disciple spoke: chicanery, opulence, mendacity, avarice. Even more common were the weapons of discouragement, disappointment and doubt.

The disciple paused, as if to let his words sink in. "Do you accept this calling?"

Though he knew what Moroni's answer would be, Mormon held his breath waiting for his son's response.

"I am honored," Moroni said quietly, "and will give my all to be worthy of the Savior's trust." At his glance, Armora came to stand beside him. He put his arm around her.

"May I ask one thing?"

The disciple nodded.

"I desire my father to stand in during the ordination."

Mormon's heart was full. He swallowed as he attempted to regain his composure. It was no use. Tears overflowed and ran down his cheeks. He stood next to the Lord's disciples and joined his hands with theirs on his son's head.

"Moroni, our Lord, Jesus Christ, has chosen you as one of His disciples. He commissioned us to ordain you and set you apart to administer in all of the affairs of His Church here upon the earth..." Mormon listened intently to the blessing. "Moroni, you are called as the last disciple in this land until the Gospel is restored in its fullness among the Gentiles who shall inhabit this land. You will be a special witness of the Savior, imparting knowledge of Him to all you meet."

At the final "Amen," Mormon opened his eyes. The three disciples had vanished. He helped Moroni to his feet, embracing him tightly, his love surging through him, warming and tingling.

Cumorah, 387 A.D.

Mormon sighed. *What joy I felt,* he thought. *Mingled with that joy was the sadness as I saw Sophrista continue to fade and finally to pass on to her reward. Why is it that so often in our lives the sorrow of death and dying tempers the joy of living? Far be it from me to know the answer to that question,* he thought. *All I know is that each of us will be judged.*

The powerful positive spirit of his son's ordination was also tempered by the disappearance, shortly after the ordination, of Bilnor, his youngest grandson. Bilnor had been in warrior training and had just disappeared, probably captured by a Lamanite patrol. Moroni and Armora had been despondent.

Why is it, wondered Mormon, *that Satan works hardest on those who have the greatest potential for success? He tries so hard to make our lives miserable. His entire thrust seems to be to frustrate our ultimate goal. Like the wars. I resigned from the army but the wars continued.* He laid his head back and thought of that time, little more than twenty years before. The Nephite armies, beaten by the Lamanites, retreated back to Desolation. While they were still recuperating from their defeat a fresh Lamanite army hit capturing Desolation.

The Lord warned us to leave Desolation. We moved our family to Teancum. But even there we were not safe. Wicked Lamanites came once again against wicked Nephites. That gave Mormon another thought. He sat up and wrote:

The judgments of God will overtake the wicked. It is by the wicked that the wicked are punished; the wicked stir up men to bloodshed.

Mormon thought of the many battles fought over Desolation and Teancum. *The Lamanites captured Teancum in the three hundred and sixty-sixth year—again, just in time, we had moved our family out of the city—offering up everyone they captured—men, women and children—as sacrifices to their gods.*

The next year the Nephites drove them out of the land of Desolation back to their own lands. A sort of peace lasted for eight years. Moroni moved his family to Mulek and strengthened the Church there. But oh, the destruction our people suffered! It is impossible for me to describe the horrible scenes of blood and carnage. Every heart—Nephite and Lamanite—was hardened. They delighted in killing. Never had such wickedness been seen among all the children of Lehi, nor even among all the house of Israel, as was among this people.

He picked up his stylus and engraved on the plate: *I write to the gentiles, to the house of Israel and to all the twelve tribes of Israel who shall be judged by the twelve whom Jesus chose as His disciples in the land of Jerusalem. I write also to the remnant of this people who shall be judged by the twelve whom Jesus chose in this land. The Spirit manifested to me that each of you must stand before the judgment seat of Christ to be judged of your works, whether they be good or evil.*

Desolation, 375 A.D.

Rain beat down in ever-increasing cadences, blanketing the warriors on the walls. Mormon looked in the direction of the city. Water ran into his eyes. He shook his head and strained through the misty rain and peered again at the wall. Anytime now there could be a horde of shiny-dark bodies emerging from the mist, attacking the city, then disappearing back into the protecting cover of the downpour. He leaned forward into the tumpline, slogging through the mud, the heavy pack dragging him down. Our Nephite warriors are already demoralized. Their commanders are kept busy just plugging the gaps, prodding, and encouraging the warriors to continue fighting. Even so, many warriors disappear—desert the battle—overcome more by fog and rain than by Lamanites. City after city has fallen.

"If I had remained as commander, could I have saved the country?" Mormon mused aloud.

"What?"

Mormon turned. Moroni, his son walked close behind him. "Nothing," he said. "I was just talking to myself."

Moroni chuckled. "That's dangerous for generals to do."

"Ex-general," Mormon said. "And even then, not nearly as dangerous as when I begin arguing with myself. How are Moronihah and Gidgiddonah doing?" he asked, serious again.

"They are all right," Moroni said. He walked a few paces and added, "But I am concerned that we will just get the plates to the city and the Lamanites will attack."

"That will be worse than if we hadn't even picked the plates up from the Hill Shim," Mormon grunted. "But you are certainly right about the outcome. The Nephite warriors are not prepared to win this battle. They are totally demoralized."

"By Lamanites and the rain," Moroni added quietly.

"The sun will be up soon," Mormon said. "Then the rain will disappear and give us a rest." He trudged on, not talking, saving his energy for carrying the plates. *I'm about to drop,* he thought, *and I am carrying the lighter load. Moroni and his sons have the heavy plates. All I'm carrying are the interpreters and my abridgement.*

As the sun peeped over the horizon the four men wound their way into Desolation. They moved slowly, burdened with their heavy packs. Refugees lined the streets, moving northward, eyes and faces showing their fright.

Merena met them at the door, a look of anxiety on her face. "Lamah and Gilgal are waiting for you. They have been here since daybreak." She had a pleading look in her eyes.

Mormon carefully set his plates down and with Moroni close behind hurried to the sitting room. The two Nephite commanders rose. Both officers had served under Mormon; both were great warriors. Gilgal had been sick for some time but believed it was his mission to save the Nephite lands before he died. "I have but a short time to live," he had told Mormon, "and victory must be won before I die." It was he, more than anyone else, who urged his warriors to take an oath to destroy the Lamanites.

General Lamah was not as easy to describe. Tough, wiry and a great fighter, he was known to his warriors as 'maneater.' His mouth, thin-lipped, topped his permanently set square jaw. He looked like a rabid monkey which refused to let go of a scrap it had been chewing on. Fear and death meant nothing to him. He stood now, watching Mormon, hands behind his back, head thrust forward. Like an eagle searching for prey, Mormon thought.

Mormon strode forward and grasped their arms. "It's good to see you. How have the battles been going?"

Lamah and Gilgal avoided his eyes. "Not well," Gilgal rasped. "The Lamanites outnumber us greatly. They have taken Bountiful and their main army is within a day's march of Desolation. We must retreat again." He coughed into his hand.

Mormon asked. "Why tell me this?"

"Mormon, the army needs your leadership," Lamah said. "Without you we are doomed.

"The men respect you and will follow you," Gilgal added. "With you as commander we may be able to save the city. We ask you to resume command of the armies."

Mormon turned to look at Merena. For years she had supported him in his calling as general over the Nephite armies, regardless of her own feelings of loneliness and frustration—not to speak of her fear at his being wounded or killed. He stepped to her, put his arm around her, and held her close. He looked back to the warrior leaders, torn between loyalty to his people and his need to be with Merena. "How much time do we have?"

"Our scouts report the main Lamanite army could be here by noon," Gilgal said lamely. "We worked all night building defenses around the walls."

Mormon sighed and walked to where the generals stood. He put hands on their shoulders, pulling them together. "I am past the age of retirement. It has been years since I led the armies. Many of your warriors are so young they wouldn't remember me. How much do you think they will respect me?"

"You are a legend among the warriors," Gilgal replied. "I am convinced you are the only one who can lead them."

"I must give it prayerful thought," Mormon sighed. "It is a decision I cannot make by myself. I know the pressure you are under, but give me an hour."

Lamah slapped him on the back. "Thank you, General. We look forward to your answer."

After the generals left, Mormon sat heavily on a cushion, looking at the floor. He didn't see the tears in his wife's eyes. "I must pray."

Moroni started to leave the room, but Mormon waved him back. "I need your help," he said softly.

Mormon, Merena and Moroni knelt shoulder to shoulder as they sought an answer, knowing the seriousness of the request.

"Father, what is Thy will," he prayed. "Should I go back on my oath and again take command of the armies?"

Minutes dragged by as he prayed. He finished and remained silently on his knees, waiting for the Lord's answer. *"Mormon,"* the whisper came, *"take care of my records. Put them in Cumorah where they will be safe."* He rose slowly to his feet and gently lifted Merena. Putting his arm around her and Moroni, he said, "I have received my answer. The Lord says my first responsibility is to the plates." Together they walked back to where his grandsons, Gidgiddonah and Moronihah, patiently waited.

"We must take the sacred records from the city before the Lamanites attack. I was told where to deposit them. After that, I will decide what to do about Lamah's and Gilgal's request."

He pulled Merena to him. Her smile was enigmatic as she looked up at him. She reached up and placed thin hands on his cheeks. He grasped them, noting how little flesh was left on them. In the last few years her health had deteriorated greatly. He cradled her grayed head against his chest, gently rocking back and forth on his heels. There was little he could say or do to still her fears. She had passed through so much sorrow: death

of Sophrista and loss of little Bilnor. This should be the
halcyon of her life—a time to relax and enjoy his
companionship—not a time for more wars and warriors.

He swiveled his head to Moroni. "We depart Desolation
within the hour. Gather your family. Take only bare
necessities."

Moroni and his sons left.

Mormon held Merena, giving her what comfort he could.
"We'd better get packed," she sighed, pulling away.

They could not carry very much with them. Merena
wandered through her home, handling every possession. Each
had special meaning for her. Almost everything would be left
behind. She watched as Mormon deftly tied their few
possessions into two packs and assigned the maid-servants to
carry them. Before she had time to grieve her departure, Moroni
and his family were back. She didn't turn to look back. She
knew she would never see her home again.

The little group picked its way through the clamor of the
city, joining other families fleeing the Lamanite threat. Moroni
walked beside his father. "We ran into Lamah and Gilgal."

Mormon looked at him without speaking.

"They said they would sorely miss you in this battle and
that they would yet need you in defense of our nation."

Adjusting his tumpline, Mormon shook his head sadly.
"The nation is already lost."

The weight of the plates forced the men to stop often.
Merena was thankful for the rests. Each step seemed more
painful for her; stops became more frequent. Her tiredness was
obvious to Mormon. He let her hang on his arm as they walked.
They stayed that night in a wayside inn so Merena could rest
better.

At the inn, Mormon hired a servant to accompany them
to Boaz. The servant carried his pack, enabling him to devote
his full strength to Merena. By the time they reached Boaz she
was totally exhausted. After sending the servant back, Mormon
arranged lodging for Merena, Armora and Greta, his granddaughter. He stood there, indecisive, reluctant to leave.

Armora put her hand on his arm. "I will take care of
her," she whispered.

He knelt beside Merena. "Dear one," he said. "I must go
now. Armora will stay with you. I will return as soon as I can."

Merena smiled wanly. "I will be fine. Just hurry back to
me after you take care of the plates."

He turned once more at the door. Merena lay on the couch. Armora sat beside her and Greta played in a corner of the room. He waved, then stepped out into the brilliant sunshine, Moroni and his sons at his heels.

Mormon didn't call a halt until night made it impossible to continue. He felt a real sense of urgency. His back ached from carrying the heavy pack but he said nothing. Sense of mission lent strength to his tired legs.

For breakfast they snacked on dried fruit and drank from a spring, then were again on their way. Mormon couldn't shake a feeling of uneasiness about leaving the women. "Please, God," he whispered, "don't let anything happen to them."

On the second day a large hill, surrounded by a wide, open valley, loomed before them. It was Cumorah.

"I have seen that mountain before," Moroni said.

"It's called Cumorah," Mormon said. "It is here the Lord wants us to hide the plates."

They struggled nearly to the top of the pine-clad mountainside. Mormon pointed. A small cave-like opening yawned before them out of a gully. The volcanic cave was tall as a man but narrow and deep—a perfect place for the plates.

"Stack the plates carefully inside," Mormon directed. "Try not to mix them up."

When the plates were deposited they placed stones and brush together until the cave's mouth was completely hidden.

"It is good," he said. "We return to Boaz. I have a feeling our women need us."

Such a feeling of uneasiness had settled in his bosom he hardly let them rest as they hurried back the way they had come. When still a half-day's march from Boaz, they met refugees streaming along the trail. They quickened their pace.

A cry came from a passing group. "Father. Father."

It was his granddaughter's voice. Moroni ran to her. Greta was covered with grime. Mormon's stomach became a gnawing ache. "Merena," he whispered, breathing quickly in his anxiety.

Greta, in Moroni's arms, sobbed with relief.

"Where are your mother and grandmother?"

Mormon knew the answer even before Greta answered. He hung his head. We are too late. Merena and Armora are dead.

Moroni set down Greta. She turned and ran to Mormon. He picked her up, holding her close, his head nuzzling her soft hair. He choked up, but he couldn't cry. Tears would not come.

"What happened in Boaz?" he asked a man walking by. The man's eyes were glazed and he leaned heavily on a stick.

"Lamanites captured Desolation and pursued the army north to Teancum," the man said. "Then they attacked again and forced the army from Teancum to Boaz." He rubbed his eyes as if to erase a horrible memory. "Our warriors stood firm for a time, but wave after wave of the attackers battered down the walls and poured into the city." He shook his head. "They cut down everyone in their path—men, women and children. No one was spared." The man cited gruesome examples of depravity then shambled on, leaving Mormon with his thoughts.

What shall I do? Mormon asked himself, his mind gradually starting to move from the paralyzing inertia brought on by news of Merena's death. He took no time to grieve but promised himself that when he had time he would pay Merena her proper respect. *I know she will never leave me. She will always be here, right beside me, strong, helpful, encouraging.* He suddenly had a sense of her presence. His eyes filled with tears and an anguished cry escaped his lips. "Merena."

Moroni, tears staining his cheeks, picked up Greta and put his arm around Mormon.

Mormon turned and hugged his son, his tears flowing freely. "I have loved and enjoyed your mother for over forty years," he said. "She and Armora are now in God's kingdom and I know we shall see them again." He pulled away and sighed.

As he looked at warriors mingled with refugees fleeing past he spotted Lamah and Gilgal. He stiffened his spine. He called and they pushed their way to him. "I am ready," he said. "Reorganize your warriors. We march to Jordan and Joshua."

Word of their new commander spread quickly. Men straightened their backs and looked more like warriors. Mormon placed proven leaders at the head of each army group. Three of those leaders were Moroni, Gidgiddonah and Moronihah.

The retreat lasted all the way to Jordan where Mormon placed the Nephites' final defensive positions. Refugees streamed past. Pillars of smoke funneled into the sky: villages plundered and burned by advancing Lamanites. Mormon knew those who had not kept up with the army would be hewn down without mercy.

He only had a few days to consolidate his defenses. He carefully placed his men: archers atop the wall, backed up by warriors with swords and spears. By midafternoon of the second day lookouts spotted the first columns of Lamanites. As the enemy approached, volleys of arrows arched through the sky. Lamanite lines broke as arrows found their targets. They retreated the way they had come, leaving hundreds of dead and wounded behind. All around Mormon the Nephite warriors cheered.

Mormon didn't cheer. He knew this was only a brief respite until the Lamanites attacked again. Watching them retreat he commented to Moroni, "The only way the Nephites can be victorious is to turn to God. If they would offer their prayers to Him for deliverance we could win this battle. The other alternative..." He didn't finish the sentence. Thought of the extermination of the Nephite people was too painful to put into words.

Cumorah, 387 A.D.

Mormon looked at the words he had written on the plate: *And so, in the three hundred and eightieth year the Lamanites did come again against us to battle, and we did stand against them boldly; but it was all in vain, for so great were their numbers that they trod the Nephites under their feet.*

"And all because the Nephites did not turn to God!" Mormon said aloud. He leaned back, hands cupped behind his neck. For two years we held the city, but finally the last defenders were driven out. *All I could do was engage the enemy in a running battle, knowing it was just a matter of time.* He sighed. Time for the Nephites had almost run out.

He picked up the stylus and wrote about their retreat. *We again took flight. Those whose flight was swifter than the Lamanites escaped. The others were swept down and destroyed.*

He shook his head. No words could adequately describe the pain and suffering of his people. He wrote: *I do not desire to harrow up men's souls by writing about the awful scenes of blood and carnage which I observed. But these things must be made known to the remnant of this people and to the Gentiles, who the Lord said would scatter this people and this people should be counted as naught among them. I speak to their seed and to the Gentiles who care for the house of Israel and know from whence their blessings come. I know they will sorrow for the calamity of the house of Israel and for the destruction of this people. Their sorrow will be that this people have not repented and that they might have been clasped in the arms of Jesus.*

Mormon wrote about the Lamanites and what would happen to them. Then he addressed the Gentiles: *Oh, you Gentiles, how can you stand before the power of God, except you shall repent and turn from your evil ways? Don't you know that you are in the hands of God? And that He has all power? At His great command the earth shall be rolled together as a scroll. Repent and humble yourselves before Him, lest He shall come out in justice against you—lest a remnant of the seed of Jacob shall go forth among you as a lion and tear you to pieces, and no one can deliver you.*

CHAPTER EIGHTEEN

END OF THE NEPHITE PEOPLE

Cumorah, 387 A.D.

There is more I must say to future generations, he thought as he looked at what he had written. His words seemed incomplete. *The spirit has manifested unto me that you may know that you must all stand before the judgment seat of Christ—every soul who belongs to the family of Adam—to be judged of your works, whether they be good or evil. I also write that you may believe the gospel of Jesus Christ which you shall have among you; and that the Jews, the covenant people of the Lord, shall have another witness besides Him whom they saw and heard. I testify that Jesus, whom they slew, was the Christ.*

Mormon tapped the stylus on the plate as he thought. He sighed and added one more sentence. *I wish I could persuade all the ends of the earth to repent and prepare to stand before the judgment seat of Christ.*

"If I could have done that," he whispered, "perhaps there wouldn't have been a last battle. Perhaps our people would not have been destroyed." Angrily he put down his stylus and stalked from the cave. He stopped at the spring where clear water poured from the mountainside. After drinking his fill he sat by the gurgling stream and thought of the events which prefaced that last battle.

Land of Joshua, 380 A.D.

Mormon, white-haired and feeling his age, sat in a corner of the command tent, brush and bark paper before him.

Gidgiddonah and Gilgal argued in one corner. Moroni sat near
the door. Mormon ignored them all. I have no fight left in me,
he thought. *I am tired of retreating and tired of losing. But what
else can I do? The Lamanites have more men; they are stronger
and are better armed. But will writing to Shoninum be the right
thing?* He chewed on his lip trying to get just the right words.

"Grandfather, may I sit on your lap."

Mormon smiled. Little Greta could always cheer him up.
He hadn't seen her come into the tent but he picked her up and
set her on his lap. Even grandpa couldn't hold the attention of a
seven-year old and in a few moments she squirmed loose. He
frowned as she skipped out of the tent. His mind was made up.
He stiffened his shoulders and looked around the tent, ready to
be done with the distasteful deed.

"Gidgiddonah," he called, "summon the tribal
commanders."

He left, followed by Moronihah and Gilgal. Mormon was
grateful. Right now he just wanted to be alone. He chose each
word carefully as he painted on the bark paper. He looked up
and caught Moroni watching him. "Son," he asked. "Do you
remember the prophecy of Samuel the Lamanite?"

"You mean when he said that in the fourth generation
from the Saviors time the Nephites would be destroyed?"

Mormon nodded. "With exception of a few believers, the
Nephites have hardened their hearts and have lost all contact
with the Holy Spirit. They are bloodthirsty and vengeful."

Moroni nodded. "They are all you say they are, and
more."

Mormon leaned back, the tip of his brush to his mouth.
"It's been four hundred years. I feel Samuel's prophecy is about
to be fulfilled." He picked up the paper he had written. "I propose
a final battle with the Lamanites where we pick the time and
place. Our people may be totally destroyed but I see no other
choice, unless we continue to retreat, picked off a few at a time."

As the commanders began to arrive he stopped talking.
He moved around the tent, greeting each of his faithful warrior
leaders. To some he gave praise, to others encouragement. When
all were assembled, he started his speech. "For almost fifty
years I have led the Nephite armies. We have won battles and
lost battles but never have we found ourselves in such a
precarious position as now. We are practically surrounded.
Many men are wounded. All are exhausted. We haven't enough
fighting men to handle one more battle." Heads nodded in
agreement. "The enemy pursues us daily with fresh armies

while our warriors become less able and willing to fight. You faithfully led your warriors as we tried to hold back the Lamanites. We always had hope in the next battle. Now I have little hope left. It is time to make a critical decision about our future."

"What do you suggest?" Lamah asked.

"I see only two possible choices," Mormon answered. "One, we can continue as we are until our entire army is destroyed, our land devastated, our wives and children killed or sacrificed to Lamanite gods." He swallowed as he thought of little Greta; it was already too late for his wife, Merena. "Or, two, we may have a chance to gather our people, have some time to heal our injuries, to make new weapons, and to see if we can gain any advantage over the Lamanites." He paused to give emphasis to his words. "We are at a crossroads."

"It seems to me that we really have little choice between the two alternatives you present," Moroni said.

"True. That is why I recommend a truce and a final battle."

Gidgiddonah spoke up. "My men right now could not fight their way out of a paper wasps' nest. They are wounded and weary. I vote for a delay."

A babble of assent greeted his words.

Mormon held up his hand for silence. "It seems most of you favor getting some breathing time. I will write to Shoninum, the Lamanite king, requesting a formal battle."

Leaders walked from the tent. Only Moroni, Moronihah and Gidgiddonah held back.

"Grandfather," Gidgiddonah said. "We support you in whatever decision you make."

Words choked in Mormon's throat. He nodded and watched as his two grandsons left the tent. He sat down in silent brooding. Moroni remained to keep him company. Mormon raised his head. "Son, read what I have written." He handed Moroni the paper.

Shoninum, we weary of fighting. We request a truce. Grant us time to gather to a battlefield for a last battle—a decisive battle which will determine for all time who will govern this land. We request four years to gather our people to the valley surrounding the hill named Cumorah.

The letter was simply signed: *Mormon.*

"Why choose Cumorah as the battleground? It is not central," Moroni said, handing the paper back to his father.

"A number of reasons," Mormon said. "It is neutral ground. It has plenty of water and fertile land to grow crops while we are gathering our people. It is also close to where we hid the plates. Most important the Lord has directed me that this should be the site of the last battle." He returned the paper to Moroni. "Please have this sent to the Lamanite camp."

While he waited, Mormon wrote more Nephite history. When Moroni returned he motioned his son to sit by him. "My time is short," he said. "When I die you must carry on as scribe. My son, will you take that responsibility?"

"You know I will, Father," Moroni said. "But I still write poorly in Egyptian."

"Spend time with me. We will practice together."

Moroni watched as his father inscribed hieroglyphics onto paper. As the sun settled just above the western hills the tent became too dark in which to write.

Someone shouted, "The courier comes!"

Mormon, followed by Moroni, stepped from the tent. He took the bark paper from the courier's hand, shook it open, and stood reading, oblivious to the stares of those around.

He looked at Moroni. "It is done," he said almost sadly. "The Lamanites have agreed to our truce."

Cumorah, 387 A.D.

No one was excluded from the gathering, Mormon thought. I disbanded my army and sent small groups of warriors throughout the land to enforce the edict. Warriors and civilians were lumped together in bands of fifties, hundreds, thousands and ten-thousands. Over each large group I put a seasoned commander, one who could give orders and make decisions. The most important time, though, was spent on

Cumorah, 384 A.D.

Mormon stood on the hillside looking over the valley of Cumorah. A huge tent city covered the ground in all directions. A pall of smoke hung over the tents of half-a-million people.

"It's a beautiful, yet sad, sight," Moroni said from behind. "I was just thinking of all the lives which will be lost," Mormon said. "Few, if any, of these people will survive."

"I've done my best to make them into an army," Moroni said.

Mormon put his hands on his son's shoulders. "No one could have done more," he said. "But how can you make an army out of women, old folks and children?" He didn't give Moroni time to answer. "Besides, even if we had as many warriors as we have people, most would still lose their lives."

"Why is that?"

"Prophecy."

Moroni sighed. "The battle right now doesn't concern me nearly as much as keeping all of those people fed, their wastes buried, and their spirits up." He laughed drily. "You have taught your commanders well."

"What do you mean?"

"Each one knows that there will be no retreat—that this is a fight to the death."

Mormon nodded morosely. "There are no alternatives. I'm just glad we prepared Cumorah. The Spirit whispers to me that we will live through the battle in order to complete the writing. Future generations will turn to what we have written as their witness of Christ and His teachings. It is imperative to finish the book."

Sounds of labored breathing came from behind. Mormon turned to see Lamah, dressed in full armor, entering the clearing.

"You are difficult to find," he panted. He stood for a moment looking at the view before him. "A glorious sight," he said. "Our army covers the entire valley."

"More than half-a-million people," Mormon mused.

"How many men will the Lamanites bring against us?"

Mormon looked at Lamah for a moment. He squinted his eyes against the glare of the sun. "When the Lamanites come, they will surround this entire valley with their warriors. Warriors, Lamah, not old men, women and children."

Lamah seemed taken back by the bitterness in Mormon's voice. "We can still beat them," he said.

Mormon didn't answer him, just turned back to view the preparations in the valley below.

"We have done all you ordered," Lamah said. "We have dug ditches surrounding our positions, have impaled stakes in the ground facing the rim of the valley, and have made weapons for any who can hold one." His voice had a plaintive quality. "Is there anything else we can do?"

Lamah had been his friend for a long time, but Mormon looked at him coldly. "You might try prayer," he said, his voice sharp.

He didn't acknowledge Lamah's salute as the old captain turned back the way he had come.

"I'm sorry, Moroni," Mormon said. "I guess I am feeling the pressure and pain of knowing what will happen in a few days."

"I understand, Father," Moroni said. "Which brings me to my concern over Greta. How can I tell her what is going to happen?"

"Say nothing to her," Mormon said, shaking his head. "Let her have peace during her few remaining days."

Preparations continued in the valley. Obsidian points were fitted to arrows and spears. Metalsmiths worked around the clock forging swords. Those without metal swords hefted wooden ones with obsidian chips implanted in teeth-like rows on the edges. Axes, scimitars and spears were issued to any old enough to hold a weapon. Mormon inspected and encouraged his people. He let Moroni supervise the vast assemblage and handle the problems.

The time came which he had been dreading. Spring had slipped into summer and days passed quickly. Indication that the time was near came when a runner appeared at his tent. "General Mormon."

Mormon stepped from the tent, shading his eyes from the glare of the afternoon sun. "What is it?" he asked.

"Lamanites," the youth said. "Captain Moroni asked me to tell you their armies have arrived." He pointed to the south where the rim of the valley rose in terraced layers towards the mountain chain that backed Bountiful.

Even Mormon gasped as he saw colored banners backed by thousands of bronze-skinned warriors stretching from horizon to horizon. The Nephite armies were completely ringed.

In the distance a lone banner waved forward. Mormon watched as the Lamanite approached. The messenger was tall and well-built. His body was mature, with full neck and broad shoulders. He moved with a smooth litheness, his muscles standing out as he carried the flag towards Mormon.

Moroni slipped up beside his father. "It must be a formal challenge from Shoninum."

Mormon nodded, not taking his eyes off the Lamanite. The man was insouciant in his bearing as he made his way between Nephite armies. Even from a distance Mormon could see his look of contempt. *I can't blame him. If I were in his place*

*and saw the sorry shape our army is in I would also be
contemptuous.*

The man stopped a dozen paces before Mormon and
planted his banner firmly into the ground. He stood beside it,
perfectly at ease. "I wish to speak to Mormon, the Nephite
commander."

"I am he," Mormon replied.

"Shoninum, commander of the Lamanite armies, has
given you ample time for preparation. He challenges your
armies to fight his armies on the morrow." He bowed, never
taking his eyes off Mormon and Moroni, stepped back two
paces, picked up his banner, and without waiting for an answer
from Mormon, made a quick about-face and trotted back
towards his own army.

"The challenge has been given," Mormon said. "We fight
tomorrow." Under his breath he added, *and die tomorrow.*

"Father," Moroni said. "My family and a few other
members will meet this evening for prayer and the Lord's
supper. We would like you to be there."

Mormon shook his head. "Thank you for the invitation,
but I must meet with each of the commanders personally and
see that preparations are complete." *Besides,* he thought, *I don't
know if I can face Greta and the rest of the family who must die
tomorrow. They must not see how emotional I am. I want them
to be strong.*

The setting sun was Mormon's signal to move from one
camp of ten thousand to another. He visited with Lamah, Gilgal,
Limhah, Joneam, Camenihah, Antionum, Shiblom, Shem and
Josh. Most were in excellent spirits—buoyant in hope of victory
against the Lamanites. He wanted to visit with the other
commanders, but there was no time. Darkness of night was
intense by the time he returned to his own tent.

In his prayers, earnest and humble, he pleaded with the
Lord to let his people live. He spent the night on his knees
imploring God to give the Nephites another chance. First light
of dawn defeated the shadows in his tent and still he had not
lain down on his pallet. He buckled on his armor, sheathed his
sword, and looked around at the few earthly possessions in the
tent. *Thank God the plates are already in the cave on Cumorah.
There is nothing here I cannot do without.*

He was calm, without fear, as he left the tent and roused
his ten thousand. "This is the day of the battle," he shouted.
"Prepare yourselves for the Lamanite attack."

By pre-agreed plan, archers moved to the front of his massed army. Behind them lined those with staffs and spears, then the swordsmen, and finally in the rear were the old men, women and children. Their weapons, pitiful in contrast to those of the warriors, were the clubs and shovels. Many were too small or too feeble to handle any weapon. Theirs would primarily be moral support for those actually fighting the battle.

"They come!" a shout from the front ranks.

Mormon didn't have to see them. Their noise, as they entered the valley was fear-producing: beating of drums and shields accompanied their caterwauling. He turned to watch the Lamanite armies marching down the valley's rim towards them.

Fear was palpable among his massed ten thousand. "It is the fear of death which fills the breasts of the wicked," he muttered. Terror continued to mount as Lamanites marched forward in seemingly endless numbers. Fear smells—sweat and urine and vomit—assaulted Mormon's nose.

Moroni's ten thousand was on his right. Mormon lifted his sword above his head and waved it. Moroni returned the wave. *That will be the closest we will get to communicating today.* He did the same for Lamah whose ten-thousand were on his left.

Within minutes the battle swirled around him. Volleys of arrows from his archers met the enemy while still paces away. Moments later spears, swords, clubs and scimitars began their violent tattoo. Mormon's sword, which had swung against enemies in hundreds of battles, began its rhythmic beat. Dodge, thrust, parry, then dodge, thrust and parry again; just one sword in an endless, synchronous beating of thousands of swords and shields.

Mormon lost track of time. A sword thrust drew blood from his arm. He slipped away from the thrust and brought his own sword to bear, chopping and hacking at those facing him. His age slowed him down. With each thrust his sword seemed heavier. Legs and arms seemed weighted. He held three Lamanite warriors at bay, dodging their swords, weaving his own in a snakelike dance.

He staggered. *What?* He looked around. A Lamanite warrior, bloodied spear in hand, prepared to thrust again. *My blood.* He looked down. Blood gushed from his side. Surprised, he turned back to the Lamanites facing him. Nephite warriors had them engaged. "Keep fighting," he cried, not realizing that weakened as he was his voice was no more than a whisper. His sword fell from lifeless fingers as he pitched forward on the ground.

Cumorah, 387 A.D.

Even now as Mormon thought of that final battle, tears rolled down his withered cheeks. His hands doubled into fists as in his anguish he whistled a soft, tuneless song between his teeth. "The record is complete—or at least as complete as I can make it," he said to himself as he busied himself cleaning the cave. As he moved around he uttered an audible prayer. "Father, I have completed the work. I yearn for Merena." Again the tuneless whistle hissed from between his teeth.

Afternoon calm was broken by sounds of complaining warriors and rustling brush. Nearness of the sounds surprised Mormon. Other Lamanite patrols had searched Cumorah, but none had come this close to the cave. *What shall I do? First, I must hide the records. Then...*

Mormon carefully placed the plates in the hiding place, but before he put away his brushes and paint he painted a note to Moroni: *My son, a Lamanite patrol searches the mountain. I fear they will discover the cave and the plates. I will lead them away. You know where the plates are. I admonish you, finish the record. I will not see you again in the flesh but will see you in the kingdom of our Father. Goodbye my son, I go now to my God and to your God.* He put away his writing tools and sealed up the hiding place. Stepping back he looked at it and nodded his head. No Lamanite would find the plates. He carefully placed the bark paper where he knew Moroni would find it. From a nearby tree he pulled a brushy branch. Walking backward from the cave he brushed out all footprints, then hid the branch in a large bush. He looked back towards the cave. The entrance was completely hidden and there was no sign of his having been there. Good!

The patrol was closer now. He sighed. *Goodbye, my son.* Dodging between trees he slipped closer to the sounds of the patrol. He waited until the warriors were almost on him, then turned and ran downhill. His old legs did not carry him very far. Breathless, a tiny smile pulling up the corners of his lips, he pulled his sword and turned to face his pursuers.

EPILOGUE

Moroni found his father's body the next morning, white hair matted with blood, his body mutilated. Mormon had died fighting.

Voice choked as tears flowed. Moroni offered a prayer over this father he had loved so much. A peaceful feeling came over him. A quiet voice filled his mind: *Do not despair. Your father has completed his work and has come home to Me. Complete the history of my people. Then I have another mission for you. There are yet some things which you must do for me.*

For the next thirty-five years, no matter where Moroni wandered over the vast continent, he felt his father with him. Mormon's body had died on Cumorah but his spirit lived on. He had completed his earthly mission. The Nephite Chronicles had a new scribe: Mormon's son, Moroni.

DATE DUE

DEMCO, INC. 38-2931